The Baron Time Forgot

Those Regency Remingtons
Book Two

Jennifer Monroe

D1566173

Prologue

Dunark, England 1797

She saw him from across the crowded ballroom.

His name was Evan, Baron of Westlake, and Miss Rose Follet had been in love with him for three years.

Rose had first taken exceptional notice of the baron whilst shopping in the village of Dunark with her mother during a day excursion.

A member of the illustrious Remington family, he had walked past her with a swagger gifted only to men of his disposition and confidence. His misty-blue eyes and waves of blond hair had her spine tingling, and his devilish grin caused her cheeks to burn with red-hot heat. After that day, she was unable to get him out of her mind.

Although they lived two hours apart—she an hour in one direction from the village and he an hour in the other—she had been fortunate enough to see him at a handful of societal gatherings. Not once did she speak with him, however, for she lacked the conviction that she would be worthy of his notice.

Even from a distance, and with no words spoken between them, Rose loved him.

It was that feeling that overwhelmed her at this very moment, just as it had those times in the past. Her heart soared, her legs became weak, and her thoughts overflowed with images of him.

The problem was, Lord Westlake knew nothing of her feelings for him. In fact, Rose doubted he even knew she existed. Most men did not.

Rose had been told often that her dark-brown hair was beautiful and that she conducted herself as well as any lady. Yet she had one distinction that set her apart from the other beautiful women.

She did not possess a thin waistline.

Her father, Mr. Ernest Follet, had told her on many occasions that she was what he deemed "unusually large." His words stung as sharp as any nettle every time he spoke them, and shame covered her like a filthy shawl draped over her shoulders. Whether with family at the dinner table or in the company of his peers, not a week passed without him reminding her of her "problem." Sometimes his comments drew a sneer or a small chuckle from whomever he told, bringing about embarrassment that burned fiercer than a winter's fire.

Whenever one of those moments occurred, Rose would sneak into the kitchen after the staff had gone to bed. Pastries, great hunks of bread, cold meats left over from that night's dinner, whatever she could find, she consumed. All in an attempt to ease her pain.

That, of course, only led to further guilt, sending her into a spiral of days so dark and cloudy, the sun seemed unable to shine through.

At eighteen, Rose was intelligent enough to understand why she was the size she was, but no matter how hard she tried, she could not stop herself. Food gave her a sense of comfort, and although the feeling was temporary, it was all she had.

Rose had spent most of her childhood in the kitchen where Mrs. Browncast, the cook, doted on her at every turn. It was there where she felt wanted, felt loved was happy. Oh, she had no doubt her parents loved her in their way, but in Mrs. Browncast's company, she felt a sense of belonging she never felt upstairs. Plus, the cook made the most outstanding and delectable foods imaginable!

Rose sighed. Regardless of how she came to be who she was today, the truth was, no man would look her way. Not even the man she loved. And she had to learn to accept her fate.

"Rose, darling," her mother said, interrupting her thoughts. Her mother was still pretty with deep brown eyes and dark-brown hair flecked with silver. Her friends often complimented her on her lovely figure, which was currently accentuated in her blue and silver gown.

Granted, her stays were tied so tightly, Rose wondered how her mother could possibly breathe.

"Why not go and speak with the other girls. The Season will begin in just a few short months. Making friends will be a prudent choice if you wish to receive invitations to any of the best functions in London."

Rose did not look forward to her first Season like the other young ladies did, for she would likely be spending her nights at home with nothing more to do than her needlework.

"Thank you, Mother," Rose replied, choosing not to voice her trepidation at doing as her mother bade. "I'll just finish my wine first."

"Do make sure it's your last. We don't need you bringing your father further embarrassment." Her mother gave her a small smile. "I must go speak to Lady Malson. I heard her niece has been up to a bit of mischief, and I wish to console her."

Rose watched her mother walk through the crowded ballroom and join a circle of ladies. Her mother's idea of consoling consisted of gathering as much information as she could from whomever she could and then turning around and repeating it.

Their gossiping would last for at least an hour, and the ladies would cover every topic and person they knew. This meant that Rose would stand alone once again at yet another party. At least the music was pleasant.

With gold-painted walls, dark-blue drapes, and numerous paintings hanging between the dozen windows, the ballroom at Tinsley Estate spoke of the wealth of the title of the Baron of Westlake and of the Remington family.

The reason for the party this night was a farewell to Lord Westlake's mother, who was leaving Dunark to live in a new estate her son had purchased for her in another part of the country. How Rose's father had received an invitation was beyond her.

When Rose had indicated her interest in attending, her father had responded with a derisive snort without even the slightest courtesy of looking up from the book he had been reading. In the end, however, he had agreed. After all, he would have to find someone to marry her eventually.

Lavinia, Baroness Westlake, was a beautiful woman, whose blonde hair was piled high atop her head and held by a gold diadem dotted with a dozen emeralds. Her green gown was overlaid with intricate white lace and showed off her exceptionally thin waistline. Rose could not help but wonder, as she often did when she encountered women of such a slim build, how the lady managed to maintain such a lithe figure.

Rose sighed and caught sight of her father walking away from the refreshment table in the company of three gentlemen. Although he had not said so outright, Rose knew he was off to play cards. Like clockwork, he would reemerge three hours later, red-faced and with empty pockets, searing at Rose's mother to make haste so they could leave.

Mr. Follet might have been a respected member of the landed gentry, but that did not save him from losing the money of which he bragged to those of the upper class. Rose suspected it was his money they respected far more than him.

Taking another sip of her wine, Rose observed one Miss Emily Garrison, an old childhood friend. Miss Emily wore a yellow dress that complemented her flaxen hair quite well and showed off a perfect waistline. Perhaps she and her friends would allow Rose into their inner circle, thus fulfilling her mother's wishes.

Yet even as she considered it, Rose pushed the idea aside. Why bother to make the attempt when they would likely reject her? Not that they had been outright rude to her, but as Rose's weight increased, her friends' availability decreased. Their schedules became full, far too full to include a moment with Rose. Even Miss Emily, the closest of her friends, ignored her. Every excuse was made, but Rose knew the truth. She had become an embarrassment to anyone caught in her company.

Well, her mother had insisted she find someone. At least she was already acquainted with Miss Emily. Therefore, Rose finished off the last of her wine and set it upon the tray of a passing liveried footman.

Drawing in a deep breath in an attempt to pull in her stomach, she summoned her courage, running her hands over the red dress as if doing so would also help hide her substantial girth. At least the high waist of the current fashion helped. And she adored this dress. It was bright and cheerful and made her feel happy.

She moved past an elderly couple speaking with another young lady. Beside them stood a gentleman of perhaps thirty with an upturned nose, who looked her over and then shook his head.

Oh, why did I not remain in the corner where no one could see me? she thought with annoyance.

Well, it was too late to turn back now.

As she approached Miss Emily, the sounds of mirth made Rose smile. They seemed quite a cheerful bunch and would make great company. If they would only give her a chance, they would see she could be as agreeable as they.

The other two young ladies were not as beautiful as Miss Emily, but neither were they homely. One had hair so light it was nearly white and eyes the color of a summer sky that matched the flowers printed on her gown. The other was at least a year older with wheat-colored hair and brown eyes. Her pink gown had an exceptionally low neckline, but she had the decency to cover it with a fichu of white lace.

As Rose approached, a familiar thing happened. Their smiles fell and they began to whisper behind their fans. The awkwardness hung in the air like an early morning fog.

"Miss Rose?" Miss Emily asked in surprise. "Truly my eyes did not deceive me. I didn't recognize you." She looked Rose up and down and turned to grin at her companions. Rose could hear their snickers. "What I mean is, it's been so long since we last spoke."

Pushing down the hurt and ignoring the sneers, Rose feigned a smile. "I sent you a letter last month. Well, I've sent you many letters since we last saw one another, but I never received a reply."

Miss Emily waved a dismissive hand. "It's my butler. He has a tendency to lose things."

Rose was not so easily deceived. Even she knew, if the butler were that incompetent, he would have been given the sack long ago.

Rather than pointing this out, she turned to Miss Emily's companions. "Hello. My name is Miss Rose—"

"Oh, look," the wheat-colored hair woman said, "there's Lord Percival. He's been occupied all evening and is finally alone. Come, Miss Susanna, before we miss him." She pulled on the arm of her companion and hurried away, leaving Miss Emily and Rose alone.

Rose's sides ached and her stomach muscles burned from the effort of holding in her middle, and her breaths came in short bursts. She had no idea what would happen if she fully exhaled. Nor did she wish to find out.

Did Miss Emily appear bored? She was halfway turned, as if searching for someone.

In an attempt to begin conversation, Rose said, "I'm very excited for the Season. To think I'll find a suitor…" She dropped her gaze. "Well, if I can find one who will look my way." The last was said with a small chuckle in hopes of breaking the tension between them.

Yet Miss Emily's attention was most definitely elsewhere. "Lord Westlake, our gracious host," she whispered. Rose followed her gaze to the very man she admired so much. "Not only is he a powerful man, but oh is he handsome! Look at that broad chest. It's as wide as a table!" The corner of her lips twitched. "And his arm muscles are wonderful to touch!"

"You've touched his arms?" Rose asked in surprise. And perhaps a bit of annoyance.

Miss Emily snorted. "Not in the way you think," she said. "But yes, I've had the occasion to accidentally bump into him. He and I have already spoken this evening, and I dare say, I'm certain he'll call on me within the week." She turned to Rose. "You don't still believe you have a chance with him, do you?"

When they were still friends, Rose had confessed her feelings for Lord Westlake—who had been Mr. Remington at the time. Inside, she wanted to do so again, to speak the truth that she still pined after him. That every night this week, she had prayed he would speak to her. Or at least remember who she was.

Yet how could she compete with the likes of Miss Emily? No man— and certainly not one like Lord Westlake—would ever consider someone like Rose when Miss Emily was anywhere near her.

"No, of course not," Rose replied. "That was just the silly ramblings of a child."

"Good," Miss Emily said with a single nod. "For it would only cause you embarrassment when he rejects you. After all, no man would want a woman in your...condition." She handed Rose her empty glass. "Be a dear and take that away. I have important people to speak with."

Humiliation coursed through Rose as she blinked back tears. With little consideration for her mother's warning about consuming too much, she grabbed a glass of wine from a passing footman, placing Miss Emily's empty glass in its place.

What would her mother care? After all, she was still gossiping with her friends. Her father was no doubt placing a bet at this very moment. Everyone in the ballroom appeared occupied, and quite content if the laughter was any indication.

Everyone except Rose. No gentleman would look her way, despite the amount of wealth her father possessed. Perhaps if she were beautiful, if she had the lovely figure of so many of those around her, they would consider her. But she did not.

Even the women considered Rose an embarrassment, and many, like Miss Emily, treated her as nothing more than a servant.

With her glass of wine in hand, Rose returned to her place along the far wall, out of the way of the other guests, to think of her life and that which would make her happy. Tonight, after they returned home, she would read her favorite newspaper, The Morning Post. If one skipped past the articles on politics and other nonsense, she could stumble across various articles on the latest fashions and where to purchase the best fabrics.

But Rose preferred the gossip columns the most.

Tales of unnamed gentlemen and ladies caught in dubious behavior made for great entertainment. An earl had recently been said to have kissed two women on the same night! How he did not live in shame for such actions was beyond Rose, but the nobility had a tendency to look past such conduct. Especially when men were the ones committing the offenses. Women did not get off so easily.

Every night, Rose sat with a bag of sweets she kept hidden in the top drawer of her vanity table, or food she had sneaked in from the kitchen, and read the columns in hopes of hiding the pain she felt inside. It was not the joy in learning of the wrongdoings of others that caused her such contentment. Instead, she would pretend it was she and Lord Westlake who had kissed in secret. Or had been caught alone in the recesses of a garden.

She could see the articles now.

Who was the handsome baron and the unusually large young lady seen with him?

The admiration an unnamed baron showed for a young lady of the landed gentry is a sure sign of an impending engagement!

Famed Remington confesses his love for a particular woman whom we mustn't name!

He cares nothing for her size!

The gentleman loves her!

Will London ever see a more worthy couple?

With a sigh, Rose took a large swallow of her wine. The dreams were pleasant, but why linger on them? Such articles would never be said about her.

"I'm glad you did not leave," a husky voice said, breaking her from her thoughts.

Rose's heart thudded in her chest, and her legs shook as she turned to find the very baron of her dreams standing beside her. He was even more handsome standing so close to her with his wavy blond hair, defined jawline, and leg muscles that tested the fabric of his tight-fitting breeches.

Her mind betrayed her as she imagined herself falling against him as Miss Emily had and touching his arm. Or to run a finger down his cheek or through his thick hair. To have his lips caress hers.

"I feared I had missed the opportunity to speak with you."

With her throat as arid as a desert day, panic overtook Rose, and she took a very unladylike gulp of her wine.

"My lord?" she managed to say.

The corner of his lip curled. There was something behind it, something Rose could not identify, but she was certain it was not disgust. That she would have recognized immediately, as often as she had seen it.

"All evening I've taken the liberty of drinking in your beauty from afar," he whispered. "It's caused me to become drunk, your beauty has. But now standing here beside you, my inebriation knows no bounds."

His breath reeked of stale wine, his words were slurred, and his eyes were tinged with red, but she did not care. He had called her beautiful, and that was all that mattered to her. No man had ever used that word when describing her, and she was left with the most wonderful feeling in the world.

"Thank you, my lord," she whispered, attempting to catch her breath. "I had thought you didn't notice me. Most do not."

He chuckled. "How could I not see you?"

For a moment, Rose cursed herself inwardly. She was not holding in her stomach! Would a joke about her size come tumbling from his mouth at any moment?

"Your beauty lights the room," he continued.

Oh, drat! He was toying with her now.

"I just may shout to all in attendance that I'm unable to look away!"

How many nights had she lain awake dreaming of hearing such words from the baron? Her dreams were coming true! The *ton* would gossip about them throughout London. She might even need to write to the newspaper herself to inform them of this wondrous news.

"My lord, you've no idea what your words mean to me." She glanced around the room and gave a relieved sigh upon seeing that her mother was still occupied. "Many nights I have thought of you."

Rose clamped her mouth shut. What had caused her to say that aloud? With a glance at her now-empty wine glass, she had a suspicion what had made her speak so freely. Or was it that her love for him was overflowing and she could do nothing to stop her from declaring as much?

Whatever it was, the baron did not take offense but instead said, "I have a marvelous idea." He looked around them and then leaned in closer. "But we cannot speak here where anyone can hear. If the other young ladies caught sight of me speaking so intimately with you, they will become jealous, and we cannot have that now, can we?"

She looked up, and indeed, Miss Emily was glowering in their direction. Well, let her be angry! Rose would prove everyone who had believed so little of her how wrong they were!

Raising her chin, she smiled. Her size did not matter. Her true love, Lord Westlake, had seen past it and thought her beautiful.

"If you go past the stairs to the first door on the right, you'll find the drawing room. I'll await you there."

Worry took over her. "My lord? I don't understand. Why do you wish to meet there?"

But he had already walked away with that confident swagger she adored.

Rose found herself in a dilemma. What could the baron possibly wish to say that he could not say here?

Then it dawned on her. Of course! He wished to confess his love for her! And he certainly could not do so in front of a hundred guests. No, a gentleman would say such intimate words in private. Perhaps they would even share in their first kiss!

Pushing aside her mother's warning that an upstanding young lady would never find herself alone with a gentleman, Rose made sure her mother was still otherwise occupied. For the first time, she was thankful no one paid her any attention.

As she approached the foyer, a tall butler with a few wisps of silver hair on his otherwise bald pate stood by the front door. Was it her imagination or did his eyes tell her she should return to the ballroom?

No, that was silly. Butlers did not give orders to the guests.

Further down the corridor, several men laughed. Her father's game was going well. For someone. One of those laughs had not been her father's.

She stopped at the partially closed door and placed a hand on the heavy wood. Her heart thudded with both fear and excitement. Just inside lay her destiny. There was no turning back.

Numerous candles lit the exquisite room. A piano sat in front of a large window beside a harp, the wood of both gleaming. Above a marble fireplace hung a portrait of Lady Westlake in her youth, just as lovely as she was today. Several marble statues sat in recesses along one wall, and a crystal chandelier hung above a sofa and two chairs, all covered in deep-green fabric.

It was a lovely room, to be sure, but she only gave it a cursory glance. For waiting beside the sofa was her baron.

Lord Westlake removed his coat and draped it over the back of one of the chairs. Then he walked over to her, a small smile playing on his lips.

Rose's breath caught when he draped an arm over one of her shoulders, trapping her in place. Never had she been this close to any man, let alone Lord Westlake, but his masculine fragrance overwhelmed her senses. As his blue eyes focused on hers, he took a step closer, and Rose heard the light *click* of the door closing behind her. Her heart beat so hard, she feared it would burst from her chest.

"I've never seen such flawless skin," he whispered as he ran a finger down her cheek. "It's like fine silk."

Heat welled up in Rose, and she thought she would burst into flames at any moment. If she did not sit soon, she would collapse into a heap where she stood!

He leaned in, his lips dangerously close to her ear. "Your lips intrigue me. If I were to kiss them, would they taste like wine?"

Rose went to reply, but before she could, he pressed his lips to hers. Without thought, she placed the palms of her hands on his chest, meaning to push him away. Yet there was no strength behind them. His kiss was far too wonderful, even better than she could have imagined. Her heart soared to new heights, and her body came to life in ways she never thought imaginable.

She had thought her first kiss would be soft and hesitant, but it was far from it. There was a possessiveness that left Rose hungering for more, and she found herself returning it with equal power.

For a brief moment, it stopped, and Lord Westlake raised a single eyebrow. Rose understood at once what he asked.

"Yes," she said. "I want another."

"Your words are pleasing to my ears," he whispered back as he trailed his fingers along the exposed skin of her arm. He lifted her chin. "Let me grant your request."

When he kissed her this time, he pressed his body against hers. Her arms wrapped themselves around him of their own accord and pulled him closer.

Much to her disappointment, the kiss ended.

"I can see you desire me," he said. "Am I mistaken?"

Did she lie and say that hunger to be held, to be caressed, to be loved did not fill her heart?

"Yes," she found herself saying instead. "I do. Very much so."

"And I desire you," he said, his voice now huskier. "Let me show you how much I care for you."

For the second time that night, Rose pushed aside her mother's warning of how men enjoyed wooing women to their beds only to leave them unwanted and unmarried later. He loved her. If he did not, he would not be with her now!

That did not mean she should not make some sort of effort, if only for propriety's sake. "But you don't know me, my lord. Do you even know my name? How can you care for me?" Her breath caught. "You do care for me, do you not, my lord?"

The baron placed a finger on her lips. "What is in a name?" he whispered. "For the rest of my life, I shall simply call you Beautiful." His smile sent pleasant shivers into her stomach. "You must understand. To say I care for you is not enough. A lady like you must be loved."

Rose nodded. This man knew her heart! All her mother's warnings disappeared as Lord Westlake walked her over to the sofa and extended his hand. "Will you let me love you?"

For a moment, fear gripped her heart.

But he loves me! Never had she thought anyone would love her, let alone Lord Westlake! Her dreams of this man had not been in vain. He was a gentleman who looked past women like Miss Emily Garrison and saw how much Rose loved him. And she could see—no she could feel how much he loved her in return.

Rose would not deny what her heart needed. For the first time that night, she exhaled, no longer feeling the need to hold her breath. She had nothing to hide. She had finally met a man who loved her for who she was.

"Yes," she said, her body trembling as she reached a hand out to him. When he clasped it, she felt safe. He would protect her, listen to her worries, and assure her all would be well.

As her eyes met his, she knew then that soon, her surname would be Westlake. That their love would grow daily. She would do everything to make him happy. Just as he would her.

"Yes," she whispered again as he wrapped loving arms around her. "I'll let you love me."

Chapter One

Dunark, England July 1803

The grand ballroom was empty.

Gone was every bit of evidence of the hundred or so ladies and gentlemen who had filled the room the previous evening. The musicians no longer played their lively music. The guests no longer drank and ate to excess.

Giving the room a final inspection, Miss Rose Follet spotted a single wineglass hidden behind a plant. The last of the wine it once held had dried, leaving a red stain at the bottom of the glass.

Why anyone would take the time to hide such a mundane object rather than place it on a footman's tray befuddled her. Befuddled but did not bother her. Rose had more important matters with which to concern herself. Such as making certain the ballroom was spotless in order to please her employer.

The man she would bring to his knees.

The man she despised.

Lord Westlake.

For six years, Rose had vowed to destroy not only the baron but every other person who shared the name of Remington, for Lord Westlake's malevolence went far beyond his title. It had deep roots in the family who made him who he was.

With careful eyes and ears, she had learned that Tinsley Estate was in need of a new maid. Although Rose had no experience with cleaning, nor any other sort of labor for that matter, she had spent several weeks studying those who did. Her maids, of course, had feared losing their positions with Rose playing their shadow for so long, yet doing so was imperative to her goal.

Once she learned what she could, Rose donned a maid's uniform and interviewed with the butler of Tinsley Estate. That was how she had gained her current position. Other than how a woman of four and twenty would be inquiring about a position as a chamber maid raised the butler's brows, gaining the position really had not been all that difficult. All she needed was a decent reference, which she designed herself. She knew quite well from personal experience that few interested parties contacted past employers, no matter how much they said they did.

For a month now, she had been working at the estate, keeping her uniform crisp and clean. The work made her back ache and the muscles in her calves strain, but as the weeks went by, she found her work—and the soreness—manageable.

During her various tasks of dusting, sweeping, washing the floor, and the like, Rose absorbed every bit of information she could from the other servants concerning the baron. She knew all too well how servants enjoyed their gossip, especially when it came to their employers, and those at Tinsley Estate were no different.

That knowledge was then passed on to her weekly gossip column for The Morning Post.

Under the *nom de plum* of Lady Honor, Rose wrote for the very same paper she had once devoured so late at night with her bag of sweets at her side. Her column had become all the rage in London since she started it a year earlier. In it, she chronicled the faults and blunders of every disgusting man who dared call himself a gentleman.

"Sadie Crawford, what are you doing?" a deep baritone boomed throughout the vacant room. "Have I not told you that idle hands bring about mischief?"

Rose had taken on a new name to hide her identity—Sadie for her favorite cat as a child and Crawford for her mother's maiden name. Although she had used it for the past month, she still found herself needing a daily reminder from her lady's maid, Leah, before she left for work each morning. It would not do to forget. Too much was at stake.

Rose lowered her head and smoothed the white apron. How she despised the fabric maids were forced to wear. She missed her muslin and cotton dresses, the layers of lace, and the smooth satin of the ribbons.

"Forgive me, Mr. Fletcher," she said, adding just enough contriteness to appease the butler. "I wanted to give the room one final inspection. And I'm glad I did. I found this glass hidden behind one of the plants."

Mr. Fletcher was not only the man who had hired her, but he was also the same who had given her a warning look six years earlier. During her interview, she inquired as to why there was no housekeeper, to which Rose was given the very same snort she received now.

"The affairs of the Westlakes—or any of the Remingtons, for that matter—are no concern of yours," he had told her.

Although Rose knew he used the word "affairs" in its proper sentiment, she knew those of the Remington family had other types of affairs, as well. The men seemed to have dozens of them. Lord Westlake was no exception.

"The room is clean enough, Sadie," the aging butler said. What was left of his hair was a deep silver, and the lines around his eyes spoke of his many years on the earth. "Before you leave for the night, you are to see to the parlor. But do take care and avoid the drawing room. His lordship is entertaining a guest there and wishes to not be disturbed."

"You mean Miss Haskett?" Rose blurted before she could stop herself and regretted it instantly. She might as well have told the butler outright that she was there to spy!

Mr. Fletcher took a step forward, and Rose braced herself for the reprimand she knew was to come.

"I find you very peculiar," he said as he frowned down at her. "Why the great interest in His Lordship's personal affairs?"

Rose dropped her gaze, donning her meekest expression. "I'm

sorry. It's just that I find his type fascinating is all. I'll mind my own business from now on."

Mr. Fletcher kept a strict regime in overseeing the servants, but Rose saw through his stoic facade to the kind heart that resided beneath. It showed most often in moments like this, when he lowered his voice and spoke to her like a father concerned for his daughter.

"It does no good to involve yourself with *his* doings," the butler said. Was that disgust in his tone? "Now, off to the parlor with you. Once you've finished in there, you may leave." He started to turn but then stopped. "Miss Moore says you refused to eat again today. Are you well? We're both concerned at how thin you are."

Her hands smoothed the apron over her stomach. "A woman must watch her figure, Mr. Fletcher," she said without looking up at him. The old wounds tugged at her heart. "If not, she'll become too large, which leads to ridicule."

Five years earlier, Rose had removed all sweets from her diet. Then she instructed the cook to plate no more than five bites of everything she made, and that only once per day. It had been difficult at first, and many days she had to stop herself from sneaking into the kitchen as she had done in the past.

It had been well worth the struggle. As her waistline thinned, men began to smile at her. She received cards requesting to call on her. The smaller her dresses became, the more letters of adoration she received.

Yet Rose refused to acknowledge any of them. She had given away her heart once, and never would she do so again. The pain was not worth it.

"Mrs. Fletcher had been what many would have termed a 'large woman,'" the butler said, his eyes taking on a far-off look. "But it did not stop me from loving her. Don't harm yourself in order to gain what society deems right, for more often than not, they are wrong."

Rose smiled as Mr. Fletcher exited the room. Mildred, one of the chambermaids, had mentioned that the butler's wife had died only a few years earlier. Although she had not been employed at the estate, many were acquainted with her, and it was apparent all loved the wife as much as they admired Mr. Fletcher.

With the found glass in hand, Rose went to inspect the parlor. Before she reached her destination, however, the familiar voice of Lord Westlake came to her ears.

A quick glance around the corridor said no one was about, so she squatted and peeked through the keyhole of the door to the drawing room.

The very room in which she had been six years earlier.

Miss Constance Haskett had an older sister by the name of Miss Katherine Haskett. Rumor had it that the sister was meant to marry Colin, Duke of Greystoke, but Rose had learned, by way of eavesdropping, that the duke was infatuated with another woman. A woman from a poor upbringing.

Although that bit of gossip would have caused all of London to come to a halt, especially given that it was about a member of the Remington family, Rose had refused to write about it. Some things in life were to be cherished, true love being one of them. She preferred to focus on the atrocities of the Remingtons and those like them. Plus, she had heard the duke was one of the good men of the family.

"My lord," Miss Constance was saying in breathy tones, "I'm afraid my mind is clouded from wine and worry. I fear I'll become just another one of your conquests."

Miss Constance appeared to be no older than twenty with beautiful red hair in tight curls. Even from her position, Rose could see the baron moving a hand down her arm. Just as he had done before...

Stop! Rose said silently, closing her eyes for a moment to push aside the memories. Now was not the time to torment herself with the past!

"Those rumors are unfounded," Lord Westlake said. "They are often started by angry women I've refused to acknowledge. Do you not see? My eyes have only been on you."

"What you say pleases me, my lord, but I cannot have my name ruined. I've taken a great risk by meeting you unchaperoned as it is." Miss Constance smiled up at him through her eyelashes. "If you have plans to announce our engagement, however, I may be willing to allow you to kiss me."

Run, you fool! Rose thought. *Run and never return!*

Rose's breath caught in her throat when Lord Westlake placed a hand on the young lady's cheek. The memories flooded her mind despite her resistance to allow them to rise.

"I'll announce how flawless your skin is. I'll declare that your beauty holds me captive. And I'll pledge my love for you so all of London hears." He kissed her cheek. "Would you like that?"

"Very much, my lord," Miss Constance said in that breathless whisper.

Lord Westlake leaned in and kissed her neck.

"But...I admit that I'm confused."

"Do you not enjoy my kisses?" Lord Westlake asked in that husky tone Rose remembered all too well.

"Oh, it's not that, my lord," Miss Constance replied. "I fear that if I abide by your wishes, you'll not look at me the same again. Will you not lose all respect for me?"

The baron pulled back and took hold of her hand. "It's because of the respect I have for you that I make my request," he drawled. "Come with me before your lady's maid returns." He brought her hand to his lips. "Allow me to show you how much I care for you."

Anger welled up in Rose's heart as Miss Constance worried her bottom lip, clearly debating whether she should agree. How she wished she could shout a warning!

"He does nothing but lie!" she would say. *"You'll be nothing more than a notch on his bedpost. Letters will go unanswered. Too many nights will be spent weeping into your pillow.*

But no. Doing so would undermine why she had taken this position in the first place. She could not afford to be thrown out of the house before she was able to complete her task.

Therefore, she did the next best thing.

Rising, she feigned a sneeze and dropped the glass. The echoing sound of shattering crystal filled the corridor.

"Drat it all!" the baron screamed.

Rose dropped to her knees and began brushing the shards of glass together with a kerchief she had taken from the pocket of her apron.

The door flung open, but she kept her gaze on the task at hand. Although she could not see him, she could feel his angry presence, warming her skin as he towered over her.

"That will come out of your wages, you fool!" he growled at her.

"Yes, my lord." She was meekness incarnate.

Then her heart leapt with joy as Miss Constance stepped past her. "I must go, my lord. But know that I'll most certainly consider your offer. I don't know you well enough to agree just yet, but I look forward to your next letter."

How Rose wanted to stand and embrace Miss Constance! To congratulate her for guarding her heart and virtue. As she watched the young lady walk away, Rose stood to find the baron staring at her. His eyes were red and his breath reeked of wine, yet he was just as handsome as she remembered. For a brief moment, her heart beat with anticipation, just as it had that night six years earlier.

No! She would not be caught in his web again.

He stared at her with angry—and a bit unfocused—eyes. Since accepting her position, Rose had feared he would recognize her the few times they had encountered one another. Yet why would he? She was far slimmer and more savvy now, a far different woman from the corpulent and foolish ninny she had been back then.

If she were honest, besides their single night alone, they had not seen each other again. She doubted he remembered anything about her. If he even recalled that night at all as inebriated as he had been.

Plus, she now wore a costume, and anyone who ever had servants knew that no one took much notice of those who maintained the home.

"Report your incompetency to Fletcher so he may punish you," Lord Westlake said with a curled lip. "Next time, I'll have you thrown out without benefit of your wages or a reference!"

Before Rose could respond, he turned on his heel and slammed the door shut behind him.

She had risked losing her position, but if it meant saving the heart of a stranger, it was well worth the risk.

As she entered the foyer, Rose watched as Miss Constance and her lady's maid left the house. Mr. Fletcher closed the door, and he followed Rose into the servants' stairway that led to the kitchen. Tilly, the kitchen maid, offered Rose a smile as she deposited the shards of glass into the bin.

"Is everything all right?" Tilly asked. A young girl of seventeen with mossy-brown hair beneath her mob cap, Tilly was a great source of gossip. The maid's big brown eyes went wide, and Rose felt a presence behind her.

"Sadie," the butler said, "a word please."

Mr. Fletcher stepped into the short corridor that led to the various storage rooms, and Rose followed. Her heart skipped a beat as the butler loomed over her.

"I find it odd that you just so happen to drop that glass in front of the very room I had warned you to stay away from." Rose went to speak, but the butler raised a hand to forestall her. "I also find it interesting that you speak far more eloquently and with far better articulation than any other servant ever employed in this house. Besides me, that is. How lucky it was for you to be taught by a tutor despite the upbringing you supposedly had."

Rose had taken great pains in looking the part of a servant, yet speaking like one had been a challenge. Years of training was difficult to hide, so instead, she concocted a story of how her mother had arranged for a tutor for a fraction of the fee in exchange for sewing. Mr. Fletcher had been surprised, of course, but not enough to believe she was lying.

Until now. What had made him take such a special interest in her background when it had not been an issue before? Perhaps she had been caught and all her hard work was now coming to an end.

"Whatever it is you're doing, stop," the butler said. "I've loyally served here in one capacity or another since the age of ten, working my way up to the position in which I am now. If you think I'll turn a blind eye after fifty years of service to this family, you're quite mistaken."

Rose swallowed hard. "Yes, Mr. Fletcher."

He frowned. "I feel as if I've seen you before. Do I know you in some other capacity?"

"I don't believe so, Mr. Fletcher."

Would he not stop staring at her?

Finally, he sighed and stepped past Rose, leaving her to grasp hold of the closest wall to keep herself upright.

"Don't pay him much mind," Tilly said when Rose returned to the kitchen. "Mr. Fletcher's always tryin' to scare the new girls. He's a big softy really."

"Thank you, Tilly," Rose said with a nervous chuckle. "I'll try to remember that. Well, I'm going home."

As Tilly returned to the last of her chores in the kitchen, Rose collected her things from the pegs beside the servant's entrance. After throwing her cloak over her shoulders, she exited the house and took the path that led to the main road. She had hired a small cottage not two miles away just before taking her position. It was a far cry from the rich home she had in London, which offered luxurious furnishings and servants of her own, but it suited her purpose well.

After the passing of her parents from a tragic accident five years earlier, Rose was left with a very healthy allowance every month. Her family estate was run by a solicitor and would be inherited by the man she married.

But at the age of four and twenty—and quite comfortable being the sole benefactor of the estate—Rose would never marry. Why give away what was hers to a man? Besides, marriage required love and that was something she would never go through again.

There were those around her who could ease her pain, and although it was not the same sort of love a husband might have for his wife, what she did have eased her darkest days.

"Miss Rose! Miss Rose!" Her young ward, Aaron, bolted from the cottage and wrapped his arms around her.

Rose could not help but chuckle. With chestnut hair and blue eyes, he was all she would ever need in life.

"Master Aaron, come here this instant!" Leah, Rose's lady's maid, called from the doorway. "I'm so sorry, Miss Rose! He tends to pay me no heed sometimes!"

"It's all right," Rose said as she squatted beside the boy. "I think it's just that he misses me." She ruffled his hair. "So is it true? Did you miss me?"

"I did, Miss Rose," the boy replied. "I-I got scared."

"Scared? Scared of what?"

Aaron looked down, and Rose shifted her attention to Leah.

Although the woman's official title was lady's maid, she had taken over the position of governess for the time being. Leah had been in Rose's life for nearly ten years now, and Rose had come to rely on her as more than a maid. They had become great friends.

"What's this about?" Rose asked of the maid.

"He was certain you wished to give him away to a new family, Miss Rose. I tried to assure him that it simply wouldn't happen, but you know how children can be."

Rose nodded, her heart going out to the boy. Taking his hand in hers, she said, "Do you remember the story of how I found you?"

Aaron nodded. "You were on the Continent with Aunt Jean, and my parents couldn't feed me. It's why they gave me to you, and now I'm your word."

Rose could not help but laugh. "You're my *ward*, not word. But that does not matter. You just need to remember that I love you now as much as I did the first time I laid eyes on you." She blinked back tears as she stood. "Now, why would I wish to give you away? The very boy who healed my heart?"

"You wouldn't," Aaron replied, now wearing a wide smile. "Because when you love someone, you don't hurt them."

"That's right," she whispered, ruffling his hair once more. "You never hurt the ones you love. Now, go and play while I talk to Leah."

Much happier now, Aaron ran toward the woods with a great "whoop!"

Rose stood and watched him as he ran in circles around a tree. "He's the greatest gift I could ever want," she said with a sigh as Leah joined her. "I never thought God was merciful until Aaron came into my life."

"It's been an honor watching him grow," Leah said. "And to see you smile is wonderful."

"It truly is," Rose said, nodding.

The three were a family of sorts. An odd one, to be sure, but one Rose cherished, nonetheless. And Leah was right. Aaron did make her smile.

"How did your day go?" Leah asked. "Did you learn anything new?"

As Aaron continued dancing around the tree, Rose considered how to respond. "The baron consumes more liquor than all the patrons in a pub. Remember when I told you about Miss Constance Haskett?" Leah nodded. "Although she'll never know it, I saved her today." She explained what had transpired, finishing with Mr. Fletcher's talk with her. "I don't know, Leah. He's growing suspicious. Perhaps this was a daft idea. Even one of the other maids mentioned that my hands are far too smooth for a maid's."

"Cheer up, miss," Leah said. "It's gone well so far. You've got dirt smudged on your face, your apron needs washing, and your hair looks as if you left without brushing it." Rose raised an eyebrow, and Leah laughed. "I mean no harm, Miss Rose. All I'm saying is that no one'll know any better."

Rose sighed heavily. "You're right."

Aaron attempted to stand on his hands but fell over and landed on his back with a sharp "Oomph!" Rose took a step toward him, but his laughter made her stop. He was not hurt. Thank goodness.

"While Master Aaron napped earlier, I read your latest column."

"What did you think?" Rose asked, smoothing her apron. "Be honest."

"I think Lady Honor's setting the tone for the women of London," Leah replied with a wide grin. "It would take a blind man not to see that you were writing about His Lordship. The women'll keep away from him now."

There was one rule all gossip columnists adhered to. Never reveal the name of the person about whom she was writing. Otherwise the newspapers could be sued for slander. Or was it libel? Well, no editor wanted to be charged with either. The writer might use a person's title and include some description, but otherwise, they could be writing about anyone. Although the clues were so blatant, everyone knew who the subject was of any given article.

"I appreciate you saying so," Rose said, the usual uneasiness at receiving a compliment washing over her. "Do you truly believe so? Was it really that good?"

"Most definitely, miss," Leah replied. "Would I lie to you?"

After that fateful night six years ago when her heart was broken,

Rose questioned whether people were being honest with her at every turn. She could not help but wonder if all who complimented her had some hidden motive. Even Leah, who certainly did not deserve such harsh judgment. Her suspicions only made her feel guilty, but she had no way of stopping them.

Rose embraced her friend. They had spilled many tears on each other's shoulders over the years. "I'm sorry," she said. "I know you would never lie to me."

"There's no need to apologize to the likes of me, miss," Leah said. "But I must ask you something. Is all this worth it? I fear the old wounds will surface and you'll be hurt again. I'd hate to see that happen. You worked very hard on healing them before."

Rose smiled as she watched Aaron leap up in an attempt to touch the lowest branch of the tree, laughing all the while. These precious moments brought her such happiness. Leah was right, of course. But Rose's anger and hurt over the last month was fuel for her writing. And now she had a new piece she would write this very night.

"London will never learn that I'm Lady Honor," she said. "Nor will they know the pain I endure. What they will know is the exploits of the aristocracy, especially those of the Baron of Westlake and the Remington family."

"And what about the duke?" Leah asked. "Have you decided what you'll do about him?"

The sound of Aaron's laughter made her turn and watch as he held up what appeared to be some sort of insect.

"If he has committed his heart to a woman because he loves her, and he cares nothing about her position, then I wish them well. I'll not harm an innocent woman for the sake of gossip." She narrowed her eyes. The taste of revenge would be sweeter than any wine. "But make no mistake. By the time I leave Tinsley Estate, the name of Evan, Lord Westlake, will be ruined forever."

Chapter Two

The bedchamber was empty.

This fact made Evan's ire boil. He had betrayed his cousin Colin, Duke of Greystoke, all so Miss Constance and he could become better acquainted. Colin had confided in Evan that he had fallen in love with a woman well below his station—a factory worker, in fact!

Upon learning this embarrassing detail, Evan had informed Colin's mother in exchange for an introduction to Miss Constance. The red-haired beauty was a marvel, a finely-crafted young women who would be a fine addition to his list of conquests. After a week of wooing her with sweet words and feather-light touches, she would become like warm butter—soft and malleable.

He had spent the past days imagining himself twirling a curl of her lovely locks around his finger as he lay in bed beside her. There would be doubt, of course. Most women had it, but he knew just the right words to have her falling into his arms. Nothing would stop him. Nothing ever stopped him.

Except a shattered glass.

That half-wit of a maid had interrupted at the most inopportune moment, creating just enough distraction to give Miss Constance time to reconsider. An entire fortnight of careful planning, of patience and restraint on his part, all brought to ruin in a matter of seconds

This morning, a week later, Evan had stared at the rumpled bedsheets one last time. Yes, he was angry about having no one beside him when he woke this morning, but his current annoyance had more to do with the letter Fletcher had delivered the previous evening just as Evan was putting away his ledgers for the day. A letter from Miss Constance. And her words were simple and clear.

I shall give you what you desire if you announce our engagement.

He had promptly shoved the letter into his desk drawer with the numerous others he had collected over the years. All came from other women with whom he had become acquainted. Most asked why he had ignored them. Some were second, third, and even fourth letters, many filled with angry words about broken hearts or other such nonsense.

Not once had Evan ever replied. Why should he? They had all served their purpose. Nothing more needed to be said. The women he conquered in his bed—or whichever room had been convenient at the time—were like a collection of sports trophies.

And he had many.

Out of all the letters he had received, however, the words of only a handful haunted him to this day. All written by one woman. She had been the only one to whom he had made any attempt to respond. Only, he never sent it.

Despite his drunken state that evening, he could recall the lovely red dress she wore. When he had caught sight of her from across the room, an odd sensation had come over him. A feeling he had never felt before and one he would readily experience again. She had glowed with such beauty that he had reconsidered everything he understood in life.

Yet he had ruined it.

The clock struck five, and so immersed in his thoughts was he, a clap on his shoulder made him start. He turned to face Archibald, Lord Caney. Two years Evan's elder, the viscount was a round man with large blue eyes and stringy blond hair on a prematurely balding pate.

"Are you still upset over Miss Haskett leaving so abruptly?" the viscount asked.

Evan scowled. "Hardly. She may be worthy of my bed, but overall, I found her a bore. If she had remained, I fear I would have been forced to endure her incessant chatter, which likely would have made me consider taking my own life. And don't forget. It was I who threw her out of the house."

Caney laughed as he walked over to lean against the unlit fireplace. "You should settle down and marry, old chap. Surely, you've proven your masculinity by now?"

Evan turned to glare at his friend. "What's that supposed to mean?"

The viscount pushed away from the fireplace. "Why would any man, let alone a baron, wish to conquer so many women if not for that reason? Tell me, did you perform poorly at a hunt when you were younger and your father humiliated you for it? Such losses can greatly affect a man's pride."

This coming from a man who was balding far too young! The man was an ignorant fool. What did he know of masculinity?

Yet it had not been a loss at a hunt that drove Evan's choices but rather any illusion to a married life. Or even love, for that matter. He had once believed love had to exist, for too many young couples experienced its pleasures.

Until he had gone for a weekend excursion to London with his father when he was fifteen years of age.

Waking in the dead of night, Evan had heard a strange cry of distress. Upon investigation, he found his father in bed with a prominent woman of the *ton*. He had been so angry! How could his father betray his mother in such an appalling manner?

When they had returned home, his father sat him down in the drawing room and explained what Evan had witnessed.

"It is your right as a Remington, a baron, and as a man to enjoy yourself with any woman you desire. When a woman gives herself to you, you are only affirming your good name." He shrugged. "That was all I was doing."

"But what about Mother? Does she know?"

"She suspects, I'm sure. Most women do. But we never speak of it. Her concerns have to do with maintaining the house and overseeing the staff, not minding a man's business. Even that of her husband. I am the master of our family, not your mother."

Confusion had washed over Evan. His father dared to justify his betrayal? But he had spoken to Evan as an equal for the first time in his life, and Evan savored it.

"Now, we'll keep this little secret between us," his father had said. Then, to Evan's shock, his father poured him a measure of brandy and handed him the glass. "You'll be a man soon enough. One day, you'll find a bride who will give you an heir. But never deny yourself the right to find pleasure with any woman you wish. If you choose to ignore your right, you'll become less a man."

"Less a man," Evan had whispered. "But am I not a man yet, Father?" He had been working extra hard on his studies. Not that his father took notice, of course.

"Not yet, but I suspect you'll be one soon enough." He clasped Evan on the shoulder. "When the day comes that you're able to prove your worth, I'll admire you as a man rather than seeing you as the boy you are now."

It was only three years later when Evan had fulfilled his father's wishes with a woman from a neighboring village. Then another. And then another. Sadly, his father died before he could congratulate him. But Evan had no doubt he was a man. And a great one, at that!

Or was he only deceiving himself?

He should have been elated by his many conquests, and in his way, he was. But with each woman he bedded, that feeling of accomplishment never came. Where was the joy his father had promised him?

Then again, his father had made no such promise.

Glaring at Caney, Evan steadied his voice and said, "I fail at nothing, and certainly not in any hunt. What? Do you think me odd for having greater aspirations than living the boring life you lead?"

Before the viscount could answer, the door opened, and Jasper, Baron Downwick, entered. Unlike Caney, Downwick was rail-thin and had a rather large nose much like a beak. The two were as thick as thieves, although no one would ever compare them to such lawbreakers. Where Evan used blackmail and coercion to get what he wanted, his friends never put a toe out of line when it came to matters of business. Or anything of importance, for that matter.

Evan had invited them to join in one of the dozens of enterprises he and his cousin Markus had developed over the years, including a boxing scheme in which they were involved. Both men had scoffed, going on about having far too much "honor and integrity" to entrench themselves in such interests.

Since then, Markus had refused to be in their company and went so far as to threaten the two men with a beating if they spoke a single word about what had been shared with them. The fact Markus was untitled made no difference to him. He was frightened of no one.

That did not mean Evan had to stop speaking to his friends, for friends they were. Even if they disagreed on how to conduct business.

"I'm sorry I'm late," Downwick said breathlessly. "The children were fussy, and Eliza needed my help."

Downwick's wife was a strong-minded woman who chose to raise their two children rather than hire a nanny. This did not make Evan dislike her. What did was the fact that she believed her opinion had value. A silly notion, that. But not as silly as the fact that Downwick often sought her counsel before making any decision. If he was not careful, his poor sons would grow to become soft men with such a reckless example of what a man should be.

"With the size of that nose," Evan said, laughing, "I'd think you need only tell them you'll eat them and they'll jump to do your bidding."

Downwick dropped his gaze and blushed as he often did when Evan mentioned his nose.

"Oh, cheer up," Evan scoffed. "Don't take offense. I'm only teasing. Here, let me pour you a drink."

"One day, Westlake, I'll have had enough of your taunting and shall never return," Downwick said, scowling. "You take your friends for granted, you know."

Evan rolled his eyes as he undid the stopper on one of the decanters. "You've been listening to your wife again, haven't you? Next, you'll be telling us about the wonders of needlework."

"If I'm to endure your constant ridicule," Downwick said, the corner of his mouth twitching as he pulled a piece of paper from his breast pocket, "perhaps I should return the same to you."

Caney sat up straighter. "What's this? Is our precious baron under scrutiny once again?"

"Indeed, he is," Downwick replied. "Eliza gave me this before I left the house. She swears the article speaks of you, Westlake."

Evan snatched the newspaper clipping from Downwick's hand as he placed the glass in the other. "I suggest you tell your wife that I've no interest in idle gossip. Besides, what does she know? The opinions of women are worth less than nothing. Especially those of the landed gentry. Is her father not a farmer?"

"Her father oversees a collection of lucrative farms," Downwick replied, puffing out his chest indignantly. "It's honorable work that pays quite well."

Evan laughed. "Then may your children be proud when you inherit his chickens on the day of his death. Now, whoever the man in this article is, I can assure you I am not he."

Downwick shook his head. "Perhaps you should read it before making such a bold statement."

"I agree," Caney said. "Read it first. I, for one, would like to hear this story."

Clearing his throat, Evan read the column aloud.

My Dear Readers,

It gives me great pleasure to share with you that a fanciful baron I shall not name has been rejected by a particular young lady from a family with a far better title than his. It appears he has lost his knack for plying ladies with fine French wines and entertaining them with fanciful words of struggling poets in order to woo them. Perhaps they have become wise to his ways, for I have learned that his once-busy bedchamber has remained empty for some time now.

As we witness the fall of a baron from one of the most prominent families in England, I shall join the other ladies in cheering his destruction. In the far future, gentlemen of honor will be remembered and the less reputable will not. I suspect he will become the Baron Time Forgot.

Lady Honor

31

Evan turned a glare on his friends. "Lady Honor?" he said with a snort. "I suspect she's no better than a prostitute." He forced back the rage as he slipped the newspaper clipping into his coat pocket. "The Baron Time Forgot? No one will ever forget me. I'm far too great." He took a large swallow of his brandy and slammed the glass on the arm of his chair.

Despite his objections, he did not doubt that the column spoke of him. Just as had the many others he had collected in the past few months. Who had betrayed him?

He glanced up at Caney and Downwick. Both were self-righteous men who disagreed with every action Evan took these days. He would not put it past them to do something this despicable in order to ruin his name.

They had once enjoyed a closeness that came from a long-lasting childhood friendship. When Evan began enjoying women like some enjoy fine cigars, however, his friends changed. In the past six months, his friends had gone from amiable allies to petty busybodies, always pointing out Evan's flaws and explaining how he should live his life.

"You should marry, Westlake," one would say.

"Don't you think it's about time you settled down?"

"You should really put these roguish ways behind you."

What began as chums giving friendly advice soon became pious dunderheads as judgmental as any vicar.

What fascinated Evan most was that no matter how much they chastised his actions—or how poorly he treated them—they remained his friends. Perhaps they needed him in some way for something far more sinister than simple friendship.

"You're leaving for the North by way of London in two days, are you not?" Evan asked with a sneer. "Perhaps you would like to stop by the newspaper office along the way and give them some more gossip to print in that rag!"

Caney threw his head back and laughed. "You think it was we who betrayed you? I can assure you we have better things to do than to entertain the gossip columns."

Downwick shook his head. "We've warned you that your ways

would get you into trouble. For God's sake, man. Stop what you're doing before your name is ruined. Find a reputable lady and settle down."

Downwick's life consisted of working and speaking of his wife in such high regard it nauseated Evan. What kind of man enjoyed spending time on a boring outing with a woman, lady or not? If the object was to woo her, so be it. But Downwick seemed to enjoy his wife's company even five years after he had married her!

"If I wish for advice from a simpleton," Evan snapped back, "I'll ask my butler. We're speaking of betrayal. Of me! Why would anyone do such a thing? Mark my words, I'll find the traitor and see his body twitching at the gallows. I'm a Remington, by God, and the Baron of Westlake! I'll not allow anything or anyone to destroy me."

And what he said was no lie. No one crossed a Remington and lived to tell about it, be he friend or family. Then again, some of his family had only brought it upon themselves. Look at Colin. He was a duke and yet he acted the dolt by marrying a peasant woman! That was the man who was to head the family in the years to come?

If Evan had his way, he would oust Colin and take his place. Colin was simply too weak for his own good. And far too soft to be a duke.

As the drinks flowed, so did the conversation, which had moved to safer topics. When the clock struck six, the anger Evan had put to rest returned when his friends announced their departure. They rarely remained for more than an hour, and he could not help but wonder if they would have preferred to stay away.

"We'll call again after we return next month," Downwick said. "Do take care, Westlake. Consider the words you use with others. You may find a day when those who have called on you will do so no longer."

"That wife of yours has you henpecked, and you've allowed it," Evan said with a laugh. "The woman bears you children and you act as if she were royalty."

To his surprise, Downwick snapped at him, "Eliza is better than royalty. She's been at my side, championing for me and has never wavered. How dare you speak of her so callously!"

Evan snorted. "You've become soft, Downwick. All over this

woman. No, that's not true. You've always been soft. She's just been able to mold you like clay."

For the first time, Downwick took a step forward, red-faced and his hands clenched at his sides. "I believe it's time for us to part ways, Westlake. You call me daft? Perhaps I am. After all, I've remained friends with you because I believed you would eventually see reason. I see I was mistaken, for now you've gone too far." He turned to Caney. "It would be best if I leave, for I may end up striking him, and I'm not a fighting man. I'll wait outside."

The door slammed in his wake.

"What did he mean about remaining my friend?" Evan asked. "Is he saying he's been charitable? Well, I need no charity!"

Caney sighed. "It's not charity we offer you but rather the bond of friendship we've shared since we were children. That's why we've remained for as long as we have." He placed a hand on Evan's shoulder. "He's right, you know. Your life will catch up to you. Do choose a better path or you may find yourself alone one day. Goodbye, my friend."

As the viscount exited the room, Evan shook his head. Had the world suddenly gone mad? When had Downwick grown a backbone? And how dare Caney try to convince Evan he was wrong!

With a sigh, he walked over and placed the newspaper clipping in a drawer with the others he had collected. They had worried him, but he refused to speak of them. Refuting what they said was as bad as admitting they were about him and would make him appear weak.

And no one dared say Evan Westlake was weak!

Pouring himself another brandy, he thought of Miss Constance. She should be in his bed not at home! Was Lady Honor's column correct? Had the ladies become wise to his ways? Surely not!

Slamming his palm on a nearby table, he thought about what had ruined his night with Miss Constance. A clumsy maid.

Clumsy, yes, but she was also quite attractive if he recalled. Though he was unsure. Who noticed the help? Plus, his mind had been too foggy after the many glasses of alcohol he had consumed that night.

He smiled. If she was decent enough to look at, perhaps he could satisfy his carnal cravings tonight. It would not be the first time he had lowered his standards. Polly Farnsworth, one of the many maids who had held a position at Tinsley Estate, had been very attractive. Attractive for a maid. He had bedded her at midnight and sent her packing by six the following morning with a ten-pound note in her hand. And he would do the same to this one. Maids were easy enough to come by.

He left the room and headed toward the main staircase, where he encountered Fletcher.

"My lord," the butler said with a deep bow, "dinner will be ready in ten minutes. Have you decided on a wine yet?"

"It can wait," Evan replied. "Have you found me a new valet yet? I'm tired of dressing myself." He had fired Floridson the previous day after Evan had caught him flirting with one of the chambermaids. He would not tolerate such behavior in his home. Not from the servants.

"My offer to act as valet still stands, my lord," Fletcher said.

Evan waved a dismissive hand. "No. You've enough to do around here as it is. I'll just continue to see to my needs until we find the right man."

"I'll place an advertisement in the newspaper tomorrow, my lord. It should only be a matter of days."

"Good. I'll be in the drawing room until dinner's ready. The maid who broke the glass. Is she still here?"

"She's finishing her chores and will be leaving for the night very soon."

Evan nodded. "Go find her. Have her meet me in the drawing room. I've matters to discuss with her."

The butler hesitated. "Begging your pardon, my lord, but perhaps you should eat first. You've consumed a great deal this evening and—"

Outraged, Evan took a menacing step forward. "What are you accusing me of, Fletcher? Are you saying I'm a drunk?"

"Not at all, my lord," Fletcher said, his eyes wide. "I only thought to mention that decisions made on an empty stomach are not always wise."

What was it with the world? It was as if everyone was betraying him! First some unknown woman in a gossip column, two men he had called friends for years, and now a butler making judgments about him!

"You forget yourself, Fletcher. You're a worm of a man and no better than that groveling buffoon, Downwick. You'll advise me on nothing, you hear? Now, get that girl for me or find a new position!"

Evan did not wait for the butler to respond before turning on his heel and storming into the drawing room. He made a mental note to write to his mother. Fletcher had been in the employ of the Westlake family far too long. So long that he was beginning to believe himself an equal. Well, Evan wanted nothing more to do with the man. If his mother did not wish to take on the oaf, he could live on the streets for all Evan cared.

"You asked for me, my lord?"

Evan turned to find the housemaid standing inside the doorway. His memory had been correct. She was a handsome woman. Dark hair, blue eyes, and more than a generous amount of bosom that the maid's uniform could not hide.

He suppressed a grin. He could have her out of that uniform in a matter of moments. Another conquest to prove himself a man.

"Close the door."

The maid nodded and did as he bade.

He crooked a finger at her. "Come here."

With her head lowered, she approached him, stopping within arm's length.

Evan inhaled her sweet fragrance, a clean smell of soap and roses. Where had a maid come by rose-scented soap? Placing a finger beneath her chin, he forced her to raise her head. Oh, she was indeed quite beautiful. In fact, she was captivating.

As he peered into her eyes, however, there was something familiar about her. As if he had known her before and always had.

It's the drink you fool! Focus on the task at hand!

"Do you recall breaking a glass last week?" he asked.

"Yes, my lord," the maid replied. "Mr. Fletcher already informed me that it would be taken out of my wages."

Removing his finger, Evan wet his lips. "I've instructed him not to do so, for it was nothing more than an innocent mistake. Am I correct in saying so?"

"You are kind, my lord."

"Indeed, I am. Which is why I would like to offer you what I know you desire."

Her eyes widened. "And what is that, my lord?"

"Me."

Without thought, he pulled her into his arms and pressed his lips to hers, and as expected, her body trembled against him. Her lips were soft, supple. "Do you wish to serve me? You will receive fine gifts if you say yes."

Such words would have most women in her position agreeing without hesitation. Yet she remained silent. Why?

Perhaps she was innocent, had never been with a man. Well, that only made it all the more alluring!

He kissed her neck. "Tell me you desire me," he whispered.

Chapter Three

Rose had been certain she was summoned to be reprimanded over the broken glass. How fatuous could a woman be in one lifetime? The baron pressed his body to hers, and his lips danced down her neck. Unwanted reactions tore through her body, and she found herself wanting to give into her desire.

But his whispered words pushed that desire away.

"Tell me you desire me."

Oh, how she wished to tell him that all she desired was to see him ruined. To have all of London—no all of England!—speak his name in ridicule. Yet she found herself in the same predicament she had six years earlier. Alone with him.

But the naive girl she had been back then was now gone. She had believed his words of love. His lies. Now stood a woman hardened by the choice she had made that fateful night.

As his kisses continued across her face, Rose stood there uncertain what to do. Any rejection of his advances would make him angry and send her packing. Yet she could not give him what he desired. Not again.

"Don't you realize I'm a baron?" he asked, his voice husky in her ear. "What I'm offering you is a privilege few in your position get to enjoy." He ran a finger down her arm. "You should deem yourself fortunate to have caught my eye."

Placing her hands on his muscled chest, she gently pushed him away. "My lord, surely there are women who are far more worthy?

I'm just a mere housemaid."

"There are, but I'm not one to indulge myself with just anyone." He placed the back of his hand against her cheek, and Rose had to fight the anger that welled inside her. "But before me stands a desirable woman, one who wants much in a man. May I tell you a secret?"

Rose nodded, fighting down the words of rebuke that filled her throat.

"I have admired you for some time now. One may call what I feel for you love. Do you wish for me to love you?"

An imagine of a girl whose confidence had always been low came to mind. Of a girl who dreamed every night to hear those very words. When all hope had been lost, a magical night occurred and she had heard this very same offer. She had given her heart—no, her very soul!—that night just so she could feel loved.

Instead of being cherished, however, she had been used and discarded.

"I wish to go home," she said through clenched teeth. The anger was so great that Rose could not hold it back any longer. "Not to serve your carnal desires, not here or in any other room in this house!"

She turned to leave, but he caught her by the wrist. "No woman rejects me, especially a servant. Do you think yourself better than me?"

It was as if the last six years came flooding into her mind. Letters sent but never answered. Many nights of weeping. A year on the Continent to try and heal her heart. And somehow she had emerged a stronger woman.

Her eyes met his, and she knew her time at Tinsley Estate had come to an end. Too bad she would be unable to finish what she started.

"I don't *think* I'm better than you, my lord," she said with a small smile. "It's a fact I know quite well. You see, I have decency and dignity, both of which I'm certain you'll never have."

Gone was the amused smile, and in its place was an angry scowl. "Fletcher!" he bellowed, his face scarlet with rage. "Fletcher!"

The door opened, and the butler entered the room. "My lord?"

Rose's heart pounded in her chest. What would he do?

"See this woman leaves and never returns!" the baron shouted. "I swear, everything is falling apart around me! Not even the servants know their place!"

"Is this how you treat your servants, *my lord?*" Rose growled, unable to keep the mocking from her tone. "Those who reject your advances are cast out to the streets?"

Lord Westlake ignored her, which only added fuel to her rage. Tears of frustration filled her eyes as she debated what to do next. She had not completed her task!

"Come with me," Mr. Fletcher said in a quiet tone as he gently took her arm. "It's time for you to leave."

With a nod, Rose left the drawing room and made her way to the kitchen. Mrs. Moore, the tall, graying cook, was plating the baron's dinner and did not look up from her work.

Rose heaved a sigh as she threw her cloak over her shoulders.

"Sadie," Mr. Fletcher said, "may I have a word before you go?"

"If you mean to reprimand me for refusing his advances, then, no, you may not." She had not meant to speak so harshly, but she could not stop herself.

Once outside, she stopped to allow the sun to dry the tears that stained her cheeks. The mid-summer sky was a vivid blue. Bees buzzed and birds sang. All was happy around her.

Rose, however, cursed herself inwardly. She could have made any number of excuses to keep Lord Westlake at bay, but she could do nothing to quell the anger inside her. Now, after all these years of planning, her chance for revenge had disappeared.

"I'm sorry for what transpired," Mr. Fletcher said as he came to stand behind her. "Truly, I am."

Rose turned to face the butler. "The fault is not yours," she said.

"No, I suppose not. But for what it's worth, he was not always this way."

"I would beg to differ, Mr. Fletcher," Rose said with a derisive laugh. "He has always been this way."

The butler tilted his head. "You do know him somehow," he mused. "I can see that now."

Rose tried to keep a stern face, but a single tear rolled down her cheek.

Mr. Fletcher produced a handkerchief and handed it to her.

"Thank you," she said, dabbing at her eye. "What you suspect is true. I knew him many years ago. It's the reason I accepted this position. I had hoped to find a way to see him suffer for what he did." She handed him the handkerchief. "I suppose you'll now go and alert him."

Sighing, the butler replaced the handkerchief in his pocket. "No, not this time. For too long I've turned a blind eye to his ways. Oh, I've tried to warn the women who have worked here. Some heeded my advice and found employment elsewhere after rejecting him. One, sadly, believed his promises and found herself without work anyway."

Rose looked away. This very man had tried to warn her six years ago, but she had ignored him.

"I'll not reveal to him your reasons for joining our staff. After all, I know very little. You've no idea how often I've considered speaking my mind and telling him that I disapprove of the man he's become."

Rose gave a sad nod. "Thank you for helping me, Mr. Fletcher. I suppose I should go now." She looked up at the large estate and sighed. "I had thought the day my leaving here would be in triumph, not defeat."

She turned to leave, but Mr. Fletcher placed a hand on her arm. "I do hope you're able to put him behind you. Best of luck to you, Sadie."

Thanking him, Rose turned and headed out the gate that led to the main road. With each step, her heart ached. Her only chance to destroy Lord Westlake had slipped away. Now, she had no choice but to return to London resigned to writing using second-hand knowledge.

At the end of the drive, she turned and faced Tinsley estate for the final time. How could a woman's heart be broken twice within the confines of the same house? And in the very same room, for that matter? Fate had reared its ugly head once more.

Accepting defeat, Rose made her way home.

Chapter Four

Mr. Nash Fletcher had first arrived at Tinsley estate at the age of ten in the summer of 1753. Having worked his way from stable hand to footman and eventually to butler, he had proudly held the position to the present.

At least for now.

When the former Lord Westlake passed away seven years earlier, Nash had given great consideration in leaving his position to enjoy a quiet retirement in a cottage all his own. He had saved a good sum of money over the years to do just that. His old bones were aching, and his sight was weakening. What better way to spend his final years? And to reward himself for his many years of service?

Yet it was Lady Westlake who asked him to remain.

"I would like someone to watch over my son," she had said. "Someone who knows him well. He can be so much more if he has the right guidance."

Never had Nash felt more pride than he had in that one request, and he swore on his good name that he would do just that.

And in his one and sixty years on this earth, never had he made such a foolish decision. The new Lord Westlake disgusted him. The way he spoke to his friends and the cruel blackmail schemes he used to extort his own family were bad enough, but the way he treated women as if they were mere objects rather than human beings made Nash's stomach churn. His Lordship saw them as nothing more than ornaments to decorate his bedchambers, often to be left discarded the following day.

When His Lordship asked for Sadie the night before, Nash had done his best to dissuade the young baron but, sadly, to no avail. Who Sadie Crawford truly was, Nash was still uncertain, but she was free from the house—and the lustful eye of Lord Westlake. She was safe.

"Tomorrow, you'll put out word that I'm looking for a new housemaid," Lord Westlake shouted from the landing at the top of the stairs, as if doing so would bring new applicants running to heed his call. "This time, you'll not hire one who is so… so, rebellious!"

It had been a day since Sadie left, and Lord Westlake had spent that time drinking and wandering around the house, just as he did most days when he had no meetings. After waking with the sun, he had replaced breakfast with another decanter of brandy. If there was a word to describe a man who was beyond drunk, Nash would have used it to explain his master's current bearing.

"And make sure she's not ugly." Lord Westlake said. "The last thing I need is ugly women in my presence." He shook his head. "If any know how to read, get rid of them, too. There are standards to maintain in this world, and servants who learn to read tend to think themselves better than themselves and spend their time pining over my books." He waved a hand in the general direction of the library, the brandy in his glass sloshing over the rim.

His Lordship's rant came as no surprise to Nash. He tended to act thus since taking his place in the barony. On these nights, Nash wished he had declined the baroness's request, but he had not. He had made a promise and intended to keep it.

Somehow.

"Yes, my lord," Nash replied. "Will there be anything else?"

Lord Westlake wobbled over to the top step of the main staircase, which descended into the middle of the foyer. On either side was a corridor that led to the main common rooms of the house. An expansive library, the study, and the drawing room were to the right. To the left were the parlor, the dining room, and the ballroom.

Last decorated by the current Lady Westlake several years earlier, Nash had always thought the entryway elegant with its white and gold marble floor and dark-oak woodwork. Tonight, however, it held no appeal as His Lordship threw back his head and downed the remainder of his drink.

"There are men who mean to destroy me, Fletcher," he said, his words slurred. "Someone's been spying on me and reporting his findings to those rags in London. Lady Honor or some nonsense. Regardless, the details are far too specific to be coincidence. I mean to learn who it is."

Although Nash typically dismissed these moments of madness his master displayed, a thought came to mind. Did Sadie not say that she wished to leave Tinsley Estate in triumph? At the time, he had not considered her words, but now...

He did not doubt she had lied about her past, although he had pushed his concerns aside. Her hands did not tell of a life of servitude, and to have a child from a family of her supposed station receive lessons from a tutor was unheard of. Even if her mother paid for those lessons with services of her own, few tutors worth their salt would make such agreements.

Could she be this Lady Honor mentioned in the newspapers? he wondered in horror. But, no. Lady Honor had to be someone else. The column had been in print far longer than Sadie's employment at Tinsley Estate.

"It's not you, is it?"

"I?" Nash asked. "Am I who?"

"Are you the spy?" His Lordship demanded.

Nash straightened his back and gave His Lordship a look of indignation. "No, my lord. I would never do anything so callous as to share intimate information about this house."

"Do you know who, then?" Lord Westlake asked.

Instinctively, Nash went to speak his suspicions but then bit his tongue. Sadie was now gone and would likely never return. There was no need to create more trouble than what had already taken place. The woman had suffered enough.

And although he felt as if he were betraying the baroness and her wishes that he watch over her son, Nash replied, "No, my lord."

Lord Westlake sighed heavily. "Then you'll dedicate your time to interviewing every servant in this house. I'll not be mocked and made to look a halfwit like my mother! Did you know she's *still* in correspondence with Mead? They have even been seen in public together!"

Nash had to force his hands out of the fists they had formed of their own accord. It would not do any good to strike his employer. No matter how much he desired to do so. "No, my lord. How would I have such knowledge?"

The truth was, he was well aware of the matter. Lady Westlake had found a friend in Lord Mead, a baron and fellow widower. From what he understood, the two enjoyed such a close friendship that marriage was likely. And Nash wished her well. Her Ladyship was a good soul and deserved a man who cared for her and treated her well. Especially in her final years of life.

Lord Westlake wobbled and caught hold of the top of the banister. "Tomorrow, I'll send word that she should cancel her yearly visit here. I don't want that trollop in my house!"

Rage erupted in Nash. There was no nobler, no kinder woman than Lady Westlake. How dare this…this *scoundrel* speak so disrespectfully of her! Every speck of good judgment, of rationality, left him and he could do nothing to silence his betraying tongue.

"Whyever not?" Nash demanded. "Your mother is a lady with an unblemished character. If she is happy, you should allow her to remain so."

The baron narrowed his eyes, and Nash knew he had crossed a line a butler should never cross.

"Because she's an embarrassment to me, that's why! She's a widow who should be mourning the loss of her husband, not a girl approaching her first Season!" He raised the glass to his lips and then cursed when he realized it was empty. "And don't ever question me again. Not regarding my mother or in any other instance. If she wishes to parade herself about as a hussy with this man, so be it. But it will not happen under my roof!"

Taking a step forward, Nash glowered at the young baron. "Never speak of your mother in such a disparaging manner again, or we shall have words!"

Lord Westlake glowered at Nash. "I warned you about speaking out of turn, Fletcher," he said, his voice resounding through the dome roof of the foyer. "Now you've destined yourself to sleeping on the streets beginning this very night! No man—and certainly not a servant—speaks to me as you have." He teetered on his feet before grasping the banister once more. "Now, be gone, you old fool, before I throw you out myself!"

Nash had dedicated his life to the Westlake family, making sure every need was met. Yet, that time had sadly come to an end. He would honor His Lordship's request, but not before having a final say. It was the right thing to do.

"A man who speaks ill of his mother as you have this night is no man at all. You, my lord, are a self-entitled brat with no more sense than a spoilt child. I wish to look back on my years here with great fondness. But to accomplish that, I must forget you. I assure you, the task will be most pleasurable."

"Forget me?" Lord Westlake bellowed. He pulled back his arm, and Nash ducked just as the empty glass flew over his head and shattered on the wall behind him. "No one will ever forget my name! Do you hear me? No one will forget the name of Lord Westlake!"

The baron took a step back but missed the top step of the staircase.

Without thought, or perhaps out of habit, Nash reached out a hand. "My lord! Please, be careful!"

With his arms flailing, Lord Westlake let out a strangled cry and tumbled backward, rolled head over heels down the stairs, and landed in a heap on the foyer floor.

"My lord!" Nash cried as he hurried down the stairs and squatted beside His Lordship. "My lord?"

Lord Westlake lay with his head slightly askew and his eyes closed. Had he survived such a terrible fall?

Trembling, Nash placed a hand on the baron's chest and heaved a sigh of relief when he felt a heartbeat.

There was the sound of hurried footsteps followed by a gasp, and Nash looked up to find Tilly gaping at them.

"I-I heard shouting," she said, her eyes wide. "Is…is he dead?"

"No, but I'm afraid he's hurt pretty badly. Find Richard and have him go for Doctor Norman. Then fetch David. Tell him to meet me here."

Tilly stared transfixed on the fallen lord and made no sign that she heard Nash speak.

"Now, Tilly!"

As if waking, the girl nodded and hurried away.

Nash looked down at Lord Westlake. What he had wanted was for His Lordship to learn a lesson, not to come to harm. And although he had been dismissed only moments before, and had been angry at his employer, he refused to leave until the man woke. A butler's honor could not be compromised by leaving an injured man alone.

"What happened?" David, the estate's gardener, asked as he entered the room. "Did he fall? He's not dead, is he?" The young man removed his cap to reveal a head of dark hair. He placed it against his heart, gaping as much as Tilly had.

"He did fall," Nash said. "But he still lives. Here, help me carry him upstairs to his bedchambers."

David had large arm muscles, which came in handy for working a hoe or shoveling great amounts of dirt. And for taking on the brunt of His Lordship's weight as they carried him up the stairs.

At the top, Nash took a moment to catch his breath.

"I can take him from here if you'd like," David said, eying Nash with concern.

Nash shook his head. "No, I'll help. He's my responsibility."

They entered the bedchamber, a masculine sanctuary with dark walls and heavy oak furniture. Brown curtains hung from the four posters of the bed, and a dark-brown rug lay in the middle of the floor.

Nash pulled back the blankets, and they placed His Lordship on the bed.

"Do you think he'll wake up?" David asked as they stared down at the sleeping lord. "Me mum told me she heard of a woman who fell asleep and never woke again. She's supposed to be sleeping still to this day, waiting for some man to return or something."

Nash shook his head. "This is no children's story, David. People cannot sleep forever only to wake when someone returns."

"Me cousin, he hit his head and didn't wake for four days."

Having no time for nonsense, Nash dismissed the gardener and made his way downstairs. After cleaning up the broken glass, he waited in a chair in the foyer for the doctor to arrive.

As the minutes ticked by, Nash hoped Lord Westlake would awaken. He may have been angry with his young master, but he certainly had not wished to see him injured in anyway.

A knock on the door made him start, and Nash opened the door to Doctor Norman. A man in his late forties with mousy-gray hair and a matching mustache, he clutched a leather bag.

"Oh, doctor, thank you for coming," Nash said, moving aside to allow the man to enter. "His Lordship is in his bed."

Doctor Norman frowned. "I was told he had a nasty fall here in the foyer. The young man who came for me—Richard, I believe?"

"Yes. He's one of the footmen."

The doctor's frown deepened. "Well, he said that Lord Westlake was frightened after seeing a ghost. What is that all about?"

Nash sighed. Why did the simplest of tasks have to become elaborate stories? "I'm afraid he fell down the stairs. A drunken fall, if you will."

"I see," the doctor replied, glancing at the staircase. "And he's been asleep since?"

"For nearly two hours," Nash replied.

A loud cry from upstairs had both men hurrying up to the baron's bedchamber.

Lord Westlake was sitting up in bed, his face as white as the sheets beneath him. "Where am I?" he asked, fear coating his voice. "Who are you? Who am I?" He touched the back of his head. "And why does my head hurt?"

How drunk had he been to have forgotten his own name? Nash wondered.

Doctor Norman sat on the edge of the bed and opened his bag. "Your name is Evan, Lord Westlake."

The baron frowned. "Evan? Lord Westlake?"

"Do you not remember?"

Lord Westlake shook his head, groaned, and touched the back of his head once more.

"Do you remember nothing of your life?" the doctor asked. "Even the smallest memory can be of help."

For a moment, the baron knitted his brow in deep contemplation but finally replied, "Nothing. I remember nothing."

The doctor stood, had the baron turn this way and that and wiggle his toes.

When Doctor Norman touched Lord Westlake's head, the baron pulled back and shouted, "Ouch! That hurts, you fool!"

"My apologies, my lord, but I must see how badly you're injured."

The baron gave a grudging grunt and allowed the doctor to exam him.

"You've not answered my question," Lord Westlake snapped.

"You've had a terrible fall, my lord. I'm afraid you'll have a sore head for several days, but that seems to be the extent of your injuries, thank goodness."

Lord Westlake gaped at the doctor. "Am I truly a lord?"

"You are a baron," Doctor Norman replied without pausing with his examination. "Can you tell me the name of your parents?"

The baron's eyes went wide. "Oh, yes! My mother, her name is…" He paused and then his shoulders slumped. "I don't recall."

"Do you have a brother?"

"Yes! No, wait. I don't know."

Nash could only watch in shock as the doctor asked question after question and His Lordship replied with the same answer.

"I don't know."

After Doctor Norman completed his examination and had given Lord Westlake a dose of a brownish liquid that smelled like seaweed, Nash helped the baron lie back against his pillows and pulled the blanket up to his chin.

"Do you think I'll be well by morning?" Lord Westlake asked, a note of worry in his tone.

Rather than answering, the doctor patted the baron on the hand and said, "What you need to concern yourself with is getting plenty of rest." And, with that, he gathered his leather bag and signaled for Nash to follow him to the corridor.

"Can a man consume so much alcohol that he cannot remember his name? Or his life?" Nash asked as he pulled the door closed behind him. "I've never seen such a thing!"

Doctor Norman shook his head. "Lord Westlake has a condition known as amnesia. I'm not a betting man, but it would be safe to wager it came when he hit his head during his fall. Such a blow can cause a memory lapse."

"Good God," Nash breathed. "And when will his memory return do you think?"

The doctor sighed. "There's no telling when it will return or what he'll recall when it does. A colleague of mine at Oxford published a study on this condition several years ago. From his research, there are those with similar injuries to the head who have lapses in their memory lasting only a day and in others a month or more. There is also the chance he never recovers it."

"What will he do?" Nash asked, aghast. "Is there anything I can do, or the rest of the staff, to help him recover his memory?"

"I would advise teaching him as you would a child. I don't mean that you should treat him as a child. He likely will remember how to do everyday activities, such as walking or reading, for they are habits that have been formed rather than moments he must remember. The best advice I can give is to take each day and concentrate on one aspect of his life and teach them to him as if they are lessons given to a student. But I warn you, you must go slowly and carefully. You don't want him overwhelmed."

"These reminders of his life," Nash said, "these 'lessons' as you call them, will they help him remember who he truly is?"

"Perhaps, but again, I can make no promises. What little I know about the ailment says that no single treatment produces the same results in two different patients."

A thought came to Nash's mind. He had hoped to teach His Lordship a lesson. Was this an answer to that silent prayer?

"If His Lordship needs training, are you meaning in aspects of his role as a baron? Would you recommend I begin with something as simple as common courtesy and the way he presents himself to others? Or would that be far too childlike?"

"If that is what it takes, by all means begin there. You'll know if what you've chosen is too simplistic. If it is, adjust your instruction as needed. I realize you are no tutor, Mr. Fletcher, but I'm sure your skills in training those you oversee will be beneficial. Furthermore, beginning with the easiest tasks may be enough to help him return to the gentleman he was taught to be."

Nash was no doctor, nor a man of science, but he understood the meaning behind Doctor Norman's words. Lord Westlake could be trained just like an obedient dog. Perhaps it was best if he remained after all. Then he could honor the promise he had made to Lady Westlake.

"Does he have anyone who can help him besides you?" the doctor asked. "Perhaps a young lady in his life? Oftentimes it is those closest to him who are the most helpful in situations such as these."

Nash could not help but smile. "I believe there is." The cogs in his mind turned as he led the doctor to the front door. "I'll inform her at once."

"Very good. It will do His Lordship good to have someone he trusts close at hand. I'll check in tomorrow, and depending on his condition, once a week from thereon. If anything changes before then, send word to me immediately." The doctor stepped out onto the portico. "I'll write to my colleague to ask if he has any recommendations, as well."

"Thank you, doctor," Nash said. He closed the door and leaned against it. If His Lordship needed retraining, Nash knew just the right person for the job.

Hurrying to the kitchen, he found Tilly and Mrs. Moore gossiping with a young chambermaid of thirteen by the name of Elsie.

"I'm tellin' ya," Tilly was saying, "he looked dead to me. His face were all white, and you could see spirits 'round him."

Elsie's blue eyes nearly covered her face. "Spirits?" she gasped. "Real spirits?"

"Enough, Tilly," Mrs. Moore said, elbowing her. "You're frightening the poor girl."

Nash cleared his throat. "Tilly, a word, please."

Elsie and Mrs. Moore hurried away, leaving Nash and Tilly alone.

"I plan to be away for a few hours," Nash said. "If by chance anyone calls, tell them that His Lordship is not in residence. Can you do that?"

Tilly paled. "You want me to lie, Mr. Fletcher?" she asked. "You said we ain't s'pose to lie. Ever."

Closing his eyes, Nash said a silent prayer. For patience. "In this instance, you must lie. It's to protect His Lordship."

"All right. If you say so. Can I go look at 'im? You know, to see what it looks like after he's come back to life?"

"No, you may not," Nash snapped. "His Lordship needs rest, not some silly maid staring at him. Now, you are not to repeat anything you've seen or heard. Is that clear? No gossiping, no telling tales. Nothing at all. Do you understand?"

"Not even to Elsie?" Tilly asked.

"No one."

Tilly sighed and dropped her gaze. "All right. I won't say nothing."

"Good." Nash walked to the servants' entrance, donned his hat and coat, and walked outside. The bright sun promised hope as he considered his plan. He had given Lady Westlake his word that he would look after her son. Now he had a chance to make him a better man, to make him into the man he was meant to be. And Nash would not pass up such a gift.

And, for the first time in many years, Nash Fletcher whistled a happy tune as he walked as fast as he could in search of the one person with the intelligence and understanding to help him see his plan fulfilled.

Chapter Five

The best gossip came from a variety of sources since Miss Rose Follet began writing under her *nom de plume* of Lady Honor. The letters that arrived via the editor were helpful, as were the invitations to parties, where the gossip flowed faster than the wine-coated lips that spilled it.

Yet all that paled in comparison to the opportunity she had lost. What she had ruined by allowing her anger to take the reins.

"Don't be down, miss," Leah said as she poured Rose a cup of tea. "You were able to accomplish far more than either of us expected." She laughed. "To think you played the role of a housemaid right under his nose, and not once did he recognize you!"

Rose slipped a hand beneath the table and ran it across her now-flat stomach. "That's true. He didn't remember me at all. No, he was like every other man in the world. He only noticed the woman I've become."

How different her life had become since that night all those years ago. Men gazed at her, their intentions written in their eyes. Other women vied to add her to their circle of friends, but Rose always refused. Despite the admiring looks and the invites to tea, Rose's life had a gaping hole. A missing piece she could not name.

In two days, she and Leah would leave the tiny cottage and return to her London home. Yet Rose wished she could remain here. She wanted it more than anything. The desire to complete her mission was too strong to dismiss so soon.

Staring into her cup, Rose whispered, "If I had been able to control my anger when he kissed me, I would not be returning home. Perhaps I should have allowed him to do so." She looked up at Leah. "I'll never love again, and I've no plans to marry. What harm would come of it if anyone learned that I had?"

"Now you're speaking like a silly goose, miss," Leah replied. "You're just as beautiful as you are smart. There's a good man out there for you. We just have to find him." She reached for the teapot and refilled their cups. "You must stop blaming yourself for the actions of others, miss. Especially *his*."

How easy it was for Leah to say such things. It had been Rose, not she, who had made a decidedly poor decision. And she had paid the price for it ever since.

Rose brought to mind one particular day six years earlier. Her father had gone out to meet with some business colleagues, leaving Rose and her mother alone. Rose had requested to speak to her mother in the sitting room. Although it had been the most painful thing she had ever done, she confessed what had occurred at the party.

Her mother had been disappointed, which was to be expected. Yet, to Rose's surprise, her mother had held her and assured her that all would be well as they both wept. It was her mother's love that had helped her through her pain.

She never told her father, although she had planned to do so as soon as she returned from her trip to the Continent with her Aunt Jean.

Yet tragedy had struck her life again.

When she arrived home, with Aaron in tow, Rose learned of her parent's fate. A horrible carriage accident during a storm had claimed both their lives at once. Despite the fact Rose had been far away when it happened, she knew it was her fault. If she had never trusted Lord Westlake, she would have been home instead of off dealing with her broken heart like a child.

But she could not take the entire blame on herself. Lord Westlake was to blame as much as she. That realization had helped fuel her desire to see him suffer.

"Now, who could that be?" Leah asked as she stood from her seat.

Rose had been so immersed in her thoughts that she had not heard the knock at the front door.

She followed the maid to the front door, and gasped when she found Mr. Fletcher standing in front of it.

"My apologies for calling so late and uninvited, Sadie," the butler said as he removed his hat and bent his head toward her. "But I would like a moment of your time if I may."

Rose nearly groaned. Had she made a mistake revealing to this man that she wished to see Lord Westlake suffer? He would not cause her physical harm, she was certain. But would he threaten her in some way? After all, he was fiercely devoted to his employer.

"I'm afraid that I'm busy at the moment," Rose replied. "I plan to return to London to seek work there, so I must pack. I've no time for idle chat."

She went to close the door, but he said, "To report to The Morning Post about your time at Tinsley Estate?"

Rose stared at him, dumbfounded. How did he know?

Mr. Fletcher chuckled. "I've come to understand that a spy has been living amongst us, one who has been reporting His Lordship's affairs to the newspaper. I've deduced that the spy is you."

"I've heard of servants gossiping about what they overhear while seeing to their duties, Mr. Fletcher. But hasn't the newspaper been printing these stories much longer than I was employed at Tinsley Estate? How can the spy possibly be me?"

"Well, that is true," the butler said, frowning. Then he shook his head as if clearing it. "To be honest, I had thought the same but wanted to inquire, nonetheless. But what does it matter anyway? I'm here to discuss what Lord Westlake wished to do last evening and what we can do to repair it."

"Excuse me?" Rose asked with a scowl. How did one "repair" outright debauchery? "The man is a scoundrel. Men such as he will never change. Furthermore, I've been dismissed, and I would not return if he got on his knees and begged." Well, that was not the complete truth. If he begged, she *might* consider it. But Lord Westlake was not the begging type. "I'll not concede to his ways, Mr. Fletcher."

She went to close the door again, but he reached out and placed the palm of his hand on it to stop her. "If you wish to exact revenge on him, I know a way."

"And what makes you believe that I wish to exact revenge on him?"

"Are you denying that fact?" the butler asked.

Rose worried her bottom lip before sighing. "No, I suppose I'm not."

"Then I suggest you hear me out."

She turned to Leah. "What do you think?"

Leah shrugged. "Can't hurt to hear what he has to say. If it were me, I'd say give him a listen and then decide."

What the maid said was true. What harm could come from listening to what this man had to say? She could allow him time to share his plan, and if what he said was not agreeable, she would decline and return to London. But if what he did have to say was appealing…

"Very well, Mr. Fletcher. Please, come in."

The butler smiled. "Thank you."

Rose led him to the kitchen, where she offered him a seat at the table. "This is my sister, Leah," Rose said as way of introduction. She certainly could not introduce her as her lady's maid! What would he think of her then?

"Ah, then this is your cottage," Mr. Fletcher said, smiling at Leah. "It's a pleasure."

They had rehearsed the story a hundred times before taking temporary residence at the cottage. Rose was a stickler for detail, especially given her need for anonymity. One wrong step, and she would end up with a foot in a bog of trouble.

"My husband passed away last year," Leah explained, shaking her head sadly. "His uncle lets me stay here without paying rent. But I didn't want to be alone, so I asked Sadie to come live with me. But enough of that talk. Let me get the kettle started."

"There's no need," Mr. Fletcher said. "I won't be staying long."

Rose took a seat and motioned to one of the chairs across from her. "Please, sit, Mr. Fletcher, and say what you wish to say."

"Thank you." He sat and cleared his throat. "For fifty years, I've been employed at Tinsley Estate. I've enjoyed my employment there, but not always. I've either seen or learned of the various nefarious deeds in which the Remington family engages, and I must admit that much of it bothers me. What His Lordship has done to the female staff—and various guests, as well—has troubled me greatly. I could place the blame on the women, of course, but with his promises of expensive jewelry, I can understand how one could be easily tempted."

Or promises of love, Rose thought cynically.

"For far too long," the butler continued, "I've turned a blind eye. After all, what right do I have as a mere butler to challenge the man who pays my wages? Regardless, I've long wished to teach His Lordship a lesson. Tonight, a means to do so has presented itself."

Now Rose was intrigued. "I'm listening. Go on."

Mr. Fletcher shifted in his seat and took a deep breath before speaking. "His Lordship took a nasty fall today and did not wake for several hours."

Rose could not stop her brows from rising in shock but then scolded herself for allowing a tendril of remorse to enter her mind. Leah outright gasped.

"And this helps you how?" Rose asked.

"Well," Mr. Fletcher said, clearing his throat again, "as it is, when he awoke, it seems he has lost his memory."

"He's lost his memory," Rose repeated flatly. "As in—"

The butler nodded. "He does not recall a single thing about is life."

"Do you mean of his recent life or...?"

"From what he had for dinner yesterday to his mother's name, all has been erased from his memory."

A thousand questions entered her mind, but none she could voice. Not yet. "Go on."

"Doctor Norman says His Lordship got the amnesia from hitting his head during his fall and that it is up to us, those who know him, to help him regain his memory. He will remember everyday activities, such as how to eat or how to walk, but when it comes to who he is and who he knows, that is where he has no recollection."

Rose sat back in her chair and stared at the butler in disbelief. "And how long does the doctor believe this malady will last?"

Mr. Fletcher sighed. "It's impossible for him to say exactly. He says it could last a week, a year, or possibly forever. But what I'm thinking is that we can use his malady to help him in a different way. We can use it to teach him a lesson. Or rather, many lessons."

"What do you mean?" Rose asked, unable to keep the suspicion from her tone. Would the butler betray his employer? She was not so naive to believe he would. Not any longer. It would be far too easy for him to turn on her and out her for who she was, and she could not have that happen.

"It's quite simple, really," Mr. Fletcher replied. "We'll have His Lordship believing he was something he was not." He leaned forward. "We can take a cruel, twisted man and turn him into a gentleman. Change how he sees his staff and those who would usually be beneath his notice. Honor will replace blackmail. Laughter will replace anger. Through this…training, for lack of a better word, he'll become a better man."

What this man offered was nothing short of madness. Yet, it was also brilliant!

"And if I agree to this plan, how much influence do you believe a simple housemaid could have over a baron? Even he will understand that someone of his station only speaks to his servants to give them commands."

Mr. Fletcher laughed outright. "No, no. Tomorrow, you'll return not as a housemaid but rather in the role of the young lady in whom he has had an interest for the past year. Come now, we both know that no housemaid speaks as you do, nor does she have your smooth hands." He had a mischievous glint to his eyes. "So, what is your real name, Miss…?"

"Follet," Rose whispered, ignoring Leah's warning glare. "Miss Rose Follet. My father was of the landed gentry."

"Just as I thought," Mr. Fletcher said with a chuckle. "You may be a mystery, but I knew you were no servant. But don't fret. I'll ask no more about your past. So? What do you think of my proposal? Will you agree to help me turn His Lordship into the gentleman he is meant to be?"

The temptation to agree was strong, but she could not appear too eager. "So, I'm to arrive tomorrow as a lady in whom he has a romantic interest? One he'll believe he can trust? It seems too simple."

Mr. Fletcher grinned. "But it is simple, Miss Follet. Granted, I've not thought through the exact details as of yet, as I've only conceived the idea an hour ago. But I'm sure we can work out the finer details as we go."

Oh, but it was a tempting offer! But how would agreeing satisfy her need for revenge? It seemed more an act of charity, and Lord Westlake was not worthy of such treatment.

Her thoughts must have shown on her features, for the butler stood, clutching his hat in his hands. "Miss Follet, allow me to give you a piece of advice, if I may. Those who seek revenge are often guided by hate or anger. Oftentimes both. What you may find is, although you may one day accomplish what you wish, in the end, you may become what you sought to destroy. If your motives are to hurt him in some way, then I'll bid you a good day. But if you're willing to aid me in this endeavor, then let us work together to turn him into a better man and pray he never remembers his past. That can be your revenge. Take something bad and make it good. That is the triumph you need."

Rose frowned. How was it that he knew that revenge was her motive? And could she truly exact revenge by changing her adversary? The pain in her heart and the anger that filled her soul had strengthened her. And both would do so from this day forward. Neither would destroy her. Not after what she had endured. Of that she was certain.

Revealing this truth, however, would make Rose lose the wondrous opportunity that had been placed in her lap. Therefore, she lied.

"Tomorrow, Miss Rose Follet, along with her ward, Aaron, and her lady's maid, Leah, will arrive at Tinsley Estate at ten in the morning," she replied. "We'll stay in the cottage at the back of the property—decorum must be maintained, after all. And together, we'll begin to work on Lord Westlake. Each day, he'll learn more about who he was—a gentleman who we hold in high regard."

"Most excellent!" Mr. Fletcher said with a wide grin. "I believe this will be the best decision you have ever made. That any of us has ever made."

"Oh, I'm certain it will be," Rose replied.

She escorted Mr. Fletcher to the door. "And what about the other servants?" she asked. "Surely they will tell him the truth?"

The butler laughed. "You're not the only woman he's tried to woo, Miss Follet. And the male servants don't care for him much either.

Sadly, I don't think even his own family really does. I'll speak to the others tomorrow, but I'm sure they'll all agree to play along. They'd prefer a more pleasant master as much as any of us."

Rose smiled. "Then I'll see you tomorrow, Mr. Fletcher."

"Wonderful!" He bowed. "We can speak later about the particulars."

Leah came to stand beside Rose as the butler walked away. "Do you think it's possible?" the maid asked. "Do you think anyone can change a man who has no memory? I've never heard of such a thing, but I have to be honest. I'm surprised you want to help him."

Rose closed the door and snorted. "Help Lord Westlake?" she asked with a laugh. "I've no plan to do that at all."

Leah frowned. "I'm confused. Did you not just tell Mr. Fletcher that you'd play the doting love interest?"

"Oh, have no doubt," Rose said as she returned to her place at the kitchen table. "To any onlookers, I'll be the committed young lady willing to do all she can to help the man for whom she cares. But while I do so, I'll also learn more about his family, who I'm certain will call on him. I'll no longer have to listen at keyholes, worrying every moment that I'll be caught eavesdropping. Now I'll be able to listen freely. By the end, Lord Westlake will be such a grand gentleman, no one will be able to recognize him. And I'll make him fall deeply in love with me."

"Love?" Leah asked with a gasp. "Miss Rose, I'm still confused. Why would you want him to fall in love with you? I thought you hated him for what he did."

Clenching her fists in her skirts, Rose thought of the sleepless nights she spent weeping, the letters that went unanswered, the time she spent slowly starving herself to become a different person. Anger consumed her as much today as it did yesterday.

"Trust me, I still despise him," she said, jutting out her chin. "But after I've finished with him, he'll understand how it feels to give his heart to someone, to make him believe that he has created a perfect world. Then, I'll destroy not only his name, but also the illusion he created. Just as he did to me."

Chapter Six

Evan, Lord Westlake. That had been the name he was told when he awoke with a splitting headache and no memories whatsoever of who he was or his life before waking.

Now, as he slowly opened his eyes, Evan—he had to remind himself that his name was Evan—recalled what little he could of the previous day. A doctor had examined him and gave him a bitter brown liquid, assuring him it would help. There had also been an older man standing behind the doctor, but he could not recall the man's name.

Sitting up in bed, Evan glanced around the fine room. Two ornate wardrobes stood along one wall. On another sat a dressing mirror encased in silver and a chest of drawers made of what appeared to be highly polished oak. He lay on fine sheets and was covered in well-made blankets.

He had been told he was a baron, which explained the wealth that surrounded him. Yes, it felt right.

Seeing movement, Evan turned to find the nameless man from the previous day enter the room. "Good morning, my lord," he said, giving Evan a friendly, and oddly familiar, smile. "It's very good to see you awake."

"Thank you," Evan replied. "I'm sorry, but what is your name again?"

"Nash Fletcher, my lord. I'm the butler. I've served in this house for so long that I knew your grandfather. Then I worked for your father, and now you. I've always been here in some capacity."

Hope filled Evan. This man knew his family and would, therefore, help him remember his life. "And where is my father? Or my mother?"

"Your father has been dead for several years, my lord," the butler explained.

Well, of course, you daft fool, Evan thought. *You would not be the baron if he was still alive.*

"Your mother lives in Rochester and is in good health. She's due to come for a visit next month. Would you like me to ask her to come sooner, my lord?"

"Tell me about her, please," Evan said. "And about me. Is this my house? Am I married? Do I have children?"

The butler smiled. "How about this, my lord? I'll have a breakfast tray sent up and then answer whatever questions I can while you eat."

"Thank you," Evan replied. "I am hungry."

It was not long before a tray laden with a silver dome and a teapot arrived. When Evan removed the silver dome, he could not help but stare wide-eyed at the amount of food there was. Eggs, kippers, buttered bread, and fruit filled the plate. Even as the butler poured the tea, Evan was scooping eggs into his mouth as if he had not eaten in days.

"So, Fletcher, how did I come to lose my memory?" Evan asked after washing down the food with a gulp of tea. "Were you there when it happened?"

"Indeed I was, my lord. You were very excited about a new charity you are sponsoring. So happy, in fact, that you missed a step on the stairs as you told me about it."

Evan frowned. "A charity?" he asked. "I work with charities?" The idea seemed foreign to him, but so did everything he currently understood about himself.

"Quite a few," Fletcher replied. "You've contributed funds and your time to a vast array of services for those in need. You're well known for being a fine gentleman with a very giving heart."

This made Evan smile. At least he was a good person.

He went to take another bite of his food but stopped. Why was the butler staring at him in such a familiar fashion? He may have forgotten many things, but men of his station don't consort on such friendly terms with his staff!

"Why are you just standing there?" Evan asked. "Do you suddenly believe that you can take advantage of me because I've lost my memory?"

The butler stood up straighter. "My apologies, my lord, but we often spend our mornings with me listening to your stories while you eat and asking for my advice. But if you would prefer to be alone…"

He made to turn to leave, but Evan forestalled him. "Wait! Please, stay. After all, if it's customary…" If he wished to regain his memory, he would need Fletcher's help. Making the older man uncomfortable would help neither of them. If he was a baron who always considered his butler a confidant, he would continue to do so now. "I'll be calling on your good graces to help me in the coming days as I try to regain my memory. Therefore, I ask that you carry on as you usually do. Perhaps the familiarity of our routines will be helpful."

"Excellent, my lord," the butler replied with a bow.

Evan returned to his food. "Now, about my parents and family. Tell me everything you can recall."

For some time, Evan listened as Fletcher spoke of the Remingtons, who were apparently the most powerful family in all of England. Yes, power seemed right.

"And you have a countless number of cousins, aunts, and uncles, my lord," Fletcher said. "Including His Grace, the Duke of Greystoke. You know him as Cousin Colin."

"A duke, huh?" Evan said, impressed. He tried to conjure an image of the man, but nothing came to mind. "No, I can't recall him. Pity that. I imagine he has quite a bit of influence being he's a duke."

"Oh, indeed he does, my lord. He's a very worthy gentleman, as are all the Remingtons. I'm sure he and others will come to see you when they learn about your condition."

Evan stabbed a kipper with his fork. "Hopefully not too soon. I'd like to remember at least a few things before taking on visitors." Stifling a yawn, he moved on to a strawberry. "And my mother?"

"She is the epitome of what it means to be a lady, my lord. I dare say no more, for I wish you to be surprised when she arrives in a fortnight. It would be far better to allow your memories to return naturally. And I've no doubt, once you set eyes on her, you'll remember her well."

"That's a very good idea," Evan replied. "That will give me two weeks alone to become better situated with my surroundings. Perhaps it would be best if you refuse anyone who wishes to see me until she arrives."

Fletcher shook his head. "But, my lord, did you forget...?" He placed a gloved hand on his cheek. "My apologies, my lord. I've already forgotten your condition. Of course, you would not remember, but you have a guest arriving today. This very morning, in fact."

"Who?"

"The young lady you've been courting, my lord."

None of this felt familiar. "And her name?"

"Miss Rose Follet."

Evan rubbed his temples in a failed attempt to stir even one memory of this mysterious woman. "Rose Follet," he whispered. "I can't seem to recall her. Please, tell me about her."

Fletcher dropped his gaze. "I'm not certain if I should, my lord. I don't wish to embarrass you in any way."

Frustration cramped Evan's shoulders. "Fletcher, you said we are close, like friends, and that I've sought your wise counsel in the past."

The butler nodded. "Yes, my lord."

"If that's true, it seems to me that nothing you say can embarrass me." He shifted the pillow behind his back. "I need you to always be truthful with me, even if you believe what you have to say may embarrass me. Otherwise I'll not retrieve my memories. Now, out with it." By the time he finished, he was forcing down anger as harshly as he had forced down his breakfast. He had no patience for incompetent staff!

He paused. Now, *that* felt truthful.

"Well, although you have been calling on Miss Follet no more than a few months, never have I seen a gentleman so happy. Each day, your smile brightens the very corridors through which you walk. That is how highly you regard the young lady."

Evan raised his brows in surprise. "So, I care for her that much, do I? But how can I care for someone I don't truly know?"

"Oh, but you've turned to Miss Follet for advice on a number of matters, my lord. Whenever you've had an important decision to make, be it in business or otherwise, her counsel has served you well."

The fork plinked on the plate as it fell from his hand. "Are you certain that I would ask a *woman* about such matters? What sort of man would do such a thing?"

He might not remember anything about this woman, but of everything he had been told thus far, this point seemed the least likely. His food felt like stone in his stomach. Evan was not a weak man, of that he was sure, but he could not stop the doubt from forming in the back of his mind.

For a moment, Evan eyed the butler. Could the man be lying to him?

Yet, why would he? What would a servant gain by lying to his employer about the woman in whom he had an interest?

"Only a man of great wisdom, my lord," Fletcher replied. "I have every confidence that Miss Follet will be of great help to you over the next weeks, for she is very intelligent. But I must offer one more piece of advice if I may."

"Go on," Evan replied. "As I said before, you are free to speak openly with me."

"Trust her, my lord," the butler said. "There is no better friend than she. You'll remember soon enough why you placed your trust in her and why you've asked her to court."

Evan considered the man's words. So, this Miss Follet was his love interest. And they were courting? That meant they would likely marry. Before he could go down this path, he had to ask one last question. The very thing that mattered most in life.

"Is she beautiful?"

When Fletcher nodded, Evan could not help but grin. It only made sense that he would be attracted to this woman's beauty. If felt right.

Then a strange urge came over him, one as foreign as any of his thoughts since he woke the previous day. Desire. But surely he would not be so forward with a woman, would he?

"And do I make her happy, Fletcher?"

"Oh, yes, my lord," the butler replied. "You make her very happy indeed."

Suddenly, the prospect of remembering his life did not seem so daunting. She was coming here. Did that mean she stayed in the house? Had she visited him in his bed?

Then he noticed a pile of clothes in the corner. "Fletcher, why are my clothes on the floor? Do I not have a valet?" Did not all barons have a valet? He could not remember.

"You did, my lord, but you gave him the sack. He was being…inappropriate with several of the maids."

"Then we must find another soon," Evan replied.

"Begging your pardon, my lord, but perhaps you should wait."

Evan frowned. "Why? I should have someone to help me dress."

"Well, your condition, my lord. You don't wish for others to learn that you've lost your memory, do you? I'm certain we can trust the current staff, but I cannot say the same for anyone else."

"Good point," Evan said, stifling another yawn. "We can put off finding a new valet, but for now, I'm tired and wish to rest."

"Very good, my lord." Fletcher retrieved the tray and left the room.

Evan snuggled into his pillow, closed his eyes, and thought back to the arrival of Doctor Norman. When Evan had asked when his memory would return, the doctor had not replied. Could it be that he would never remember his life?

At least he had a loyal butler and a woman who cared for him. Both would serve him well, he was sure. It would be interesting to meet her today and hopefully take another step toward remembering who he was.

A sudden gasp made Evan start. Had he fallen asleep? He sat up in bed and turned to find the most beautiful woman he had ever seen standing in the doorway. Her hair was the color of polished oak, her face perfectly sculpted with high cheekbones and a slender nose. Her rich-blue muslin dress accentuated her feminine form quite well. He had a sudden primal urge fill him, and he had to grip the covers to keep himself from throwing her on the bed and having his way with her.

"Oh, my lord!" she cried as she approached the bed. "You poor, poor thing. Mr. Fletcher told me you took a nasty fall and can't remember a thing. Is this true?" Her gray-blue eyes glistened with unshed tears. She truly did care for him!

And here you are acting like a cad with your indecent thoughts! he scolded himself inwardly.

Before Evan could respond, she leaned over and kissed his cheek. Another primal sensation coursed through him as he inhaled her sweet fragrance of the flower after which she had been named.

"Miss Rose?" he asked, and she nodded. "So, what Fletcher told me is true? I'm sorry, but I don't remember you. But don't fret. I don't really remember Fletcher, either."

She sat on the edge of the bed and placed a gloved hand over his. Her closeness caused his heart to race. Oh, but the woman was beautiful. All he could think about was kissing her.

"Don't worry, my love. I'll do everything I can to help you recover. I'll be staying in the guest cottage until that day comes." Her smile made his throat go dry.

"I told Fletcher that I'll be relying on the two of you in the days ahead. I'm pleased you decided to remain here to help me." He raised her hand to his lips and kissed above her knuckles. "Tell me, Miss Rose. How is it that I'm so fortunate to have met such a lovely woman?"

She giggled. "Oh, darling, we both know it's not proper for me to remain here in your bedchambers alone. I made an exception because you're ill, but I really should leave before we are caught together unchaperoned."

She went to stand but he refused to release her hand. "Wait! Don't worry. No one will know. Fletcher explained that I've shown great interest in you. Is that true?"

A blush crept into her cheeks. "Yes."

"And you share this interest?"

She smiled. "I cannot lie. I cannot recall a day since we first met that

I have not thought of you."

What was it about those words that made doubt cloud his mind? There was something in her smile that seemed...forced.

Evan, you numskull, she's here to help you and you doubt her intentions? Stop thinking such nonsense! Plus, will you throw this beauty out into the streets? Not hardly.

"Before you leave," he said, still holding her hand, "tell me how we met."

She glanced at the door. Was it his imagination, or was she making an escape of some sort?

Then, to his relief, she settled back onto the edge of the bed. "I'll tell you this one story but no more. At least until you've gotten some rest. Your memories really should return naturally."

As Miss Rose began, Evan found concentrating difficult. He knew nothing about this woman, but that did not matter. She would help him in his recovery, and in return, he would allow himself to indulge himself with her.

Yes, *that* felt right.

Chapter Seven

The baron had the most pitiful expression on his face. He was so desperate to learn anything about his life, and for a brief moment, Rose had felt pity for him.

Drat it all, Rose! He deserves no mercy!

What Lord Westlake deserved was to suffer for all the hurt he caused so many. That had been her one and only reason for accepting Mr. Fletcher's invitation. She had no time for anything else.

Sitting on the edge of the bed, she stared at the wall. "Six years ago, you hosted a party, a farewell to your mother, who was moving away to live in her own estate. It was there that we first met, but it was not until recently that we began seeing one another. Over these past months, we've grown quite close, as you've said."

That thought made her want to stand up and break into mocking laughter. Close, indeed!

"And what do you find humorous?" she asked when he began to chuckle.

"Fletcher shared a funny story with me. He said that I often go to you to seek your advice—both personal and in business."

Rose held her breath. He might not recall much, but he had not lost his ability to test people. And she had no reason to believe that testing her was something other than his intention now.

"Oh, that was no joke, my love." She pushed out her bottom lip. "I'm shocked you would consider any part of our relationship humorous. Perhaps it's I who you think is a joke."

Lord Westlake sat up straighter. "No, please. I'm sorry. Of course I don't see you in such a terrible light. After all, how can I not confide in someone as lovely as you."

Well, it appeared his roguish ways had not disappeared either! He had the same sparkle of mischief in his eyes she had seen before. His playful smile, his sweet words, all of it made her thankful she did not retch on him.

"I suppose," he said, yawing widely. "I suppose there's much we should discuss, but not now. But thank you for being here with me. I truly do appreciate it."

He raised her hand to his lips once more, and she swallowed back bile. How pathetic he was! At least she was wearing gloves. The thought of his lips touching her skin made her cringe.

"Perhaps I should get out of bed," he said, smiling.

Pulling her hand away, she stood. "Yes, I imagine you would like to explore the house. I'll leave and allow you a moment of privacy to dress."

"Miss Rose," he said, and she stopped at the door. "Will you join me?" He laughed. "Not to dress but in my exploration of the house?" His words were an invitation, but the tone was a command.

Reminding herself to keep her temper in check, she offered him the sweetest smile she could muster. "Of course, my lord. I'll meet you in the foyer."

Without waiting for his response, she stepped out into the corridor and closed the door behind her. Oh, but he was an odious man!

When she arrived in the foyer, Rose found Mr. Fletcher pacing.

"Well? How did he receive you? What did you tell him?"

"I said that we met six years ago, which was true, and that we only began seeing one another in a more romantic situation in the past few months. I informed him that I would remain to help him recover, and he was delighted."

A smile crossed Mr. Fletcher's face. "This is good. Very good, indeed. If everything goes according to plan, even if he recalls his former life, it will not matter in the least. For a new man will stand in his place."

"I agree, Mr. Fletcher," Rose lied, for her idea of a good outcome was far different than his. "Are the rest of the staff in on the charade."

"All the inside staff are, yes. The others won't matter, as they've never met you. I have to admit, Tilly thinks it a wonderful idea."

Rose smiled. She would make certain Tilly was rewarded for all she endured in the past.

"And did your young ward and lady's maid settle into the cottage?" Mr. Fletcher asked.

Rose nodded. "Aaron will dine with me tonight here. Do you mind sending a tray over to Leah?"

"Don't you think that a bit bold, Miss Rose? Will Lord Westlake not think it strange that your lady's maid eats the same as you?"

"Lord Westlake thinks nothing that we don't tell him. If we wish to make him a better man than he was, you must trust me to do what must be done."

Mr. Fletcher seemed to be working out some sort of dilemma in his head.

"If you believe simply telling him he was a good man, one who gave to numerous charities and such, if you believe that is all that is needed, what am I doing here? We must show him that charity begins at home if we are to be successful. If we can't convince him of something as insignificant as a lady's maid eating the same as any guest, of what *can* we convince him?"

The butler gave a small nod. "I suppose you're right."

Rose glanced up at the empty landing at the top of the stairs. "Would you please go check on Aaron and Leah? I'm to wait here for His Lordship."

With a nod, Mr. Fletcher left her alone.

Rose drew in a deep sigh. What was she doing here? Her charade was well worth the information she would gather, but the baron's lustful gazes made her wary. She had believed that his lack of memory would be like dealing with a blank piece of parchment, yet his roguish ways seemed to have remained.

Just her luck.

Growing impatient, Rose made her way to the grand ballroom. As she entered the room, memories washed into her mind. She could almost hear the orchestra playing. There, across the room, stood her mother, gossiping with her friends. Her father had gone off to play cards with his.

Along the far wall stood a girl in a red dress, hiding away from everyone else. Her heart ached for that girl. She was ashamed of her size and the lack of any positive attention.

This brought to mind another memory of another party. She had overheard two young men whispering that she belonged in Astley's Circus. Their hateful words had been like a fist gripping her heart. The remainder of the night had been spent hiding behind a bush in the gardens, weeping and wondering how anyone could be so hurtful. Did they not understand that their words caused damage to her soul that lasted for years?

If she could comfort that girl today, she would. And she would hold her and tell her that she would be all right.

But, sadly, that girl no longer existed.

"There you are!"

Rose turned with a start as Lord Westlake entered the ballroom.

He frowned at her. "I thought we were to meet in the foyer."

Her anger rose to match his tone. "It's clear that I'm here and not there." Then she paused. She could not lose control, not before she even began! "Forgive me for speaking so harshly. I'm just tired from the long journey, and I've been terribly worried about you."

"Say no more," he said with a dismissive wave of his hand. "I believe we may all be at our wits end, and no thanks to me." He laughed and then looked over the room. "This is a very impressive room, isn't it? It's too bad I don't recall anything about it."

"You will in time," Rose said, forcing a smile on her lips. "Shall we go and explore?"

"Yes, but first I must tell you something. Although I don't recall anything about my life, I'm already certain I'll come to care for you as I once did. You are undoubtedly a beautiful woman, and I can see you're also highly intelligent. You must be if I seek your advice as often as Fletcher says I do." He offered her his arm. "What great fortune that we met and you're now here to lend me your aid."

His words sounded so sincere, Rose nearly found herself taken in by them. But common sense prevailed. This was Lord Westlake.

"Shall we begin in the study?" she asked, taking his arm with great reluctance.

The study was a significantly masculine room with a polished desk, a small bookcase holding his ledgers, and two high back chairs. Lord Westlake walked over and perused the bookshelf.

"It appears I'm quite the businessman," he said as he returned a ledger after flipping through its pages.

Rose would find time to explore the extent of his trade. Such information would likely give her a good bit of gossip for her column.

"This desk seems familiar," he said as he ran a hand over its top. He pulled on one of the drawers and frowned. "It's locked. Do you happen to know where the key is?"

"I'm afraid not," she replied honestly.

Lord Westlake pursed his lips. "I must reiterate that I find the fact that I consulted you on matters of business odd."

Rose smiled at his uncertainty. Not only was he unsure what to believe, but it also gave her the perfect excuse to be in the room later without him. "You always trusted my judgment, my lord." She sighed and trailed her fingers across the desktop. "I spent many long hours poring over your entries, looking for mistakes. We've laughed so often because you always wanted to remain in the library while I worked. You feared what I would find."

Rather than smile, the baron frowned. "Again, I find it highly unusual."

"I don't see why," Rose countered. "After all, you've never been one for numbers."

"You've made that clear twice now," he snapped. "Why did I not hire someone from an accounting firm? Why entrust such things to you?"

Drawing in a deep breath, Rose replied, "It's a very long story. If you wish to spend two hours so I can explain it all, I shall. Or you can simply understand that men sought to harm you, financially, of course, and I offered my services. I've always been terribly clever when it comes to sums, you see, and you trusted me above all others. If you prefer that I no longer see to that task, I'll agree." She walked over and trailed a finger down his chest. "But I'll miss our laughs together alone in the library after I completed my work."

She could see the hesitation in his eyes. This was proving to be harder than she first thought. He should have been docile by now.

To her relief, he heaved a sigh. "You must understand. I'm finding all this quite frustrating. But if that is who I am, so be it. Of course, I'll continue to trust you with the ledgers."

The game Rose was playing was a delicate one. She needed to remain in control at all times but allow Lord Westlake to believe that the choices he was making were his own. Otherwise, he would become suspicious.

Once again, she allowed her fingers to slide over his broad chest. "My lord, I fear you wish to do things your way." She pushed out her bottom lip. Playing the simpering ninny was not in her nature. "If you don't wish me to help you, then simply tell me. After all, you're a man and I'm a woman. What would you want of me?"

The corner of his mouth turned upward, and he moved to stand in front of her. "You're so beautiful, Miss Rose," he said.

She batted her eyelashes at him and his grin widened.

"If you wish to look over my work, then do so." He placed the back of his hand on her cheek. "Carry on as you always have."

When a woman needed a simple-minded man to bend to her will, she needed to only play the right game. "So you admit that you need me?" she asked, running a playful finger down his arm. "Just like you did before?"

For a brief moment, a flicker of pain crossed his eyes. "I need you now more than ever."

The desperation in his voice made her smile. "Oh, you most certainly do," she replied.

"I think more than you understand."

His voice clearly relayed his intention, and Rose had to put a stop to it. He moved to take hold of her waist, but she took a quick step to the side. She was not so oblivious to her situation that she would fail to notice he wanted to kiss her. Delaying any form of intimacy took priority.

"Come, my lord," she said with forced elation. "There is so much more to explore."

For the following hour, they went to every room, and much to her relief, Lord Westlake recalled nothing. With each room they explored, he appeared all the more frustrated.

Finally, they entered the ill-fated drawing room. The room Rose detested most.

Lord Westlake frowned in thought as he ran a hand along the back of the couch. "This seems familiar. I must have spent a great deal of time on it." He turned toward her. "Do you think it holds any significance?"

Rose smoothed her dress. "It's just a couch, my lord, and nothing more."

The sound of footsteps made them turn, and Mr. Fletcher entered the room. "My lord, Miss Follet, dinner is served. Your guest is waiting for you."

Lord Westlake's brows knitted in irritation. "Guest? What guest? I specifically said I was to have no callers but you."

Rose gave him a small laugh. "Perhaps you'll remember when you see him. Come and see."

When they reached the foyer, Leah stood beside Aaron, who was gawking at the room. With her chestnut hair and simple beige dress, Leah was quite pretty. And Aaron looked adorable in his little suit.

"Miss Rose!" Aaron said, running over and wrapping his arms around her waist. "I'm hungry. Can we eat now, or do we have to wait?"

Rose laughed and adjusted the collar on his coat. "We'll wat in just a few minutes." She turned to Lord Westlake. "This is my ward, Aaron, and Leah, my lady's maid."

"It's wonderful to see you again, my lord," Leah said with a curtsy. "And I'm so pleased to see you up and about."

"Hi, Lord Westlake," Aaron said, putting out a hand for the baron to shake. "I don't remember you."

Rose laughed. "Oh, children. They can say the silliest things."

Lord Westlake ignored Aaron's hand. "It's nice to see you again." He did not sound as pleased as his words might have conveyed. "Or rather…that is…well, to be honest, I don't remember either of you." He glanced at Aaron. "At least we have that in common."

Rose placed her hands on Aaron's shoulders. "Come. Let's go to dinner. Leah, we'll speak later."

When they reached the dining room, Evan drew in closer and whispered, "I don't remember the boy. Is he well-behaved?"

Far more than you were, she thought wryly. "Oh, he's a delight. You'll see."

As Rose took her seat, she gave Mr. Fletcher a sly wink. The table could seat ten, and the dark wood was polished to a high sheen to the point that one could see her reflection. A candelabra sat at one end of the table where three places had been set. This would be the first formal dinner Rose was to enjoy in well over a month.

Lord Westlake raised his glass of wine. "I would like to propose a toast. To my lovely Miss Rose, who has come to my aid. My gratitude to you can never be put into words."

Rose responded by lifting her glass and taking a sip. The wine was tart but pleasing to her tongue. This first dinner would be a stepping stone to those that followed, so she had to tread carefully.

"Is Lord Westlake my friend?" Aaron asked in what was meant to be a whisper but was much louder.

Before Rose could respond, the baron said, "I believe we are. After all, I do like children."

A sudden bolt of worry tore through Rose. The last thing she needed was to have Aaron developing a relationship with this man. The idea of having him join them for dinner had seemed wise, but now she realized she had put the boy in harm's way.

"Friend is a very strong word," Rose said. "As you said before, my lord. You don't have time for children."

Lord Westlake frowned. "What a cruel thing to say. Well, it's about time I put that way behind me. What do you say, young Aaron? Shall we be friends?"

Rose's stomach clenched when Aaron voiced his approval. She would need to make sure the two were kept apart as much as possible. Otherwise, it would be a disaster.

Mr. Fletcher and Richard the footman returned and began serving the first course, giving her a moment of reprieve.

As luck would have it, they ate their soup in silence. Rose could feel the awkwardness roll off Lord Westlake in waves. Any attempt at conversation fell flat. He played with his spoon more than Aaron did. It was clear he was uncomfortable.

Good. Let the man suffer!

"What shall we do tomorrow?" the baron asked as their bowls were taken away. "Should we go into the village? Perhaps there are people there I may recall."

Rose placed a hand on his arm. Going into the village meant encountering people who *would* recognize him. It was far too early to take such a risk.

"Oh, my lord, the last thing you need is to overwhelm yourself by leaving the house. I think it would be best if you begin with reacquainting yourself with your surroundings here, and once you're comfortable, we can go into the village. Would you not agree, Mr. Fletcher?"

The butler bowed. "I think you are very wise, Miss Follet. There is no reason for His Lordship to overburden himself."

Lord Westlake sighed. "You're correct, both of you. I must focus on this house first and my duties within it. The problem is, I've no idea what those duties are! Where do I begin?"

"I suggest you just rest, my lord. I've already sent word of your accident to the estate manager." When doubt crossed his features, she leaned in close and lowered her voice. "I believe your energy should be saved for more *important* matters."

This made Lord Westlake rub his chin. "Very well. I'll spend the day in leisure."

As dinner continued, Rose studied the baron. He was clearly lost, and for a moment, she had a twinge of sadness for him. What he was enduring would terrify the strongest of people.

Yet she was not here to pity him. She meant to exact her revenge. It would be a slow process, but it would be well worth the trouble when he finally crumbled.

"Why are you not eating more?" Lord Westlake asked when she pushed her plate away. "You hardly touched your food."

"I prefer smaller portions," she said, instinctively drawing in her stomach. "Is that unusual?"

The baron smirked, and her ire grew. "I suppose not. But still, you should eat more."

He and Aaron resumed their eating, and Rose forced calm into her breathing. Eat more? Did he not see that she craved the food set before her? That she had not enjoyed a true meal in years? And he was the reason for it!

"Is everything well, Miss Rose?" Lord Westlake asked, breaking her from her thoughts.

Gripping her fork so tightly she thought it would snap, she forced the smile back onto her lips. "It's wonderful, my lord. I doubt I have ever been better."

Chapter Eight

As Evan walked the halls of the grand estate, he hoped for the slightest, the most minute glimmer of a single memory to come to mind. Yet as the last three days had proven, he recalled nothing. He had taken it upon himself to touch every object in sight in hopes of any recollection, but still, no memories came to mind.

After the tour of the house with Miss Rose, Fletcher had assembled all the staff to make introductions. Yet Evan had recalled none of them.

Making his way to the kitchen, he found Mrs. Moore wiping off one of the counters. She was quite tall and had a dome of graying hair pulled back into a tight bun at the back of her head. Whistling a tune Evan did not recognize, she turned and gasped, dropping the rag she had been using.

"My lord," she said with a quick curtsy. "You startled me. Was there something served at dinner tonight you didn't like? I'd been wanting to try a new recipe I got from my sister for the veal, but if you didn't like it, I won't make it again, I swear!" Her voice was shaking. Strange, that.

"Forgive me for intruding, Mrs. Moore," he replied and then paused. No man apologized to any woman let alone a servant. He was not sure how he knew that, but it seemed right. Yet he wanted to confirm a suspicion. "As to your dinner, it was just as perfect as every other dinner you've served."

The cook beamed. "I'm pleased, my lord." She gave him an expectant look before asking, "Er...is there something you wanted, my lord?"

"I'm doing what I can to recall anything about my life, but nothing seems to be helping." He touched the counter and shook his head. "I don't suppose I spent much time here."

Mrs. Moore's smile was sympathetic. "No, my lord. Have you tried the parlor? Or maybe the drawing room?"

A younger maid—Tilly? Yes, her name was Tilly—entered the room, came to an abrupt stop, and dropped into a curtsy. "If the wine sauce was off, milord, I made it, not Mrs. Moore. I'll do better next time, I promise."

Evan frowned. "You—both of you—act as if I spend a great deal of time complaining about your cooking."

The cook began to nod, but Tilly said, "Oh, no, milord. You don't complain 'bout nothing. You used to come down to thank us all the time. Ain't that right, Mrs. Moore?"

"Oh, yes," Mrs. Moore replied, her apron twisted around her fingers so tightly the tips were white. "You're always gracious, my lord. Your compliments always make us feel better." She gave a fervent look at the maid. "Isn't that right, Tilly?"

What a strange and peculiar pair! Did Mrs. Moore not just say that he rarely came downstairs? Had he caught them in a contradiction?

No, of course not. They were simply nervous. After all, he was the baron and they his servants. Were not all servants a bit disconcerted around their betters? Yes, that was it. Evan was being nothing more than a suspicious goose.

"Well, I'll continue to come down and thank you," Evan said, smiling at the two women. "Good evening to you, Mrs. Moore. Tilly."

As he walked away, he did not miss the quick glance the women gave each other. They were whispering before he reached the staircase that led to the main floor.

When he returned to the foyer, he heard a faint noise and stopped in the open doorway of the study. Miss Rose sat at his desk, a ledger opened in front of her, and a quill flicking in her hand as she made an entry. A warm glow emitted from her, far brighter than any chandelier he had ever encountered.

Not that he remembered any other than those that hung in his house...

He shook his head. One day, he would recall every one of them. At the moment, all he wanted to do was gaze upon the stunning beauty before him. How lucky he was to have claimed such a lady!

Then a thought came to him. He had yet to kiss her since she arrived. Surely, they had shared in such intimacies given their current relationship? Well, he would right that wrong this evening!

"Oh!" Miss Rose said with a gasp. "Why are you still up, my lord? I thought you had retired early. You really do need your rest, you know."

Evan leaned against the door jamb, crossing his arms over his chest. "I decided to explore the house in hopes of recalling something."

"And did you?" Miss Rose asked as she returned the ledger to the bookcase.

"No, but it led me here to you." He smiled. "Therefore, in the end, it was well worth the loss of sleep."

Miss Rose gave him a small smile and returned to the chair behind the desk but said nothing.

"And how are my accounts looking?" he asked.

"Quite good," she replied as she folded a spare piece of parchment that was lying on the desktop. "You're very wealthy."

"So I've come to understand." He glanced at the window behind her and an idea came to mind. "Would you allow me the honor of walking you back to your cottage?" When Miss Rose stood, she clutched the parchment to her chest. "What is that?"

She waved a dismissive hand. "Minute details of some of your holdings of which I wish to keep note." She tilted her head. "Would you like to see for yourself?" Her voice had an accusatory tone to it that nettled Evan.

"Don't talk to me as if I've no wits, Miss Follet!" he barked.

Miss Rose took a startled step back. "Why are you acting like this?" she asked.

Confusion filled Evan. Speaking to her thus seemed...natural. But why? A kind man did not use such harsh tones, did he?

No, of course not.

He hurried to her and reached for her hand, but she pulled it away.

"What has come over you?" Miss Rose shook her head. "If my being here makes you uncomfortable..." She offered him the piece of parchment. "But it's more than that, is it not? You don't trust me." Her eyes glistened with unshed tears.

Evan felt as if he were in a standoff. Although he had doubts about her ability with his ledgers, accusing her of wrongdoing would do no good. Especially if he wished to kiss her plump lips.

"I see no need to see your work," he said. "And, please, treat this study as your own."

Hesitation remained in her eyes, but she said, "Very well. If that is what you wish." Her gaze dropped. "But I must admit, I don't understand why you feel the need to be angry with me. I'm merely here to help."

Evan had to purse his lips to keep himself from snapping at her, to command her to keep quiet and not question him. Instead, he studied the pattern on the wallpaper. That, at least, should have been familiar.

Yet it was not. Would he ever enjoy the luxury of remembering?

"Perhaps it's my frustration with my current situation that pushed me to speak so harshly. Learning from others who I am is not coming easy to me. So little of it feels right." He sighed. "I've never felt so alone."

He looked at Miss Rose and for a fleeting moment thought he caught sight of a small smile on her lips. Had it been one of sympathy? Yes, he had been far too harsh with her.

"Well, you are not alone," Miss Rose said, taking the candelabra in hand. "If you wish to walk me to the cottage, you may." A bit of pink crept into her cheeks. Oh, but was she a beauty. His integrity had apparently paid off quite well if he had landed such a lovely creature.

"Wait," he said, taking hold of her arm. "There is something I've been wanting to do. Something I must do."

Before she could respond, he grasped her around the waist and pulled her into him. He hushed her small gasp with his lips. At first, she resisted him, but it was not long before she was returning the kiss with equal fervor.

And those lips! They were soft and delicious—and somehow familiar. Her feminine fragrance caused a stirring inside him. Having her in his embrace felt right, and he wanted to lift her into his arms and carry her to his bed.

No. Gentlemen did not do such things. Did they?

He could not help but wonder if they had been intimate, but now was not the time to ask. Why would he even consider that? Ladies simply did not do such things before marriage.

Did they?

"There," he said, his voice husky as he released her. "That is much better. Tell me, Miss Rose, did you enjoy it as much as I?"

She gave him a small smile and walked to the door. "You know I did," she said. "Now, if you wish to walk me to the cottage, hurry along."

The desire that had built flowed out of him, and he clenched a fist. He was no dog to be commanded!

Well, the fault is your own, he thought. *Was it not you who had spoken harshly and upset her earlier?* His kiss had not been enough to quell her anger. Next time, he would tame her wild ways. For now, however, he would say nothing.

They exited the study and made their way to the door at the back of the house. Clouds covered the sky, creating a darkness that would have had them stumbling if it were not for the candelabra. A lantern would have been more appropriate for the outside, but as there was no breeze, they could make do with what they had.

"Allow me," he said. As he took the holder with his left hand, his right hand fell to his side, brushing against her arm. The touch of her skin was warm and smooth. An image of a bright light came to mind.

Confused by what he saw, he said nothing as they approached the gate that separated the guest cottage from the main gardens.

"I can walk alone from here," Miss Rose said.

But Evan was not ready to leave her side. It was as if allowing her to go on alone would cause him pain. The thought sent his mind and body into turmoil, and he could not have said why. On one hand, he considered his behavior proper. What man did not wish to spend time with the woman he was said to love? On the other hand, he could not help but feel as if this was all foreign to him. As if none of this was real.

"If you would like," he said, "we can talk for a few minutes. I know I would like that." And he found that this was a true statement. Was it because she was one of the few familiarities in the otherwise alien world? Or was it because he truly did care for her and simply did not remember that he did?

Miss Rose glanced at the gate. "Well, I see no harm in that. What would you like to discuss?"

His mind went blank. He had no idea what to say. "Let's speak of the kiss I gave you."

A look of sadness crossed her features. "If I'm to be honest—and I do strive to always speak my mind—I found your anger this evening upsetting. But then you have the indecency to grab me and kiss me without the benefit of asking if I wished to be handled in such an uncouth manner." She pulled a handkerchief from her reticule and dabbed at her eyes. "Do you see me as nothing more than an object? I pray that you do not."

Evan could not say why, but this was not what he had expected to hear. Why did taking hold of a woman as he had in order to indulge himself seem natural?

"I thought—"

Miss Rose placed a hand on his chest. "Perhaps, as with everything else, you should ask permission beforehand. After all, you're a gentleman, not a rogue."

Confusion filled him. Something about that statement did not seem correct, but he could not have said what it was. Yet, who was he to argue? Perhaps the fall had somehow changed his character. He would have to ask the doctor about that possibility.

"What you say is true," he said, although conceding to her a dozen times a day was tiresome. "Let's speak of your ward, Aaron. How did he come to be with you?"

For a moment, he thought she would not answer. She would not keep such information secret, would she? Not from him.

"My Aunt Jean thought it would be wonderful to skip the Season and instead spend time on the Continent. We stayed in numerous hotels, visited museums, ate food in lovely cafes. We had a most splendid time. While in Denmark, we stayed at an inn where we encountered a disheveled couple. I felt pity for the mother, for she held a tiny baby in her arms. When I spoke to her, she said that they had seven other children at home and could barely feed them. Eight was simply too many mouths to feed."

Evan shook his head. The idea of having children held no appeal to him...

Or did it? Even so, he did not wish to see any suffer. "How terrible," he murmured.

Miss Rose nodded. "That same night, they made an appeal to my aunt and me, asking us to take the baby and raise him as our own. My aunt and I spoke about it at length, but our decision is obvious."

How had he landed such a lovely and kind young lady? "What a brilliant tale," he said. "To take on a ward at such a young age must have been difficult."

"My aunt has been helpful. And Leah."

"I imagine your prospects have lessened," Evan said with a chuckle.

"What does that matter?" Miss Rose asked, frowning. "I'm here with you, am I not?"

Evan could not help but clench his fist to keep from shouting at her again. "I'm only curious why the woman in whom I have an interest has never married. Why is the question so upsetting?"

He had put up with playing nice long enough. A woman's role was never to question a man, let alone a baron! Yet, Miss Rose believed herself worthy enough to do so. It was about time he proclaimed such nonsense ended!

Before he could make his proclamation, however, she replied, "Because there were no true gentlemen to be found, at least not until I met you. Now I'm suspecting that my initial assumptions about you were all wrong. It's clear that I've upset you, though I'm uncertain how."

A myriad of sensations bombarded him. How could this woman make him feel guilty and frustrated at the same time? He had arrived at another crossroad. Either he could make amends and keep her near or allow his rage to overtake him and send her fleeing from him.

He knew which he preferred.

"What suitors you've had in the past makes little difference," Evan said, smiling down at her. "You're here with me now, and your help is appreciated." She glanced toward the cottage once more. "Do you not wish to talk for a little longer?"

"I really must return to put Aaron to bed and check my own finances," she said. "I was meaning to go shopping later this week, and I like to see how much I can spend. Shopkeepers tend to frown on extending credit to ladies. Good evening."

The gate creaked as Miss Rose opened it, and Evan felt a sudden emptiness in her leaving. "Wait, please," he called out to her. What was this battle inside him to chastise her in one instant only to be kind to her in the next? "I would like you to shop to your heart's delight. Place any purchase on my bill."

A small smile formed on her lips, and he wished he could see it fully realized. "There's no need, my lord."

"I insist," he said firmly.

"I appreciate the gesture, but I receive a very generous allowance from my father's estate. Therefore, I must refuse. Although I'm very pleased that you offered."

He bowed to her. "The offer is there if you change your mind, Miss Rose. Goodnight to you."

"Goodnight."

After the light disappeared behind the closed door of the cottage, Evan found himself alone in the dark. As his eyes adjusted to the surrounding darkness, the footpath appeared, the white stones a stark contrast to the surrounding black.

On his way back to the house, he considered the last few days. Although it frustrated him that Miss Rose knew more about him than he did, he had come to accept one fact. A woman's anger was most certainly something he preferred to avoid.

Plus, leaving her to potter about his ledgers and other affairs made his life all the easier. What harm could she possibly cause?

Chapter Nine

Playing the doting woman Lord Westlake supposedly loved was becoming far more difficult than Rose had anticipated. Between his infuriating behavior and the exasperation she experienced at every turn, the thin partition she had created to protect herself was beginning to crumble.

How would she ever be able to hold his interest without exasperating him at every turn? And without stoking her annoyance? It was not as if they were friends who could easily work through their differences.

"That's it!" she said, startling Leah so she pricked herself with the needle she was utilizing. "We must work on our friendship. We have none."

Leah's brows leapt up toward her hairline. "There's a problem with our friendship?" she asked, her voice filled with anxiety. "If I've done anything wrong, please tell me so I can fix it!"

Rose could not help but laugh as she stood. "No, not *our* friendship but rather that of Lord Westlake and me. But I'll explain it all later. If Aaron wakes before I return, tell him I'm just out for a walk and shan't be long."

Throwing her shawl around her shoulders, Rose walked outside. Dew clung to the blades of grass, and birds sang in the trees, but Rose took little notice of the early-morning beauty around her.

Why were the best solutions so often the simplest? She had approached this situation in the wrong way. Kisses would only get her so far. She also needed to create a bond with him. A bond so strong, when it broke, it would leave him as shattered as a vase that had fallen off a table.

The maids were bustling about the ground floor of the house as Rose entered, seeing to cleaning the fireplaces, drawing the drapes, and dusting the various figurines that decorated the tables—all those chores Rose did during her short sojourn in service at Tinsley Estate. They no longer greeted her with hearty hellos but instead treated her as they would any guest of their master's family. Rose was pleased they held up the ruse so well.

Fletcher was speaking to a footman as she entered the foyer. When the younger man bowed and hurried away, Rose approached the butler.

"Good morning, Miss Follet," Fletcher said. "You're looking especially pleased this morning."

"Indeed, I am," Rose said. "I've found new hope in our plan for our baron. Is he in the drawing room perchance?"

"No, miss. He's been out front for about an hour. May I get the door for you?"

Rose nodded and then stepped past the butler. Indeed, Lord Westlake stood outside, leaning against one of the tall pillars that held up the large roof of the portico. For a moment, this pose brought to mind a function years earlier where he stood just as he did now. Her mother had been aghast at his terrible posture, but Rose had thought it a part of his dashing qualities.

"What an embarrassment to his family," her mother had whispered. "What would compel a gentleman to present himself in such a slovenly manner?"

Although Rose had not responded, she knew well the answer. A man as handsome as Lord Westlake cared nothing for what others thought of him. He had a rebellious heart that made him all the more attractive, for her heart had not a drop of contumacy.

Or so it was then. Now was a far different matter.

"Miss Rose," Lord Westlake said as he turned at the sound of the door closing behind her, "for what reason am I favored with your presence at such an early hour?

Uncertain if his tone had a hint of sarcasm, Rose presented her best smile. "I've been spending a great deal of time thinking about us. As a couple."

He moved as fast as a cobra to clasp her by the arms. "Have you? And what have you determined. Tell me every detail." His voice had a hint of urgency to it, as if he were asking for a drop of water upon entering an oasis.

"I think we should start at the beginning," she said. "We must redevelop the friendship we once had. Only last night I realized we've somehow lost that important step in our relationship."

"Friendship?" he asked, dropping his hands and gaping at her. "But we're courting. You say we've already become enamored with one another. Surely, a friendship has already been formed?" His eyes narrowed. "What are you playing at, Miss Follet? Or is this some ploy to leave me?"

How quickly he becomes enraged! she thought with exasperation. Her next words were vital to her plan, so she had to choose them carefully if she was to succeed.

"How could I ever leave you, my lord?" she asked as she took a step closer. "You've been thrust into a world you don't recall. You're a baron who's courting a woman you no longer know." She placed a hand on his arm. "Not only will rekindling our friendship help your memory, but it may also help *you.*"

He frowned. "So, we'll no longer be courting?"

Rose sighed. "Of course, we'll still be courting. But if you'd rather..." She paused and looked away. Would he believe her next words? "I had just thought that by being friends...well...never mind. It's a foolish notion. Just forget I mentioned the idea."

She made to return to the house, but he said, "No, wait. There is wisdom in your words."

"Do you mean that?" she asked, batting her eyelashes. How she despised the girlish trick, but if it helped her achieve her goal, she would do whatever it took, girlish or not. "I was worried you no longer wanted a friendship like the one we had before we began courting."

The baron sighed. "I want you near me, Miss Rose. Therefore, yes, we will become friends again. But how will we start?"

Inwardly, Rose cheered. This was going far better than she had anticipated. He had become desperate, for his tone reflected that.

She dropped into a deep curtsy. "Good morning, my lord. My name is Miss Rose Follet. It's a pleasure to make your acquaintance."

His laugh made her breath catch, for it was the first she had heard since this charade began that was not filled with malice. And it sounded wonderful.

"Evan, Lord Westlake," he replied with a bow. "And the pleasure is all mine. Would you like to enjoy an activity with me today? But you must help me because I've no idea what activities I enjoy."

Wetting her lips, her mind raced. What she chose had to be innocent yet also intimate enough to move things along quickly. "The library," she said. "We often read together. Would you like to do so today?"

"Are you available now?" he asked. "I would like to begin as soon as possible. I've a memory to reconstruct." The eagerness in his voice pleased her.

"I must return to Aaron, but we can meet in an hour if you'd like."

"An hour it is," he said with a smile. "I think I'll remain here for a time." He turned to lean against the pillar once more.

With her hand on the door handle, Rose stopped and turned back toward him. "Why do you stand out here? Are you expecting someone?"

Lord Westlake shook his head. "I'm hoping to remember something. Anything." He sighed. "Do you think I will ever regain my memory?"

Rose grinned as she opened the door. "Oh, you'll remember everything soon enough, and I'll be here to make sure you do."

***

Evan was growing more frustrated but not because of his inability to recall his life. Now, he struggled to select a book to read. For someone who spent a great deal of time in the library reading, the act felt foreign to him. Not that he did not know how to read but rather that he found no enjoyment in it. Yet, if Miss Rose said it was an activity they delighted in together, he had to trust her word.

Miss Rose, on the other hand, had found a book within minutes and was already curled up on the sofa with it in her lap.

"Books on warfare seem boring," he murmured as he looked over the shelves in front of him. "And the sciences seem even worse." Shoving the book he had just looked through back onto the shelf, he sighed. "It's hopeless. Perhaps I should just sit and watch you read."

A tinkling laugh filled the air, and Evan found the sound beautiful. "You've always been indecisive when selecting a book because you hope to find a new interest. Yet you continually return to your favorites."

She went to a far shelf and motioned to him to join her.

He inhaled the scent of rose soap as he stood beside her, and a familiar desire washed over him.

Behave yourself! You're meant to be her friend not some rogue wishing to kiss her at every turn.

Her suggestion to take a step back and work on their friendship had initially made him angry, for he had thought it was her way of distancing herself from him. The last thing he needed was the one person who could help him recover his memory leaving him to grapple with it alone. Once she had explained her reasoning, however, he found the idea appealing. Even if it meant he had to wait to kiss her plump lips again.

Stop that!

"Here," she said, taking a small, brown leather-bound book from the shelf. "Try this one. It's always been one of your favorites."

"*Prose of the Wayward Man?*" he asked in horror. He opened the book to a random page. "This is a book of poetry! Men don't read poetry. Do women not prefer reading it?"

"I'm not asking you to recite it to the entire village," she replied. "And it's written by a man. If men don't appreciate such writings, why would it be men who pen it? But the decision is yours. I just thought you would appreciate a book from what has been your favorite genre for as long as I've known you."

Evan closed his eyes to quell the familiar annoyance that bloomed inside him. "Very well, I'll read it. But I just don't understand why I feel such an aversion to doing so." He forced a smile. "If you say this was what I enjoy, then I suppose I'll enjoy it once I take the time to read it."

Miss Rose returned to her seat and patted the place beside her.

He joined her, leaving a great deal of space between them, and opened the book to the first poem. It was simple enough, about a man on a journey thinking of the love he left behind. He nearly groaned. How could anyone enjoy such drivel?

Closing the book, he considered searching for another. But when Miss Rose gave him a curious look, he opened the book once more, this time choosing a different poem.

Fletcher gave him a blessed interruption by bringing in a tea tray. There was something…off about the smile the butler gave Miss Rose, but it was gone so quickly, Evan considered it had been his imagination.

You're seeing conspiracies everywhere, Evan Westlake! It was no wonder he was making little progress toward regaining his memory if he became suspicious of the only people he should trust.

He took a sip of his tea and turned to Miss Rose, whose eyes darted across the page of the book in her lap.

"What are you reading?"

"It's called *The Warrioress*. It's a fascinating tale about a woman who fought in the Four Years' war."

Evan snorted. "It must be a work of fiction. What woman wishes to go to war?"

Miss Rose slowly closed her book and turned toward him. "Are you saying that women are incapable of fighting?"

"Not at all," Evan said with a laugh. "But you have to admit that the possibility of such a frail creature using a broadsword is highly improbable."

Miss Rose pursed her lips. "For your information, she murdered one of the leaders of the opposing army."

He frowned. Now he knew for certain the book was rubbish.

"And she did so without a single thrust of a blade."

Evan could not help himself. His curiosity was piqued. "How did she do it, then?"

Miss Rose shook her head. "I'll not say since you'll only mock me again."

"I promise to keep my mocking at a minimum," he said, grinning.

She sighed. "Oh, very well. If you insist. Edward Lamarre, who fought under Charles de Bourbon in 1522, sent an invitation to Henry the Eighth in hopes of bringing peace. When a woman arrived rather than the King, Lamarre flew into a rage. Lady Norwich, indignant at his treatment of her, poisoned his tea when he was not looking. He then drank the tea and died." She smiled at him over the rim of her teacup. "Do take care with what you drink, my lord. You never know what I may do if you insult me."

Evan glanced at the cup in his hand. She would not poison him, would she? Then he looked up to see a mischievous grin on her face, and he roared with laughter. "Well played, Miss Rose. Well played, indeed."

As she returned to her book, Evan finished the rest of his tea and returned to his.

After flipping past several poems, Evan found a piece of prose that intrigued him, and soon he was engrossed in his reading.

The rustling of Miss Rose's skirts made him look up to find that an hour had already passed. "I really must look in on Aaron," she said, standing. "Thank you for a lovely time."

"Wait," he said, rising, as well. "This poem, it reminds me of you."

"I appreciate you saying so, but I really must go. I worry about Aaron being alone for so long."

"But he's not alone," Evan said. "I'm sure Leah can watch him for a few more minutes. I'd really like you to listen. It won't take long."

She gave a small nod. "Go on, then."

Smiling, he opened the book and began to read.

Where shall my next step take me?
The void, it draws so near.
Will it engulf me?
Yet what hope is there in despair?
I cannot fail, for she fights at my side.

I shall prevail.
Because of her.

Closing the book, Evan placed it on a side table. "What you said was true, Miss Rose. Reading the book was what I needed." He took a step closer. "Like the author, I find myself balanced on the edge of a void." He placed the back of his hand on her cheek and smiled at her audible gasp. "I'll prevail in this. Because of you."

"That...that was beautiful," she whispered.

A sudden urge came over Evan, and without thought, he pressed his lips to hers. As wonderful as the kiss was, however, it came to an abrupt end when she took a step back.

"As much as I enjoy your kisses," Miss Rose said, her face flushed, "we already go well beyond the boundaries of propriety by me being unchaperoned here with you. To engage in such intimacy is taking things too far. Now, I really must go."

Feeling somewhat foolish, Evan scolded himself inwardly. He needed to refrain from taking advantage of her whenever the urge presented itself. Doing so was proving more difficult than he imagined. No matter how hard he tried, that desire to do as he pleased bubbled inside him. The battle ahead lay not only in remembering his former life, but also in his ability to show her the respect she deserved.

The problem was, he was unsure which would be more difficult to achieve.

Chapter Ten

If there was one thing Rose enjoyed above all else, it was spending time with Aaron. He was a joy to be around and had a way of making her laugh, even at the darkest of times.

Second to her time with her ward was her love of shopping. It did not matter what she purchased, be it new dresses, hats, gloves, jewelry, all of it brought her happiness.

Today, however, she found herself disconcerted rather than joyful. Lord Westlake's impropriety the previous day had been nettling. After her talk of friendship, he had used the poem to weaken her resolve. And for a moment, she had become so enthralled that she had forgotten who was reciting the prose and thus fell for his charm. Again.

The poem had reflected his current predicament, to be sure, yet what baffled her was Lord Westlake's eagerness to have her listen to his recitation. He had read it with such passion, with such feeling, that there was no doubt of his authenticity. Which led to her readily accepting his kiss.

Such a fool!

Yet her shame went beyond that. Her reaction to that kiss had left her in an odd position. Those feelings she had long since buried had attempted to escape, and that was the very last thing she needed. More kisses were inevitable—she was playing the part of his love interest, for goodness' sake!

But alongside those intimate moments, a friendship was forming.

Or so Rose hoped he believed. What she needed was for him to fall for her in the same way she had him, and a new dress would help her do just that. Thus her reason for today's outing.

Leah and Aaron sat across from her in the carriage as they drew closer to their destination. Dunark was a mid-sized village with a substantial number of shops that offered a variety of goods. Today, her main destination was a dressmaker's shop.

She had never realized how easy it was to manipulate a man. Then again, never had she desired to do so with anyone but Lord Westlake. Other men had been rude to her. They had ignored her. But none had used her in the way the baron had. None had broken her heart.

Lord Westlake's old ways still showed through, but with each gentle touch, each tiny smile, each soft word, she had him bending to her will. The power was alluring. The same power she would use against him as she had. And with each planned step, he would draw closer to her—and thus closer to his eventual destruction.

"Why didn't the lord come with us?" Aaron asked as he tugged at Rose's dress. "Doesn't he like us?"

"He needs to rest after his terrible fall," Rose said, gathering the boy into her arms. "We must give him time alone, which is why we're going shopping."

The village of Dunark came into view, and the carriage came to a stop in front of the first shop. The footman opened the door and offered her a hand.

"Thank you, Richard," she said with a small smile.

The footpath was busy and peopled jostled her as she waited for Leah and Aaron to alight. A governess chased after her two charges, both boys laughing with delight with each glance over their shoulders. Unlike those boys, Aaron was not of the mischievous sort. He had always been a good boy, thank goodness.

After her time in the country, the village seemed busy and loud. Not as loud as London, of course, but certainly busier than Tinsley Estate.

"You'll not eat until tonight," a man was saying in a nasty tone to a young lady who appeared to be his daughter. "If you become any fatter, we'll have to add extra horses to the carriage!"

The young girl was no older than fifteen. Although she was not twig-thin, neither was she exceptionally big. Still, she hung her head in shame as she walked past.

Rose wanted to comfort the girl, to tell her that she was no burden. That her father did not understand the harm he was causing her.

"Miss Rose?" Leah asked. "Are you all right?"

"Yes, of course," Rose replied, pushing the poor girl from her mind. She could do nothing to help except pray that she made better choices than Rose did. "I say we begin at the dressmaker's since that's the reason I wanted to come into town." Upon seeing Aaron's frown, she laughed. "When we're done with our shopping, we'll see that you get a new toy. How does that sound?" How quickly such a promise made him smile!

Soon, the trio was entering Madam Trudeau's dress shop. Once the door closed, the din of traffic was gone, replaced by the sound of ladies flipping through the various catalogues or exclaiming over a particular fabric.

"Good morning," said a woman, her chestnut hair streaked with auburn. "I'm Mrs. Fluer. How may I assist you?"

Rose nodded to Leah, who ushered away Aaron. Then she turned to the clerk. "I'm visiting from London and would like to purchase a new gown."

The woman beamed. "You'll find our selection here among the best. Are you new to Dunark? I don't recall seeing you before, Miss..."

"Follet," Rose replied. "An old friend recommended your shop. Lady Westlake?"

Mrs. Fluer's eyes widened and her smile nearly cut her face in half. "Oh, yes, the baroness was a frequent visitor to our shop before she moved away. I'm sure we can meet all your needs."

During her investigation into the Remington family, Rose was always amused at how people groveled at the mere mention of any of its members. Two years earlier, while traveling to Cambridge, she mentioned being acquainted with the Duke of Greystoke and was offered the best room at the inn in which she stayed. A year later, she stopped at an inn in the village of Wilkworth. When she happened to make an inquiry into Mr. Markus Remington, the barkeep had been more than accommodating. Until he realized she was sniffing out information. Then he closed up like a frightened oyster.

"For now," Rose said to the waiting clerk, "I'm looking to purchase a gown in a particular style with which you may not be familiar."

Mrs. Fluer raised her chin indignantly. "We may not be London, Miss Follet, but I can assure you our seamstresses are quite capable of producing clothing as good as—if not better than—the best shops on Regent Street."

"I imagine so," Rose said. "Let me explain what I need." She leaned in and whispered what she desired.

"I see. I believe you may find exactly what you describe among our newest plates." She walked over to a counter and flipped through a book of plates. "Yes, here we are. Does this meet your needs?"

"That is exactly what I would like," Rose said, smiling.

"Wonderful! Now, we must take your measurements and get one of the seamstresses on it right away. Have no doubt it will be a lovely gown."

"How long will it take?" Rose asked.

"Typically when we have a new patron, a dress like this can take up to three, or even four, weeks. But as you're an acquaintance of the baroness, I can see it completed in two. Will that be sufficient?"

Rose beamed. "Most certainly. Thank you."

"Will you follow me?" Mrs. Fluer said. "Nancy will take your measurements." She snapped her fingers, and a young woman with blonde curls hurried over to her. "Nancy, this is Miss Follet. She is a valued client, so I want you to take extra care in her fitting."

"Yes, Mrs. Fluer."

As Nancy completed her work, Rose's mind began to wander. Although the gown itself was not the pinnacle of her revenge, it would be a very important part of it. In order to make him fall in love with her, she first needed to make him desire her. To wish to hold her. To want to kiss her lips. All while she controlled him. He had slipped through and stolen the kiss that had gotten the better of her.

Well, she would not allow it to happen again. Not without her say so. This time, she would have complete control of her feelings and actions.

Playing her part as the caring interest, the new dress, all was meant to send him down a path where he would fall in love with her. And when that day came, when he professed that undying love, she would destroy him!

"Miss?" the young assistant said, breaking Rose from her thoughts. "You can get dressed now. Unless there's something else you need?"

"No, thank you," Rose replied.

Nancy dipped her head and helped Rose with the buttons on the back of her dress. A few minutes later, Rose returned to the main room, where Aaron was turning the pages of one of the books, a sullen look on his face.

"Is this young man your younger brother?" Mrs. Fluer asked.

"I'm not her brother," Aaron said. "I'm her word. Miss Rose gave my mum and dad food so she could keep me."

Rose laughed. "Aaron is my family's ward. Unfortunately, his parents were unable to properly care for him, so my aunt and I took him in."

"How very kind of you, Miss Follet. And it's clear the boy has taken a great liking to you."

Looking down at Aaron, Rose's heart was fit to burst. she loved him more than anything. More than the single night she had stood at his bedroom door, silently weeping as he slept.

"He is a dear," Rose replied. "A miracle that came into my life during its darkest days."

Rose glanced over to where Leah stood by the front window, her hands gripping her skirts. "Will you excuse me?" she said to the clerk and then hurried over to Leah. "What's wrong?" Rose asked, looking through the window for any sign of trouble.

"Should you be doing this, Miss Rose?"

Rose frowned. "Doing what?"

"Tricking His Lordship like you've been doing. I don't mean any disrespect, miss, but what if he works out your plan and gets really angry and does something terrible?"

"Have you forgotten what he did to me?" Rose demanded, finding her maid's reluctance more than a bit inconvenient. But rational thought returned. Leah was more than a maid. She was family and had nothing but worry for Rose.

Taking a calming breath, Rose said, "I know you care about me, but

I assure you, what I'm doing is more than justified. And I'll be careful. Am I not always?"

Leah sighed. "Yes, you are. And he does deserve to learn a lesson."

"Indeed, he does," Rose said, smiling. "And I promise, once I've completed my mission here, once I've collected what information I must, we'll be on the first coach back to London. You'll simply have to trust that I'm doing the right thing."

"I've always trusted you, miss," Leah said. "And I'll never leave your side."

"I know. And for that I'll be eternally grateful." Rose turned and called out to Aaron, who came running over immediately. "I say it's time to purchase your toy. I know! I saw no signs of the necessities for shuttlecock at Tinsley Estate. Why don't we search out the nicknackatory and see if they have what we need?"

Aaron grinned and nodded. "I'd like that!"

As they exited the shop, Rose could not help but wonder. Why could Lord Westlake not be as formidable as Aaron? Well, she would see that he was. One small intrigue at a time.

***

"Do you think Lord Westlake'll wanna play dogs with me?" Aaron asked as they made their way back to Tinsley Estate. Although the boy had been disappointed that the shop did not have rackets for the shuttlecocks, he was thrilled when he found two wooden terriers, each carved in exquisite detail.

Rose found her response stuck in her throat. The last thing she wanted was for Aaron to become attached to the baron. Not for the baron's sake but for that of Aaron.

"I'm afraid he cannot," Rose replied.

"But why?" Aaron asked as he looked up at her with his innocent blue eyes. "Doesn't he like dogs?"

"I'm afraid Lord Westlake doesn't have time to play," Rose said, pushing back the wave of hair that had fallen over his forehead. "But Leah and I shall play with you."

Aaron's shoulders drooped. "But you're not boys. It's not the same."

The youngster spoke with such a disheartened tone, Rose's heart clenched. He may not have been able to communicate it clearly, but he needed the support of a man in his life, a mentor of sorts. No charade would ever end with Lord Westlake being that person.

The mere thought frightened her so terribly, she wrapped her arms around Aaron and kissed the top of his head. She could do nothing to stop the lone tear from escaping her eye at the thought of ever losing this boy. Aaron and Leah were the only family she had left.

Well, there was Aunt Jean, but she was in poor health. She had aged considerably over the last few years, and Rose feared the woman's days on this earth were drawing to a close.

It was a relief when they returned to Tinsley Estate.

"I trust your excursion was pleasant," Mr. Fletcher said as they entered the foyer.

"Quite," Rose replied. "Where is His Lordship? I'd like to say hello to him."

"As a matter of fact, he's waiting for you in the ballroom, Miss Follet."

She turned to Leah. "Take Aaron to the cottage to rest. I'll be along soon."

When Rose reached the doors to the ballroom, she stopped to observe the baron pacing back and forth, his hands clutched behind his back.

When he caught sight of her, he smiled. "Miss Rose! I'm so glad you're back. I've been waiting for you. I have some wonderful news, news that I cannot wait to tell you! I recalled something while you were gone!"

Rose's stomach felt as if it were filled with lead. The strange look of innocence in his eyes pulled at her heart in a very strange way. He was suffering. A sliver of nostalgia flittered into her mind, but she used the images of six years earlier to push them back to their hiding place. Whatever she had hoped they would share would never come to pass. Not if she could help it.

"How wonderful!" she said, forcing a smile. "Do tell me everything!"

Chapter Eleven

With each passing moment, Evan found his frustration growing. Not a single memory had returned to give him any indication of who he truly was. There were moments of familiarity, such as the couch in the drawing room, or a vase in the parlor he somehow knew he had purchased. But in regard to any specific memories, a wall as strong as any fortress kept them from him. It was the same sensation one gets when he knows a particular fact or the name of an acquaintance, but it refuses to emerge.

What was strangest of all, however, was that although he wanted to remember for his own sanity, he found he wanted to do so for Miss Rose, as well. Why that would seem strange was beyond him. He could not deny that he found her attractive. Even a blind man would recognize her beauty. And he was eager to explore the wonders beneath the layers of clothing she wore.

Yet something was amiss with her. There were times when they kissed and she had not reciprocated his passion. Yet in the library, she had.

He was so confused!

This malady, this amnesia, was a thorn in his side! All his thoughts came in confused knots. He wished to care for Miss Rose as he once did, but not knowing to what extent those feelings went made doing so all the more difficult.

The doctor had called earlier that morning. When Evan had expressed how frustrated hew as, the doctor had instructed him that he should simply be patient. That was easy for him to say! He was not the one waging this battle. If everyone had not informed him that his name was Evan and that he was a baron, he would not have known who he was at all!

He stood in the library, a finely decorated masculine sanctuary filled with leather tomes and leather furniture. Paintings hung between the tall bookcases, one depicting men on horseback chasing after a fox.

"They seek the fox for a trophy," he mumbled.

A shiver went down his spine. Trophies. There was something in that word. But what?

He pushed against that invisible wall, but it was as solid as if it had been built out of stone.

The door opened, and Fletcher entered.

"I've a strange feeling that I have many trophies," Evan said to the butler. "Do I have a collection of pelts or other objects to show the spoils of sport? Mementos of the hunts I enjoyed?"

"You've certainly participated in several hunts, my lord, but I'm not aware of any winnings—or, as you say, trophies—from any of them."

Evan frowned and looked up at the painting once more. "I've a feeling inside me, something telling me that collecting trophies brought me joy. If they were not from fox hunts, what could they be?" He heaved a heavy sigh. "Fletcher, it appears I may never recall a single thing in my life."

"Worry not, my lord. It's not been a full week yet since your fall. I have a firm belief that in time, your memory will return and you'll be a better person for it."

Evan glanced at the butler, his frown deepening. How did losing one's memory make him a better person? That made no sense whatsoever!

"Perhaps you and Miss Rose are correct in your beliefs," he said aloud, not wishing to cause an uproar. He had to either trust the two people in his life or go it alone. And the latter was far too daunting. "I'm going to the ballroom. Inform Miss Rose that I would like to speak to her when she returns."

After Fletcher left, Evan looked up at the painting once more. The more he tried to remember, the angrier he got. Loneliness was becoming a constant companion despite the number of servants who walked the halls and the presence of the woman he was supposed to love.

Evan attempted to imagine the ballroom full of people. They would be talking and laughing. Yet where would he be? Was he the type of host who moved from person to person, engaging in delightful conversation and making them each laugh at one humorous antidote after another? Or was he a more formidable man, one who preferred serious conversation? Neither seemed right. Maybe he was somewhere in between the two extremes.

He walked around the large room, closing his eyes every so often to imagine himself standing there surrounded by guests. What fragrances did they wear? What colors were their clothes?

"This is insane!" he said in a harsh whisper as he crossed his arms and leaned a shoulder against the wall.

When he looked up, he paused. A single memory flashed into his mind. He had stood here before, in this very spot, observing a woman in a red dress!

His pulse quickened. Yes! She had a glow about her that had intrigued him. He could not make out her face, but the memory caused an odd stirring in his heart. That must have been the moment he and Miss Rose met!

Closing his eyes, Evan replayed the fleeting image in his mind, hoping to conjure more. But to no avail. All he knew was that the woman had most definitely been Miss Rose. Who else could have made sweat bead on his brow and dampen his palms? It had to be her!

Excitement coursed through him and he began to pace, praying that more memories would appear. He could not wait to share this good news with Miss Rose!

He turned to find the object of his thoughts standing in the doorway, and he hurried over to her.

"Miss Rose! I'm so glad you're back. I've been waiting for you. I have some wonderful news, news that I cannot wait to tell you! I recalled something while you were gone!"

He took hold of her gloved hands, wishing to touch her bare skin, to see if it would help the memory to deepen, but he could not ask for her to do something so improper.

"How wonderful!" she said. "Do tell me everything!"

Evan could not say why, but he had a sense that her reaction was forced. He could not push aside the cloud of suspicion that filled him. Her smile seemed strained. Why would she not be as exhilarated as he with this fantastic news?

"You seem bothered," he said, taking a step back, rage pounding in his temples. "Nothing is keeping you here, Miss Follet. You are free to go whenever you wish. I don't want you to see me as a burden." He was uncertain from where the words came. All he knew was he was angry she did not share in his elation.

Her lower lip trembled and her eyes filled with tears.

He sighed. Why had he lost his temper again? This was not who he was, or at least not according to Fletcher and Miss Rose. Yet he became angry so easily.

"Forgive me," he said, choking out the words. Apologizing made his mouth feel as if it were full of dirt. "Since you left, I began the arduous task of walking through the house again in search of any memories, and one came to mind. Please, follow me, and I'll tell you about it."

Evan took hold of her hand and led her to the place beside the wall. "I remember standing here during some sort of function—a party or a gathering of sorts. I don't recall for certain, but I get the sense that the room was filled with people. I saw a woman across the room, although I cannot remember who she was." He turned to her. "Miss Rose, it had to be you, for I felt something inside me. A need of sorts. It was more than attraction, it was the need to know her. She had to be you. What other woman would make me feel that way?"

At once, the word "weak" came to mind. Why would he confess aloud such feelings?

Because it's the truth.

He had hoped she would throw her arms around him and congratulate him. And dare he say, even ask for another kiss. What he did not expect was for her to pull her hand away.

"I assure you, that was not I," she said with a hint of annoyance in her tone.

"But who else could it have been? You told me we met at a party six years ago. A party hosted here. What I remember must be that night!" His excitement dwindled further upon seeing her frown. "Are you not pleased for me? Even if it was not you, at least I have recovered one memory. A small one, to be sure, but still one, nonetheless."

"You are correct, we did meet here in this ballroom. And I would be happy if you were remembering our first encounter. Unfortunately, I believe know exactly which party you've brought to mind, for that was the night you met Miss Betty Hollingsworth. You and I spoke only in the foyer while you greeted each guest, but Miss Hollingsworth had your eye the entire night. You spent so much time in her company that you ignored the rest of your guests."

Upon realizing his mistake, Evan shook his head. "I truly believed it was you."

"Well, it was not, I can assure you of that," she said, smoothing the front of her dress. "You didn't even look at me twice that evening."

"Now I feel foolish," he said. "I didn't realize."

"And how could you?" Miss Rose said. "Although, perhaps next time, you should consider what you wish to tell me, my lord, for I'd prefer not to hear about feelings you once had for another woman. Now, if you'll excuse me, I have matter to which I must attend."

And with that, she turned and marched out of the room.

Evan squeezed his hand into a fist in frustration. Not at Miss Rose, for she had every right to speak as she had, but rather at himself. Speaking of feelings for another to the one he was supposed to admire most? Complete folly, that!

No wonder she resists your kisses, you fool! You're supposed to be rebuilding a friendship, not pushing her away!

With a need to see that she was not too hurt, he threw open the double doors that led out to the gardens in hopes of clearing his head. Just going around a hedge was Miss Rose, her dress swishing around her ankles in her rush toward the guest cottage.

"Miss Rose!" he called. "Wait, please!" He broke out into a run, taking hold of her arm just as she reached for the latch on the gate.

"Please, I must speak to you."

When she turned, he took a step back in surprise. Her eyes were rimmed in red.

"What I said back there...it was not my intention to hurt you."

Evan paused. That was one thing he knew for certain.

Miss Rose shook her head. "Well, I can assure you, my lord, that was exactly what you did. Far more than you will ever know."

A single tear escaped her eye, and he reached up to brush it away with his thumb. "I truly am sorry," he said. "Here we've made a great deal of progress and I've ruined it."

With a sigh, Miss Rose said, "Perhaps I overreacted just a bit."

Hoping to ease the situation, he offered her a smile. "It appears my temper is contagious."

"Was there anything else you wished to say, my lord? I must return to Aaron."

He had much he wished to tell her. That he thought well of her. That he...

How could he name what he felt for her?

Well, it did not matter at the moment, for now was not the time for proclamations of any sort.

"Just one more thing, if I may. I don't know about the past, but I can say that at this very moment, seeing your cheeks stained with tears saddens me. This person I've become—this person who is angry all the time, who lashes out at every turn—I don't like him. I'm doing my best and will not stop trying." He placed a hand on her arm. "And like the man in the poem, I need you. I want to be the man you knew me as, a gentleman who keeps his temper in check. You told me I once cared for you. Give me time and I'll care for you again, and in the way you deserve."

For a moment, he thought she would not respond. Had his plea made him appear weak in her eyes?

Just as the anger began to settle into his jaw, she said, "I appreciate your apology and accept it," she said finally, a smile forming on her lips. Lips perfect for kissing.

She took a step back from him when he leaned in closer to her, and once again, his frustration grew. Was he not deserving of a reward?

"I really must be going," she said. "Aaron is waiting. Shall I see you tonight at dinner?"

A thought came to him, one that would allow them a private moment together. "What if we dined alone tonight?"

Miss Rose stopped and turned. "I would like that."

He watched her walk up the footpath and sighed. Who knew friendship—or whatever it was they had—was so difficult?

With a growl, he kicked at a stone. What had begun as a memory giving him hope had returned him to frustration. It was as if regaining his memory would drive Miss Rose away if he were not careful.

He could not for the life of him, however, explain why that bothered him as it did. He could not name a single feeling for her save one. Necessity. He needed her presence, for it eased his anxiety, made him feel more secure.

Yet surely there was more? Had Miss Rose and Fletcher not said as much?

Returning to the house, he considered returning to the ballroom but instead went to the library.

"Poetry," he mumbled as he selected another book from the same shelf Miss Rose had found *Prose of the Wayward Man*. "It still seems so odd."

With a sigh, he settled into a chair and opened to the first page, but he struggled to keep his mind on what he read. His thoughts kept returning to Miss Rose and the mysterious woman the ballroom. So much was missing in between.

Chapter Twelve

Too often, Rose had lost her temper with Lord Westlake. Now, however, that emotion was replaced with hurt. If she continued to allow the hurt of her past to drive her actions and words, her plans to make him fall in love with her were doomed.

At his initial mention of recalling a memory, she had felt a twinge of happiness for him. But that was quickly replaced with concern. If he recalled too much too soon, all her plans would unravel.

Although she had kept her anger in check, it boiled beneath the surface. How could she have been so naive to believe they could have built any sort of romantic relationship? If Lord Westlake had possessed even a shred of decency six years earlier, he would have reciprocated the love she had for him. Instead, he had used her.

As the old dreams attempted to resurface, a single tear had rolled down her cheek, for her stupidity, for her naivety, for her weak-minded decisions. And he had clearly misconstrued her moment of weakness as something else.

Well, let him, she thought. It only helped in seeing her scheme realized.

Sighing, she dabbed a bit of perfume behind her ears and on her wrists and gave herself one final look in the mirror. Her green dress was one of her favorites, for it had lovely ruffles and did not cling to her body as her clothing had done in the past. She would have to be careful with how much she ate tonight. Too much, and the dress would no longer fit her and she would have to buy a new one. Then she would return to the woman she once was.

Her father's words echoed in her mind.

Unusually large.

Another reason she had chosen this dress was because she knew Lord Westlake would approve. Not because she valued his opinion, for it mattered little to her. But she had to gain his attention, and this was the very dress that would do that.

She shivered. The thought of his lips touching hers had disgusted her, but she was beginning to enjoy them. If she was to keep up this ruse, however, tonight she would have to allow him to do just that.

As long as she maintained control.

"Are you sure you're well, Miss Rose?" Leah asked. "You seem to be more agitated than normal these days."

Rose sighed and turned to face the maid. "Yes, I'm quite aware of this fact. But I mean to put an end to that tonight."

Leah hugged her. "All will be well, Miss Rose. I know it will."

A knock on the front door made Rose start. She went to answer it and found Lord Westlake standing there wearing a stern expression.

"Is no one else joining us?" he asked as he looked past her.

Rose frowned. "I thought you wished to dine alone. Would you like Aaron join us? I can see he is dressed—"

"I've no idea what I want," he said in a harsh tone. I fear a memory, or any request I make, will upset you. You claim that my earlier words did not bother you, but I'm no fool. As much as the thought saddens me, I'm beginning to wonder if it would be best that you leave so as I don't upset you again."

Panic welled up in Rose. Her plans were falling apart, all because she could not keep a tight rein on her emotions. "Here," she said, offering him her hand and a small smile. "Let's walk."

The low sun hid behind a bank of clouds to the far west as they made their way down the short path that led to the gate. They came to a stop beneath the boughs of a large tree.

"I want to be here with you," she said. "I admit that I've been out of sorts as of late, but I'm frightened."

Lord Westlake arched an eyebrow. "Frightened? Of what?"

She had concocted a plan to get not only herself back to where she needed to be, but Lord Westlake, as well. That meant burying her emotions. At least for the time being. Once all this was over, she could do whatever she wished. For now, some semblance of kindness was in order. She could not make any more mistakes or she would be thrown out on her ear.

"I fear for us," she said. "I do believe your memory will return, but what if you no longer care for me as you did? What if we lose everything we built together?" She placed a hand on his arm. "Is that possible? Will you stop caring for me?"

He drew in a deep breath as she moved a hand across his broad chest and batted her eyelashes at him. Yes, this was the way to always handle him. He would become soft clay in her hands, and she would mold him, form him, like wet clay.

Once he dried, she would break him.

Like he broke her.

He took her hand. "I'll never stop caring for you," he said huskily. "My outburst earlier…I only meant to give you the opportunity to leave if you so choose. I don't want to hurt you."

This made Rose smile, for she could hear the sincerity in his voice.

"Do you truly wish to remain?" he asked.

Now was the moment to convince him she did. Bracing herself, she placed a gloved hand on the side of his face. "Let's make an agreement of sorts," she whispered. "You will continue to work on being the gentleman who does not lose his temper, and I'll no longer be frightened of our future together." She snaked her arm around his neck and smiled. "Now, kiss me."

No sooner than the words left her mouth than he pulled her in close and did as she asked. Hunger filled that kiss, and Rose had to push back the desire that filled her, the same desire she had felt when he had pressed her against the door six years earlier. His masculine fragrance, his very being made her heart pound and her body to weaken. Her body tingled just as it did in the past, and she so desperately wanted more.

He hurt you! she thought, forcing herself to remember why she was here.

When the kiss ended, Lord Westlake pulled her close. "Your kisses are wondrous," he whispered in her ear.

No, she could not allow him to ruin everything!

Rose went to push him away, but he frowned at her. "Your kisses are as wonderful as they have ever been, my lord," she said. "Although, I do wonder if we should go to dinner. I'm sure Mr. Fletcher is waiting to serve us."

Evan's frown disappeared and he smiled. "Indeed." He offered her his arm. "Shall we?"

Placing a hand on his arm, they walked to the house together. When they entered the dining room, the baron pulled out a chair for her before taking his seat. A footman poured their wine, and Rose raised her glass.

"To Lord Westlake. The gentleman I adore."

The baron lifted his glass, as well. "To my Miss Rose, the woman I'm thankful is here with me."

As Rose took a sip of the wine, she could not help but feel a sense of pride. Disaster had been diverted. Now, all she had to do was keep it that way.

"It has occurred to me," Lord Westlake said as a footman offered him a platter filled with sliced beef, "I've been focused on remembering my former self that I've ignored learning more about you and your past. It would be wonderful to meet your parents.Or meet them again if I already have."

"They are both dead," Rose replied. *And you played your part in their deaths!* "A tragic accident I would prefer not to discuss."

"I'm sorry to hear that," the baron said. "Do you miss them?"

Rose had to loosen her grip on her fork and knife. "Every day I think of them. But I would rather know if you've had a chance to enjoy any more books in the library."

"Oh, yes. Very much so. I've even taken one of the books of poetry to read in bed."

As Lord Westlake shared the various titles he had read, Rose feigned interest, nodding and exclaiming "how wonderful!" at what seemed like appropriate moments.

"It's odd. At first, I thought I didn't enjoy reading—especially poetry of all things. But now, I find that I do. Perhaps it was the injury to my head that jumbled my brain." He chuckled as he cut into his beef. "I plan to read in the library this evening. Would you care to join me?"

Rose pushed a potato with her fork. "I would love nothing more. But I do wish to do a little work on your ledgers beforehand. If you don't mind waiting, of course."

The baron put down his utensils. "What if I observed you while you work?" He nodded as if giving himself permission. "Yes, I insist on it. I really should become acquainted with my accounts. Or reacquainted, as the case may be."

It was not what she wanted, but any argument would likely make her lose what little ground she had gained. "I think that is a splendid idea."

As they talked about other matters, Rose nibbled at her food. Although the beef was succulent and the potatoes and peas lovely, she forced herself to eat only a few. If she gave into her desire to eat the entire plateful, she hated to think where that would lead her.

"She is already unusually large," came her father's voice in the back of her mind. He had been speaking to her mother as Rose listened from outside the room. *Do make sure she does not eat at the party and draw the attention of every guest there. She can be such an embarrassment."*

Rose set her utensils on the plate. She would not embarrass her father, nor herself, tonight by eating far more than she should.

"You really should eat more," Lord Westlake said as if he had been listening to her thoughts. "We would not want you wasting away." He said the last with a small chuckle before taking another drink of his wine.

Most of her food remained, just as it always did since her return from the Continent. And like every other time anyone made such a statement, she replied, "I've always had a small appetite."

The baron frowned as the plates were removed but made no comment.

Then a footman placed a slice of cake in front of her. She pushed away the plate. "None for me, thank you."

"Mrs. Moore is going to think you don't like her cooking," Lord Westlake said with a grin. "Go on. Just a small bite will not hurt. I promise you'll enjoy it. It's one of her specialties."

Did he not understand that her desire to eat the delicate cake was akin to the strength of fighting off his kisses? Changing the way she ate had not come easy. Returning to her old ways were far too tempting. "Thank you, but no."

"Send it back," Lord Westlake commanded with a wave of his hand. His chair scraped the floor as he stood. She had angered him again, she was sure of it.

Yet, to her surprise, when he pulled out her chair for her, he was smiling. "Now, show me how you've saved me from bankruptcy."

Entering the office, Rose selected the ledger she had perused the previous day while the baron slept. She sat in the chair behind the desk, and the baron stood behind her.

She opened the book. "You own a farm just outside of Flemming, two villages over." She ran a finger down one of the columns and stopped at a figure. "This is your profit from a venture in sheep. As you can see—"

He placed his hands on her shoulders, sending a shiver down her spine. Not in terror, nor even in annoyance. His touch was somehow...soothing.

She chose to ignore his familiarity. "That scheme has been profitable for several years."

His fingers began working at the knots in her shoulders. She closed her eyes, enjoying how relaxing his touch was. Her thoughts floated away as the tension eased.

"Your hands," she whispered. "They're wonderful."

So lost in the moment was she that her eyes flew open when Lord Westlake pressed his lips to hers. She had to force herself to calm as she put a hand to his chest. "My lord, we really should not be so...intimate."

The frustration she pushed down was more at herself than him. Why had she not stopped him when he first touched her shoulders?

He sighed. "Yes, you're right. Shall we go to the library?"

Rose stifled a frown. She wanted more time with his ledgers, to gather more information for her column. Yet how could she do so without drawing suspicion?

"Allow me to look through one more," she said, running a finger down his cheek. "Then I'll join you." Annoyance clouded his eyes, and she added, "But you must promise me that you'll save one more kiss for me."

His eyes glazed over with what she could only name as lust, but his words did not match what she saw. "Miss Rose, you're an enigma."

"An enigma? How so?"

He motioned to the ledger. "The way you speak of numbers, there is an excitement to your tone. From where does that come?"

A memory came to mind that made Rose smile. "My father would often leave his ledgers lying open on his desk. Being the inquisitive child I was, I would sit in his chair, pouring over his entries and testing to see that his calculations were correct." She let out a small laugh. "He never caught on to what I was doing."

Lord Westlake joined in her laugher, and for a fleeting moment, she thought the sound wonderful.

"Before I leave you," the baron said, "I've one more question to ask."

Rose tilted her head. "Go on."

"I don't wish to know why you've refused other men, for that is your business and not mine, but why me of all people?"

She frowned. "What do you mean?"

Lord Westlake walked around to the front of the desk and placed his palms on the desktop. "You're a beautiful woman, Miss Rose. But there is much more to you than simple beauty. You're patient and kind. A wonderful human being. Far better than I've been as of late. So, what did you see in me that made you accept my offer of courtship rather than those of other men?"

Rose drew in a deep breath as she recalled the man she had known all those years ago. Or rather the man she believed him to be. "You were confident and cared nothing for what others thought of you or with whom you spent your time. Such a man could cause an impressionable young woman to fall in love with you if she's not careful. That is why."

The baron pushed away from the desk. "Thank you for telling me," he said. "I'll continue my pursuit in finding that man. I'll see you soon."

Rose considered what she had told him. It had been a confession of the very thoughts that had consumed her before. But those days were gone.

With a sigh of relief, she pulled a second ledger from the shelf. After scanning the various entries she growled with aggravation. Nothing of interest. She returned the book and removed another.

This time, she smiled the moment she opened the cover. Inside was a letter, one that would be of use to her. It appeared Lord Westlake and his cousin Master Marcus were patrons of boxing. That in itself was of no importance. Many gentlemen found the sport riveting. What caught her attention, however, was that their interest included fixing fights.

Taking a piece of parchment, she jotted down the most important points, returned the letter to the book, and continued her perusing. She was by no means an accountant, but the baron's entries did not make sense. It seemed that he owned a tavern in London that brought in an income far better than such an establishment should earn. Furthermore, he had annotations that implicated himself in several underhanded deeds!

Twenty minutes later, Rose returned the ledger to the shelf. Folding the parchment, she slid it into the pocket of her dress. She would write up a new article and send it off to Nathaniel Green, her editor. By the time Lord Westlake fell in love with her, all of London would see him for who he was! A cheat and a swindler!

Standing in the doorway to the library, she watched the baron as he sat in a chair reading, one leg crossed over the other. He was as handsome today as he had been six years earlier.

And as devious. He did not remember that fact, but it did not matter, for he believed all was well.

And that was what made her smile when he looked up at her.

Chapter Thirteen

Evan stormed down the corridor and paused at the door to the study. He had spent the better part of yet another morning doing all he could to recall anything of his past life to no avail. For a moment, he considered seeing to his ledgers, but business was the last thing on his mind. It could wait. But the memories he sought could not.

The question was, why did they allude him so?

"My lord," Fletcher said as he approached, "the marquee you requested has been erected."

Evan smiled. He had asked Mrs. Moore to put together a selection of food appropriate for a picnic as a surprise for Miss Rose. He had to make up for his recent misdeeds somehow.

"I've requested that Richard join me in serving."

"No, I'll see to it," Evan replied.

Fletcher bowed. "As you wish, my lord."

The butler went to walk away, but Evan called out after him, "Wait."

"My lord?"

"It's been nine days since my fall, and I find myself...angry a majority of the time. Yet this seems to go against who I once was."

The old butler frowned. "I'm not sure I understand, my lord."

"What if the injury to my head has altered who I am? What if I remain this way forever?"

Evan had stayed awake into the late hours the previous night

117

considering this very question. How would his life change? Not that it mattered, he supposed, since he could not remember what it had been like before. Yet it was one thing to go from an angry man to a kind one—something that would please many people. But it was quite another to do the opposite.

"Ah, I understand now," Fletcher said. "May I offer a bit of advice, my lord?"

"Please, do."

Fletcher smiled. "I hope you don't think me impertinent, my lord, but given your current situation, you've placed a great deal of expectation upon yourself. I suggest you stop trying so hard to regain your memory and allow them to return in their own time. Enjoy yourself as you are now. Your home and finances are in order. Your staff is happy. Perhaps it's time you were, as well."

Evan considered his words. "I appreciate your honesty, Fletcher. I truly do. I'll give it some thought."

Despite the butler's wise counsel, the doubts remained as Evan made his way to the foyer. As soon as he saw Miss Rose, however, they flitted away like the seeds of a dandelion. She wore a dress of dark-blue muslin that showed off her perfect figure. Her hair was neatly piled atop her head. The desire to kiss her again erupted inside him.

No, he wanted to do more than simply kiss her.

A twinge of guilt tickled the back of his mind. Why would he have such coarse thoughts? He was a gentleman, not some rogue who devoured women like sweet cakes. Women should be adored, prized, revered. Not looked upon as objects. Or so he had been reminded.

This thought brought about a new dilemma. How did one treat a woman for whom he cared? Should that not be one of those habits Fletcher had mentioned? Like eating, drinking, and talking.

Blast this wall that kept him from his memories!

"My lord?" Miss Rose said, breaking him from his thoughts. "Are you well?"

"Yes. Yes, of course." Hiding his frustration was difficult.

Without waiting, he walked past her. As Fletcher opened the door, however, Evan thought he saw the butler give Miss Rose a small, mysterious smile. Now, why would he do that? What sort of secret could his butler and the woman who had captured his attention share?

No, that was absurd. Fletcher had a smile for her every time they met. He was simply being polite. Yes, that was what it was—politeness of his staff for one of her station. He would have to thank the man later.

The marquee had been set up beneath a large oak tree, a table and two chairs beneath it. The corners of the tablecloth flittered in the warm, light breeze, but clouds fought for dominance in the early afternoon sky. He had hoped for better weather.

At least it's not raining, he thought ruefully.

"This is lovely," Miss Rose said as they approached the picnic area.

He pulled out a chair for her and began to unpack the basket.

"Drat!" he said, slamming shut the lid. "That deuced woman forgot to include a knife! I'll go for one."

Miss Rose placed a hand on his arm. "Stay. I'm sure we can fare without it."

Evan pinched the bridge of his nose. "Are you certain?"

"Most definitely," she replied, smiling up at him.

He sighed as he dropped into his seat, the legs of the chair sinking into the soft ground. "I find my mood rising and falling at every turn. The frustration I feel at not remembering gnaws at me. Fletcher advised me that I should stop trying, but I cannot." He pulled the stopper on the crystal decanter and poured Miss Rose a glass of wine. "At least I can remember some things, such as how to pour wine."

She arched an eyebrow. "Do you wish me to kiss you again? Is that why you're plying me with alcohol?"

"No," he said with a laugh. "What I wish is for you to be near me. That is all I need in this world."

He clamped shut his mouth. What had made him say such a thing? He pondered how that statement made him feel. It felt...right, somehow. Perhaps his old feelings for her were returning.

Yet, Miss Rose did not smile. Not at first. Then the doubts that budded in him fell away as she reached over and placed a hand atop his.

"I'm here for you, my lord," she said. "Never doubt that."

Evan sighed. "I doubt many things, but you seeing me through this difficult time is not one of them."

"Then you trust me more than you did last week?" she asked. "You're no longer concerned that I'm seeing to your ledgers? Or having you read that ghastly poetry?"

She pushed out her bottom lip and the oddest sensation came over Evan. Since he had first seen her, not a moment passed when he did not wish to kiss her. Yet now there was something more. He wished to hold her. Not bed her, although that thought was pleasant, but to simply hold her close, to whispers sweet words in her ear.

He had hurt her with his questioning of her motives, and that troubled him. The thought of her being hurt, especially by him, put his nerves on edge.

"I insist you continue doing what you always have," he said, staring into his glass. "I've no desire for seeing to whatever enterprises in which I've entangled myself. I trust you to see to it until I'm able to do so on my own." He looked up at her. "Did I lose my temper often with you? Before my accident, that is."

Miss Rose smiled. And what a lovely smile it was! "Every man loses his temper from time to time, but any harsh words, any disagreements were settled quickly."

"This friendship you say needs to be rebuilt. Was it the reason we were able to settle matters so quickly in the past?"

She nodded. "And it was through those disagreements that I came to adore you even more. You're a gentleman through and through."

Evan sighed. "I don't see myself as such." He reached for the bottle and poured another glass. "Tell me about our time together. When did you know I first cared for you? And you for me, for that matter?"

She threw her head back took a rather large, unladylike gulp of her wine, emptying the glass in one go. "May I have more, please?"

Stunned, he poured more wine into her glass. When he stopped at a measure, she tapped the rim of the glass, and he poured more. It was not until the glass was full that she indicated he should stop.

"Well?"

"Forgive me," she said with a laugh. "I forgot to answer. But I believe it should wait for another day."

"Why? Is this not a wonderful time to discuss us? No one is here to overhear." He frowned. "Why are you avoiding the question?"

Miss Rose gave a small nod. "I'm not avoiding it, I assure you. I was being selfish, I suppose, enjoying this time with you. I would rather not want to cause you any undue worry. After all, you'll likely not recall anything I say."

Evan stared into his glass and growled. What she said was true. That did not mean he liked it. "Let's forget about it, then."

As he raised his head, Evan thought he saw a fleeting smile cross her lips. But, no, it had to have been an illusion created by the shade of the marquee.

"One day," she said, patting his hand, "you'll care for me as you once did. And when that happens, it will create a new memory that is far better than the old."

"You're as wise as you are beautiful," he said. "And I've no doubt that I'll care for you as I once did."

As he spoke those words, an odd feeling came over him. It was as if he could recall caring for her, although to what extent remained to be seen. That had to be something, did it not?

As they spoke about a variety of topics, Evan listened with interest. With each word Miss Rose spoke, he understood one thing. At one time, he had been a gentleman and had cared for this lady. What seemed strange was that the challenge to have that relationship return outweighed the desire to kiss her again.

Chapter Fourteen

Rose found her worries easing with Lord Westlake's trust in her building, so she returned to the study to poke about. Any tidbit of information would be enough to cause a lovely scandal and his eventual condemnation from society. As to hear heart, that was hers alone to break.

Admiring the finely-bound leather ledgers, Rose selected one at random. Perhaps she would be lucky and this would be the one with the most damning evidence.

As she sat in the chair behind the desk in his study, she opened the ledger and began her perusal. If anything could get her mind off what she had just heard, learning more about Lord Westlake's unscrupulous enterprises would surely do it. Learning about the fixed fights had been revealing, but there had to be more, surely.

Tracing a finger down the columns, however, she had no will to peruse them. Doing so felt wrong somehow.

Slamming shut the book, she pushed it away and dropped her head into her arms. She needed a moment to collect her thoughts. Had Leah been correct? Had Rose taken this too far? Lord Westlake had mentioned feeling lost, and no matter how hard she tried, she could not stop that feeling of pity for him.

With a sigh, she stared down at her skirts without seeing them. Then, a piece of black metal sticking out from beneath the desk caught her attention. Leaning down, she slid her fingers between the bottom drawer and the floor and pulled out a key from a small pocket. She turned it in her hand. She knew where it belonged.

Her hand shook as she slid it into the keyhole in the top desk drawer she had previously been unable to open. A sharp *click* told her that it had unlocked, and she slid open the drawer.

Inside, she found stacks of papers. Clippings from a newspaper proved to be her column. So, Lord Westlake had been aware of Lady Honor before his memory loss. Although Mr. Fletcher had made the connection between the column and Rose, he had not discussed his suspicions with the lord of the house. Or so she hoped.

She placed the scraps on the desktop. Beneath them were at least a dozen letters, and Rose sifted through them.

"I fear I have been used," one said.

"Why do you not reply to my correspondences?" said another.

A third said, *"You swore your love to me, but I know better now. It no longer matters, for I've found a better lover than you ever were."*

Then Rose covered her mouth when she came across one of her letters, sent in desperation.

"I leave for the Continent in ten days and wish to speak to you before I go. Please, I beg of you, whatever has caused you to turn away from me, give me the opportunity to rectify it. Send word as to when and where we can meet, for I have so much I wish to say.

All my love,
Rose Follet

Tears filled Rose's eyes as the letter fell from numb fingers. Oh, how she had waited in hope he would send word that he wished to meet. That he wished to explain. Every day she waited. Until the day Aunt Jean arrived. It was that day when Rose finally admitted that Evan, Lord Westlake would never respond. Nor would he ever acknowledge her if she saw him again.

Would he remember what she looked like? They had known one another less than an hour, and she had given herself to him like some harlot, a hussy. Perhaps she should have requested payment for the time he had spent with her! After all, she was no better than any prostitute who sold her body for a pittance! Even if she had done so out of a delusional sense of love for him.

He had made her promises he never intended to keep. And as foolish as she had been, he should have known better than to play with her heart as he had.

It was the first night on the ship, when a man frowned at her, that Rose made a promise to herself. Her dress sizes would shrink. Her round cheeks would slim. She would do everything to make herself beautiful in Lord Westlake's eyes. When he begged for her to love him, she would reject him. And she would walk away in triumph, allowing him to wallow in his own misery, just as he had done to her.

Yet with each passing action, Rose found herself miserable, not he. Even before she came to this house, no dress made her feel beautiful. She was just as ugly now as she had been six years earlier.

Wiping away a tear, she thumbed through the remaining letters. She did not have the heart to read any others, for they likely carried the same message of heartbreak and loss.

When she came across one, unfinished, she paused, tilting her head in stunned awe.

Dear Miss Follet,

You must forgive me for ignoring your letters. Although I know you will never understand, I must confess what I have done and why. First you must know, when I saw you standing alone across the ballroom at the party where we met, I was mesmerized by you.

Your last letter spoke of the fear you have due to your appearance and that you believe I have turned away from you because of it. I can assure you, that is nowhere near the truth. That night, you did something to me, simply by being you.

Though those around you may not have noticed you, I can say with utmost certainty that I did. Not only did I find you beautiful just as you are, but I also saw a glow around you that drew me to you. In that moment, I wished I weren't the man I was, for I wanted to be a man worthy of the lovely woman I did not even know. Yet, like a fool, I wasted my only opportunity to know you by using you for my own pleasure.

I spoke words that I knew would satisfy your heart, that would lure you to give me what I wanted. Even now, as I know you are to go abroad, I cannot help but think of you. I imagine us together, as a couple, and for the first time, I see myself happy. But that is nothing more than an illusion, for I would only destroy you, just as I have everything else around me.

What you will see is that I'm a man who deserves to be forgotten. Discarded like an old rag. Thus, I implore you to find a gentleman who will cherish you, for I lack the decency to do such a thing.

The parchment was torn where the quill had scratched out the last lines of the letter.

Rose's hands shook as hurt and anger swirled in her heart. Why had he never sent the correspondence? Why had he not stopped her and proclaimed his feelings for her?

Yet it was his words of asking her to forget him that caused her heart to ache and the tears to spill. Did he not know that a woman could not simply forget? That once her heart belonged to a man, it remained there in one form or another?

Did this mean that, after all this time, he truly cared for her? In his way, of course, but still, he cared?

No! she thought as she swiped at the tears on her cheeks. She refused to believe these lies. He had likely written to her as a way to alleviate his own guilt.

But why had he not posted it?

She collected the letters and replaced them in the drawer—save the one he had written to her— followed by the newspaper clippings. What she wanted to do was toss them all into the fire, never to be seen again! The fact he had never posted his apology—if one could call what he wrote as such—said that he was doing nothing more than placating any regrets he may have had once the effects of the liquor wore off.

For a moment she stared at the letter she never received. Then she placed it inside the ledger and returned it to the shelf. Just as she leaned down to slide the key back into the pocket beneath the desk, the door opened, and Mr. Fletcher entered.

Rose kicked the key beneath the desk and sat up straight. She would have to replace it later.

"Miss Follet," Mr Fletcher said, "with his Lordship resting, I thought I would come to ask about his progress? Is the gentleman we both desire to see emerging yet?"

Taking a deep breath to stave off the emotions of what she had just read, Rose said, "His temper is still quick, and his lack of patience is trying, but I'm beginning to see the smallest of improvements."

Mr. Fletcher smiled. "Wonderful! I must go and begin preparations for dinner, though I must say, your endeavors thus far are astounding. I'm so pleased you agreed to help him."

Rose thanked him and waited for him to leave he room before glancing at the ledgers again. Should she take the letter with her or leave it until another time?

As her eyes scanned the room, an unsettling feeling came over her. Was she justified in what she was doing?

For the first time since this endeavor began, true doubt began to rise inside her. Yet those memories from six years earlier forced her to push away the uncertainty. The baron could have sent that letter and at least made an attempt to right his wrongs. The fault was his, and whatever revenge Rose exacted on him was justly due.

Just then, Lord Westlake entered the room. "You were not working, were you? Surely, you must rest like everyone else?"

His kind words nearly fooled Rose, and she laid a hand on his arm. "My lord, I'll never rest until my work with you is done."

Chapter Fifteen

Rose peeked around the corner to the corridor that led to Lord Westlake's bedroom. A chambermaid entered the room across the hall, and she knew she would be there for a better part of twenty minutes.

She had left the baron alone in the library to read, allowing her a moment to go in search of anything that could spark an idea for a future article. Her readers wanted something more delectable than what she had found in his ledgers. Fixed fights would only give her so much fuel for the fire she wished to build. She needed more.

As expected, Lord Westlake's bedroom was a place of luxury with its heavy wood furniture and large silver-rimmed standing mirror. She stopped in front of it to study her reflection. Although she had done all she could to make herself appear more desirable, she had not reached her ideal of what was pretty. Yes, she had high cheekbones, a small waist, and a bosom that caught many men's eyes, yet she still felt as she had in her younger years.

Alone.

Scared.

Ugly.

No amount of attention, no matter how many requests to call she received, she felt no better than she had before. Like the dress she ordered the previous week, the satisfaction would be temporary. Would she never be happy?

Running a hand over her stomach, she sighed. There was no time for self-pity. She had investigating to do.

She went to the dresser, pulled open the top drawer, and moved aside the clothing. A silver flask, a few coins, and a bundle of notes. But nothing of interest.

Moving to the next, she did the same, sighing when that drawer, too, yielded nothing. Perhaps the information she had gathered thus far from his study was enough to bury him. She had already sent a collection of articles to Mr. Green, each revealing a tiny piece of what she had found during her investigation. By the time the last was released, his name would be ruined!

As would be his heart.

Since his brief recollection in the ballroom, Rose had doubled her efforts, all so she would not lose her temper. They continued to dine alone, and last evening, they had discussed going into the village together.

A glance out the window had her stop and stare at the tree under which they had shared in their picnic.

"What I wish is for you to be near me. That is all I need in this world."

His words had seemed desperate. And for good cause. He knew nothing beyond what Rose told him. And her attempts were working. He was more polite and kind. And although he was still prone to sudden outbursts of anger, they occurred less often than before.

Then there was the letter she had found, words that had remained with her since reading them. A confession of sorts that she wanted so much to believe. Yet she could not do so. She had a purpose for being at Tinsley Estate, and that did not include giving him a second chance.

Her job was far from over. Each time she reminded him of his distrust of her, every time she stepped away from his ire, he tried harder. She had no doubt that he was learning to rely on her. Soon, he would care for her, and eventually fall in love with her. Then her endeavor would be complete.

"Miss Rose?"

Startled, Rose turned to find Lord Westlake staring at her.

"What are you doing in my bedroom?"

Fear coursed through her as she glanced at the dresser. Why had she not closed the drawers?

"Why are you searching through my things?"

Rose's heart skipped a beat. She had made a mistake and now was caught. Her mind searched for any excuse, but none would come. "I've no excuse," she said as she went to stand before him. "I *was* searching through your things."

"But why?" he asked, scowling. "What do you hope to find?"

"Miss Follet?" Tilly called from the doorway. "There's no need to look anymore. I found His Lordship's cravat. Thank you for helping me."

With her heart thudding in her chest, Rose walked over to Tilly and took the offered cravat. "I'll put it away for you, Tilly." Then she leaned close and whispered, "I'll speak to you later." She would repay the girl whatever she wanted for saving Rose from Evan's wrath.

When she turned back around, she nearly jumped out of her slippers. Lord Westlake was standing behind her, a wide smile on his face.

"How is it that you're willing to help even the servants?" the baron asked, his voice filled with awe as he took the cravat from her. "Truly, you're an amazing woman." He placed the back of his hand to her cheek, and Rose found it comforting. "If my tone was accusatory, I'm sorry. It's just that I didn't expect to find you here."

Rose was stunned. Did he just apologize? Not the forced words to placate her but a true acknowledgment of wrongdoing? Perhaps her hard work was giving better results than she realized.

"I know you meant nothing by it," she said, giving him a sad smile.

"Now, I must show you something," he said as he pulled her toward the bed.

Her eyes flew open. "Surely, you cannot mean to..." She swallowed hard. Perhaps she had convinced him of their mutual attraction far quicker than she thought!

"I find this room in need of a change," he said. "It needs a lady's special touch."

Rose had no idea how to respond. It was as if the words she needed teased her tongue and then bounced back into her throat. She had to put a stop to whatever he was considering, and soon!

"Will you help me redecorate the room?"

"I...I beg your pardon?" Rose released the lungful of air that she had been holding.

"It feels gloomy and dark in here. I would appreciate whatever suggestions you can give. Just no ruffles or flowers, please. Or lace. I would like the room to retain its masculinity." He said the last with a laugh. "I say we go into the village tomorrow. I believe there is a shop that can order what we need. If they don't carry it themselves, of course."

Relief washed over Rose. She could not have been more wrong about his intentions! "I would be happy to help," she said. "But perhaps it would be best to wait until after your mother arrives."

When he had shared with Rose that his mother would be arriving soon, he had done so with a mixture of excitement and worry. She could not help but feel as conflicted as he. Would the baroness prove to be as cruel as her son? And would she even recall meeting Rose or her parents all those years ago? Lady Westlake would have a barrage of questions for Rose, but if Rose kept to the story she and Mr. Fletcher had concocted, there was no reason for concern.

If I don't panic and forget, that is!

Lord Westlake frowned. "But why? What does Mother's visit have to do with my bedchamber?"

"Nothing whatsoever," Rose replied. "I'm only saying that it's likely far too soon to go into the village. Seeing old friends may prove difficult. Remember, you must take small steps if you're to have your memory returned."

The truth was, Lord Westlake had made many enemies in the village. According to Mr. Fletcher, most of the townspeople despised him. Oh, they would take his money as readily as a cat drinking milk, but that did not mean they did not wish to scratch his eyes out when he had no milk to offer. If the baron learned this truth too soon, it might deter her plans.

Despite her suggestion to wait, however, Lord Westlake appeared as if he was going to object again. So, Rose placed her hands on either side of his face. And kissed him.

At first, he stiffened, but then he wrapped his arms around her and pulled her close. Soon, he was returning her kiss with fervor. What was meant to put him at ease sent her heart into a flutter she had never felt for anyone else. Her insides warmed and her knees grew weak.

When the kissed ended, she could do nothing but stare at him.

He smiled down at her. "I must say, I do enjoy how you settle arguments. I'll remain home. For the time being." He grasped her hand and pulled her toward the door. "Now, come with me. I have a surprise."

"A surprise?" she parroted. "I don't care for surprises, my lord." Plus, she had endured enough turmoil for one day!

"You'll approve of this one, I assure you."

A small laugh of anticipation erupted from her as she hurried after him. As they descended the stairs, Mr. Fletcher waited at the bottom.

"What does he have in mind?" Rose whispered to the butler as he helped her don her coat.

"I suggest you wait and see," Mr. Fletcher replied. "Cheer up, Miss Follet. Not every day is meant for work."

Nodding, Rose stepped out onto the portico where Lord Westlake stood beside two horses, one with a sidesaddle. "I thought a nice ride was in order."

"But I'm not properly attired. And the weather appears…" She looked up at the clear blue sky. That excuse would do her no good.

They could not do this! The thought of being near him and finding she enjoyed it unnerved her.

"You've done so much for me," Lord Westlake said. "If anyone deserves a reward, it is most certainly you."

A tug of guilt played at her heart, but she pushed it aside and allowed him to help her mount the horse. Mr. Fletcher handed her a bonnet, which she tied beneath her chin.

She watched Lord Westlake mount, finding herself admiring his masculine form. The sun highlighted his perfect jawline, and the muscles beneath his breeches tightened as he hugged the horse's flanks with his legs. He truly was a specimen of a man.

Turning away from the tempting sight, she chastised herself. *You are here for one reason only. To see him pay. Remember that!*

"Do you not like my surprise?"

She forced a smile. "I do. Thank you. It's lovely."

"Mr. Fletcher told me we went riding several times in the past, and although I don't recall those outings, I thought it would be a good idea to trust his word."

Rose's surveyed the area as they rode past the stable and entered the green field beyond. It was filled with magenta corncockles and yellow lady's bedstraw. She inhaled deeply. "There is no better smell."

"I cannot argue that," Lord Westlake replied. He was staring at her. And grinning.

"What are you gaping at?" she asked, her tone far more playful than she had intended.

"You, this field, the flowers, the clouds and sky. It's all so beautiful. You belong with beautiful things, Miss Rose, for that is what you are."

A flush in Rose's cheeks made her look away. His words should not have such an effect on her. But they did.

"I must confess something," he said, drawing his horse closer to hers. "I've made a promise to myself not to try to steal any more kisses from you. I want to get to know you better, but the more I learn, the more a strange myriad of emotions rise in me. It's as if there is something familiar aching to break through that wall that blocks my memories. The only answer that makes sense is that whatever I felt for you before is returning."

Rose could not help but smile. Her guess had been correct! What she was doing was working. "How wonderful!" she exclaimed. "Today has become even more special."

Lord Westlake took her hand in his. "When I kissed you in my bedchamber, just know that I hadn't intended to take such liberties. It simply...happened." He chuckled. "I don't know what came over me."

She nearly laughed. It had been she who had initiated that kiss, just to silence him.

The sudden image of Miss Constance Haskett and what Rose had seen through the keyhole to the drawing room invaded her thoughts. There was no reason to believe there were not other women he had seduced in that room. On that couch. There were likely many others.

When she looked at Lord Westlake again, she knew why he had laughed. He was mocking her.

Or was he? There was such an innocence in his eyes, Rose was uncertain what to believe.

"Why do you wish to kiss me, my lord?" she asked. She needed to know!

The baron shook his head. "It just happened. As if it were meant to be. As if it were a natural occurrence. Is that not what people who care for one another do?"

What was natural was this man speaking sweet words and using his lips to convince women those words were true. Just as much as his ignoring her. As his allowing her to weep every night as she prayed for just one response to her many letters.

With trembling hands, she gripped the reins, unsure if she should leave. Why could this moment, these words, be real? This could have been their life!

As she looked at him, the smile he wore made her heart ache. It was a pure smile that had her doubting everything she felt.

"Yes, that is what people who care for each other do," she said. "They read in the library, eat outside, go on rides together." She sighed. "That is what they do."

Lord Westlake placed a hand atop hers. "If that is what we did, then we'll do so again. Our entire lives are before us, Miss Rose. Granted, it may include you giving me reminders for the remainder of mine, but at least we'll be together. Is that not what we both want?"

Rose nodded and then stopped herself. This imaginary life with Lord Westlake was nothing but a dream concocted by the young mind of a naive girl!

But the words he wrote! What of them?

He did not mean them.

"This outing has been wonderful," she said, glad to have her thoughts back where they belonged. "But I wish to return to the house. I must dress for dinner."

Rose turned the horse around and rode away, her emotions in a knot. She had meant to fool him, not the other way around! He had tricked her again, and she had no one to blame but herself. *She* was the one who had kissed *him* earlier! And all because she had allowed those old dreams to return.

Fool, fool, fool! She screamed at herself in her head. *You are nothing more than a half-witted goose!*

As she drew near the cottage, she paused and drew in a calming breath. There was far too much to accomplish, and Lord Westlake was no longer the main obstacle. It was herself. She had given in to feelings before but without understanding the consequences for them.

Well, that would not happen again!

Chapter Sixteen

The Morning Post, 19ᵗʰ of July 1803

News of the Ton

Our favorite baron has come down with quite the ailment, one in which he believes he is absolved of all his past sins. Not only does he believe he has the right to ignore his past transgressions, but he also believes that he has gained the ability to be a gentleman. Many a gossiping tongue tell me that scorned women are coming in droves to exact revenge on him. Only in a children's tale would a man return from his past to emerge a better man. But a wise woman knows, once a man acts like a dog, so shall he forever be.

If you are curious as to business dealings of a deceitful nature, I shall share what morsels I have been given. Do look for more later as I uncover more on this unscrupulous man.

Lady Honor

Rose set aside the newspaper and leaned back in her chair to look out the window. Aaron played outside, using a stick as a sword as he battled the trunk of a trees. Rose smiled. The boy could always make her smile.

They had been at Tinsley Estate for nearly three weeks, and Lord Westlake had yet to recall anything more than what he had in the ballroom.

Thank heavens! she thought.

The idea that she was the woman he recalled was unsettling. After his countless conquests, after all the lovely women he had taken to his bed, why would he remember her? After all, she was not the type one readily remembered. Not in the way he had described.

Few people noticed her enough to remember. And when they did, all they recalled was how many yards of fabric the dressmaker must have used to make her dress.

Yet there was the letter she had encountered during her search through his office.

No, I'll not think of that anymore. He never posted it, so it does not exist!

Plus, her sights were set on something far greater.

Glancing down at the two-day-old newspaper, she frowned. On most occasions, reading her column gave her a sense of pride. Of accomplishment. This time, it did not. Now it gave her the feeling of having traipsed through the mud in her new slippers.

"It's just your mind playing tricks on you and nothing more," she whispered.

The clock struck five. It was time to change for dinner.

Her new dress had been delivered earlier that afternoon. The timing could not have been more perfect. Lady Westlake was scheduled to arrive tomorrow—she had put off her visit by a week for reasons unknown—and Rose was thankful to have another opportunity to spend time with Lord Westlake before his mother arrived.

Signaling to Leah, she and Aaron followed Rose into the cottage.

"Can I go play with my dogs, Miss Rose?" Aaron asked, referring to the wooden toys they had purchased on their visit to Dunark.

"Yes, of course," Rose replied, ruffling the boy's hair. "I'll be eating dinner again with Lord Westlake tonight. Promise me you'll behave yourself for Miss Leah. And don't argue with her when she says it's time for bed."

"I promise," Aaron replied before hurrying to his room.

"He's growing every day," Rose said. "He'll be as tall as me in no time."

"I know his stomach grows every day," Leah said with a laugh. "How can a child always be so hungry?"

The bedroom where Rose slept was decorated with fine gold drapes, an ornate four poster bed with gold fabric curtains, a wardrobe and matching chest of drawers, and a vanity table. On the bed lay the pale-green dress she had ordered.

"Let's get started," Rose said. "I want this night to be memorable."

Each layer of clothing was of the most luxurious fabrics, but the gown she had ordered from Madam Trudeau's was the most exquisite. Made of the softest cotton, it had a bodice that allowed just enough cleavage to tantalize. The skirt was covered in intricate red lace, and the short, puffed sleeves were hemmed with lace. A satin ribbon accentuated her waist.

When she had fastened the last button, Leah turned Rose around and gasped. "Oh!"

Rose could not help but grin. "It is lovely, isn't it? Mrs. Fleur was correct. The seamstresses do very good work, indeed."

"It's lovely, yes, miss," Leah said hesitatingly. "But if you don't mind my saying, I certainly hope you don't plan to ever wear this out in public. It's nearing indecent!" Her cheeks went from pink to red. "I don't mean any disrespect, miss."

"I promise to only wear it this one time." She turned this way and that and giggled at the way the dress accentuated her feminine form. "Mother would have been downright apoplectic if she saw me in this! But I have a specific reason for wearing it, and tonight, it will serve that purpose."

"I don't understand, miss," Leah said, frowning. "What's the purpose? To make his eyes go big?"

Rose let out a small laugh and took hold of Leah's hands. "Tonight, I'll lead His Lordship to the very room to which he led me six years ago. Unlike that night, however, I'll emerge the victor! Do you not see?"

Leah shook her head. "I'm sorry, miss, but I don't."

Giving Leah's hand a gentle squeeze, Rose replied, "It's like stepping back into the past, but this time I'll not be hurt. Instead, I'll rebuff his advances, leaving him confused. As he falls in love with me—as I did him all those years ago—I'll be the one to break his heart. 'Revenge is sweeter than live itself.'"

"'So think fools'," mumbled Leah.

"What was that?" Rose asked.

Leah shook her head. "Nothing, miss."

Rose gave a firm nod. Nothing, indeed. Lord Westlake would be left muddled in the mind once he saw her in this dress! "Tonight is the beginning of the end for him. And I'll finally have the peace I deserve. No longer will I feel unwanted or...or disgusted with myself."

Glancing in the mirror, however, she could not help but believe those feelings about herself would always remain. Becoming thin had not changed how she saw herself in the least.

Stop that! she thought. It was about time she saw herself in a better light, and Lord Westlake would be the key to her doing so. It was a plan worthy of a thousand smiles.

Leah's smile, however, did not return as she pulled the brush through Rose's hair.

"Do you not agree with what I'm doing?" Rose asked the maid.

Leah paused and bit at her lip. "It's not really for me to say, miss."

"You know I trust your judgment, Leah. Go on."

"Well, I understand your reasons, miss, I really do. But you've changed since you first arrived here. You've become so consumed in seeing him hurt that you're hurting yourself. Your words, your actions, they're a far cry from the young girl I first met."

"That young girl," Rose said through clenched teeth, "she was naive."

Leah nodded. "But she was happy, miss. Even when people were cruel, you were happy in your way. Much more so than you are in seeking this revenge."

Rose considered the maid's words. There had been a time when she was happy—before that party. She had not been thin, and her father had been unkind, but she still had happiness in her life.

"I know His Lordship's hurt you, miss, but don't let what happened destroy you. When will it be enough? How long will it take? There must be a point when he'll have suffered enough."

Rose clenched a fist. "There will be no stopping point, not for him. If you wish to leave, you're welcome to do so. Return to London. But I'll remain and see this to the end."

Leah stopped brushing and sighed. "I'd never leave your side, Miss Rose. You know that."

Tears welled in Rose's eyes as she recalled returning home after the party six years earlier. She and her parents had stayed at a local inn and returned home just after noon the following day. As Leah helped Rose undress for the night, she had confided her deepest, darkest secret to the maid.

"Last night, I became a woman," Rose had said.

Leah's face lit up. "You mean that a gentleman has asked to call on you? How wonderful!"

Rose shook her head. "No. I mean that I'm a true woman." When the maid covered her mouth in shock, Rose said, "Don't worry. Lord Westlake loves me. I expect him to call tomorrow, or perhaps the next day, to speak to Father." She placed a hand on Leah's. "Don't be disappointed with me."

"No, of course not, miss," Leah whispered. "It's just...I'm just worried is all. I fear for you."

Leah had always been protective of Rose, but she assured the maid that all would be well.

Four months later and still no replies to her letters, however, had left her sobbing into Leah's shoulder.

"My life is ruined," she had cried as Leah held her. "I'll lose everyone. They will leave and I'll be all alone."

"Oh, no," Leah had said, gently rocking her. "No matter what happens, I'll never leave you."

Now, blinking back tears as she had that day so long ago, Rose looked at the reflection of the maid—her only true friend. She placed a hand on top of Leah's. "I know you're here for me. And thank you."

Once her hair was piled high in a perfect chignon, perfume dabbed on her skin, and a touch of color added to her cheeks and lips, Rose took one last look in the mirror. Yes, she was ready.

There was a knock on the front door. Rose's heart thudded in her chest. Tonight would prove to be among the most important in her life. Tonight, she would go further than she had since her arrival to give him a glimpse of what could be. And like before, at just the right moment, she would pull away, all for the sake of "propriety." He would think the fault was his and therefore try all the harder to prove he was a gentleman. And he would be one step closer to falling in love with her.

"Don't forget your wrap, miss," Leah called as Rose went to leave the room.

Rose took the wrap with a sense of relief. She might have wanted to shock and intrigue the baron, but that did not mean it was easy. Despite the inches lost in her waist and stomach, she remained uncomfortable in her own skin. Would she have the nerve to go through with this?

"I'll see you tonight," Rose said, smiling. "And don't worry about me. I'm in complete control and shall remain so."

When she opened the door, however, she was not so sure. Lord Westlake stood there in a black dress coat and matching waistcoat that fit him quite well. His white cravat was tied perfectly around his neck, and his beige breeches showed off very fine leg muscles. The early evening sun caught the gold in his blond hair. His smooth jawline looked stronger than ever, and his smile matched the twinkle in his eyes.

How often as a young woman had she lain in bed with these same thoughts about this gentleman, her heart thudding with the love she felt for him?

Drat you for thinking him handsome!

"Miss Rose," he said, taking a step back, "that dress, your hair...I dare anyone to tell me there is a more beautiful woman in all of England. For I can prove to them there is not."

Rose smiled and gave him a curtsy. "You are just being generous," she said, smoothing the fabric that lay over her stomach. "You really should not say such things."

"And why not? Do you not enjoy the truth?"

For a moment, Rose allowed the words to comfort her broken heart. Hearing him say such things was a delight.

She nearly snorted. The entire reason for this evening was to execute her plan, not to believe that he had made such a drastic change in no more than three weeks. What had come over her?

He put out his arm. "I would hate for you to walk alone."

Rose, unable to bring forth words, nodded and took his arm.

"I must admit, I've been looking forward to this evening all day."

"As have I," Rose said as they approached the gate that led to the gardens. "Dinner with you is worth the anticipation."

Lord Westlake opened the gate and ushered her through it. "I would disagree. The honor of dining with you is worthy of giving up everything."

He must be drunk, she thought wryly.

"Will we be having drinks in the parlor first?" she asked in some attempt to change the subject. "A glass of wine would be lovely."

"Whatever you wish. Let me find Fletcher."

"Oh, leave the poor man to his duties, my lord. I'm sure you are capable of pouring wine."

The baron frowned. "But he's the butler. It's not as if the task is unexpected." He stopped and searched her face. "Is something wrong? You seem to be carrying a burden. Is there anything I can do to help?"

If he only knew the burdens she carried!

"Not at all," she said, forcing a smile. "Forgive me. I'm just tired is all." She returned her hand to his arm. "Come. Let's go have that drink."

Once inside, Rose sat on the couch, and Lord Westlake poured their wine. She considered removing her shawl but thought better of it. Now was not the time.

"Thank you," she said as she accepted the glass from him.

Lord Westlake sat in the place beside her. "We've an entire hour together. I would like to hear more about you."

"Oh," Rose said before taking a rather large gulp of her wine. "Well, let's see. We share many of the same interests. And...I'm not sure what else to say."

He brushed back a wave of blond hair from his brow, and Rose took another drink. Would she never get her nerves under control? This should have come far easier to her. She had planned this out to the minutest of details. Or so she had thought.

"Tell me anything," he said, smiling. "Whatever comes to mind."

What was she supposed to say?

And why was it so hot in here?

She went to take another drink and was horrified to find her glass empty.

"Here, allow me to pour you another."

"Yes, please," she replied. She needed something to give her courage. And to help her create the false past she so desperately needed at the moment.

"Why not start with the most recent," he said as he handed her the new glass of wine. "A moment that might be memorable to me."

"Well, a month ago, we laughed over an idea I had, a business proposition of sorts in which we were to participate." Her mind raced as she concocted the story. "I wished to purchase a millinery on Regent Street. You thought the idea silly. 'What baron wishes to be involved with such matters?' you had said."

Lord Westlake chuckled. "Yes, well, it is a peculiar enterprise for any man, I'm sure. But it's not unheard of. What did I agree to in the end?"

"That you would purchase the shop for me as a gift," she replied with a nervous laugh.

What had made her say such a thing? A millinery? What would she ever do with such a business? Purchasing hats she enjoyed, but she did not know the first thing about running a shop! Nor did she truly wish to learn.

The baron frowned. He likely thought it as ridiculous a notion as she did!

"I'm sure it has already been sold by now," she said with a small smile. She placed a hand on his arm, a bad idea, that. He had well-formed muscles beneath that coat that left her mouth as dry as a desert. As if burned, she pulled back her hand. What was wrong with her? She was acting like a silly goose.

Yet the act had its desired effect on him, for he smiled in very much the same way Aaron did when he was promised a sweet.

"I say we purchase it for you," he said, rising. "If that shop is indeed sold, we'll find another location. Whatever you want, Miss Rose, I'll give it to you."

"There's no need, my lord," Rose said. "I get a reasonable allowance that can pay for anything I want."

"Keep your money. It will be my pleasure to do this for you."

A sudden regret for what she was doing filled her. She had no idea from where it came, and it felt foreign to her, but it swarmed over her as thickly as bees in a hive. "Please, don't buy me a shop. Besides, you don't know me. Not truly."

He laughed. "I may not know you now, but I did at some point. And you must admit that I've better control over my temper these days. I'm confident that my memory will return as time goes by. In fact, I'm feeling like a new person and that can only be attributed to you. To you and your confidence in me. That gentleman you once knew, he'll return soon enough, and this angry man I've been lately will be gone once more. I'll be a better man, Miss Rose. I promise you that."

Rose's heart raced. Seeing true sorrow in him was a strange encounter. Could there be a gentler, kinder man inside him? Mr. Fletcher had alluded to as much, and the letter showed it, too. What if a better man had emerged? What then? Would she still want to hurt him?

Her confidence began to wane.

As the baron returned to his seat Rose turned away. *What you had hoped for all those years ago never existed,* she reminded herself. It had been nothing more than an illusion. She was here to see him suffer, and she could not lose sight of that.

Taking the new glass of wine, she settled back into the couch. Soon, she was relating all sorts of tales—all stemming from long-ago dreams—of their make-believe life together. Gone were the palpitations, replaced by calm assurance.

And a lighter head than she wanted.

"And that's why I remain in London with Aaron and you are here," she ended.

"When did we discuss courtship?" Lord Westlake asked, catching her off-guard. "Or rather, how long have we been courting?"

But Rose had endured enough of stories for one night. If she forced her mind to concoct another lie about their life together, she would pull out her hair! She had a task to complete, and now was the time to take the first steps to seeing it done.

"My lord," she whispered as she fanned her face with a hand, "it's getting awfully warm in here. I must remove my shawl."

Lord Westlake frowned. "I don't find it hot," he said, taking her glass. "I hope you're not falling ill." He turned to set aside the glasses as Rose removed her wrap. "Are you certain..." He paused. and the hunger in his eyes betrayed his thoughts as they focused on her revealing neckline. "...you are well?" he completed his sentence.

"Oh, yes, I feel wonderful," Rose purred. "My wrap was far too heavy, but I'm much more comfortable now." She leaned forward and lowered her voice. Oh, but she felt giddy! "Can I tell you a little secret?" The baron nodded. "I considered purchasing a new necklace, one with a lovely pendent that will nestle very nicely right here." She touched the tip of her finger to where the valley between her breasts began, and Lord Westlake swallowed visibly. "You look tense, my lord. Are you sure it is not you who is unwell?"

The warmth she had been feeling traveled through her body, and she found herself needing to be held. Caressed. Loved.

He ran a finger down her arm, and she trembled at his touch. "You are so beautiful, Miss Rose."

The desire in his voice pleased her. "I remember a wonderful evening we shared right here no more than a few weeks ago." She leaned in closer, and he drew in a short, haggard breath. His masculine scent made her head swim. "Your kisses were so hungry, I begged for more." She placed a hand on his chest and looked up at him through her lashes. "Your kisses are so passionate that they bring out the desires in a woman. How can that happen?"

"You enjoy my kisses that much?" he asked huskily.

Rose smiled at his confusion. "Oh, my lord, I cherish each and every one of them."

He stared at her as if in a trance, and a thrill ran through her. She controlled him this time! And she found she wanted more. "I prefer the strong possessive ones you place on my lips. The tender ones behind my ear."

Without warning, she was in his arms, his lips pressed to hers. The kiss was powerful, demanding, and Rose's body betrayed her.

Push him off, you halfwit! her mind urged. Yet she lacked the ability to do so. If she had it her way, she would allow him to kiss her thus the entire night!

Then he was kissing her neck, whispering words that made her weak. "Miss Rose, you make me feel alive! I'm lost without you."

Rose closed her eyes as he kissed her cheeks, her forehead, behind her ear. Breathing became difficult and her body trembled at his touch.

"I need you," he whispered.

I need you, she thought but did not say aloud.

There was sincerity in his tone, and confusion filtered into her thoughts. What had come over her? This was not how the evening was meant to end!

You've a plan, Rose! You must…

He lifted her chin and bent her head back to place a kiss in the hollow of her throat. Of its own accord, her hand went to the back of his head to draw him closer. She could endure his kisses forever!

For a moment, Rose imagined them together as the couple they should have been. In that image, she was there truly to help him be the man she once believed he was. That man who had expressed his feelings in a letter. Yet this time, he would share it rather than hide it away.

His hand moved down to the buttons on the back of her dress.

Just as she wished to give in to his loving ministrations, she opened her eyes.

And took in the room. The very one where her life found ruin.

Her mind cleared as quickly as a summer storm. Now was the time to take control!

Pressing her hands firmly against his chest, she pushed Lord Westlake away, leaving him gasping for breath and with confusion on his handsome features.

"Would you like to hear what else you did?" she asked in those same purring tones.

"Yes, tell me," Lord Westlake said, leaning in to kiss her again.

She lightly pushed him away once more. "You took me in your arms. I all but begged you to carry me to your bedchamber and kiss me all night long. To lie in your bed. To be in your arms. For that is what those in love do."

"I'll do that now," he said. "Tell me that is what you want and we'll leave at once."

Rose suppressed a small smile. The lust and desperation in his eyes pleased her. She placed a hand to her breast and said, "But to my surprise, you refused. Instead, you walked me right over and sat beside me on this very couch."

"Did I?" he asked, the disappointment clear in his tone.

"Oh, yes," she replied. "You said you would not violate me in such a horrendous way, that such actions should be reserved for the marriage bed. You even made it clear that we should follow propriety and remain virtuous until the day we are married. That is, if we were to marry."

Lord Westlake closed his eyes and fell back against the couch.

Returning the wrap to her shoulders, she stood in victory. Or rather relative victory. This would be the last time he ever saw of her in that state! She did not like playing with fire, for she would be the only one burned.

"Forgive me for nearly giving into temptation once again," she said. "Do you understand now why I must abstain? How I struggle to remain a lady when I am faced with such impropriety?"

The baron buried his head in his hands and grunted what could have been taken as agreement.

"I assure you that I'll honor your request. You do wish me to honor it still, do you not? Surely, you were only testing me when you said we could go to your room together?"

"Yes…yes, of course," he stammered, standing, as well. "We must refrain…yes, we must refrain until the time is right. I only meant to test you, as you said."

Rose let out an exaggerated sigh. "That is why I adore you, my lord. Only a true gentleman would refuse a woman as you did." She smiled upon finding his eyes on her. "Even if we were to go through with it, you don't love me. How can a woman agree to such improprieties with a man who does not love her?"

Lord Westlake stood. Something had replaced the fire that had sparked in his eyes, but she did not recognize it. Gently taking her hands in his, he said, "Miss Rose, I wish to make a pledge to you. In the days ahead, I'll honor and cherish you and search for the love I once had for you. That is my mission, to give you the love you deserve.

Rose tried to form words, but her breath was caught in her throat. In his eyes was sorrow and a desperation to please her. Although he had said the very thing she had hoped to hear and this time was able to refuse him, she was filled with sadness.

"Miss Rose?" he asked. "Is that not what you want? For me to love you again?"

A single tear rolled down her cheek. "It's all I've ever wanted."

But she was unsure if it was truth or a lie.

Chapter Seventeen

Evan paced the study with frantic energy. Last night with Miss Rose had come close to being a disaster! When she removed her wrap, his body had taken on a mind of its own, and the spark of desire soon became a raging inferno. Her lips were soft, her skin flawless. Oh, but how she tempted him! He had wanted to carry her to his bed where they would share in the sweet agony of love.

How strange it seemed that they had been in that very situation before. Learning that he had far better control over himself than he realized had been a relief. And a triumph. He truly had been a gentleman!

Although Evan was seeing himself as who he previously was, he could not shake the feeling that they had been intimate before. How else did one explain how much he wished to be with her? To hold her in his arms. To have her rest her head on his chest. To whisper in her ear and proclaim her beauty. If they did nothing more than held one another, he would be pleased.

Yet his mind played tricks on him once again. He would respect her wishes, for she was deserving of such respect. That was the reason he had pledged to search for the love he once had for her. What he had failed to ask was if she still loved him.

Of course she does, you dolt! Why else would she be here?

Yet, for reasons he could not explain, he wished to hear her say so. It was as if he needed it more than air to breathe or water to drink.

Although he wished to consider love and what its implications in his life, he had no time to linger on that topic. His mother was due to arrive this morning, and he had no idea who she was. That did not mean he did not anticipate meeting her.

"My lord, your mother has arrived."

Evan stopped his pacing and turned to the butler. "My mother. Good." His heart was fit to burst. "Fletcher, I remember nothing about her! I don't wish to hurt her, but..." He shook his head. He had a strange sensation that he had somehow caused her pain, but he simply could not remember. Well, no matter what he had done, Evan swore to never do it again.

"All will be well, my lord," the old butler said with a kind smile. She is aware what to expect. You'll find her both gracious and understanding."

Evan nodded. He had asked Fletcher to write to his mother, explain about his condition, and ask that she wait an extra week for her visit. Knowing she knew what to expect did little to calm his nerves, however. This was his mother, the woman who gave birth to him. Although Fletcher had assured him that they had been close, like Miss Rose, it would be a relationship on which he would have to work.

The door opened and a woman of perhaps fifty entered the room. She had his same blonde hair and friendly blue eyes. Her brown traveling dress spoke of wealth, as did the large emerald ring on her gloved finger.

For a moment, she stared at him, leaving Evan unsure as to what to do.

"Oh, my handsome boy," she said finally, wrapping her arms around him and hugging him.

Evan closed his eyes and relished in her love for him. There was a sense of healing in that embrace. Yet, a healing from what?

"You do remember me, do you not?"

"I'm sorry.... Mother," he said. "I do not."

She waved a dismissive hand before pulling off her gloves. "I've every confidence that you will," she said. "Patty, you may return to your old room once you've unpacked my things."

The woman, who could only be his mother's lady's maid, curtsied. She had tawny hair hidden beneath a mob cap and wore a shy smile.

If he were to guess, Evan would have said she was older than he but only by a few years.

"Yes, my lady," the maid said before hurrying away.

"Ah, Fletcher, it's so good to see you again. I hope you are well."

The butler gave her a deep bow. "My lady, it's an honor to have you grace this estate once more. As to my wellbeing, I'm as fit as I ever was."

His mother laughed. "I don't doubt that one bit." She turned her smile on Evan. "Fletcher has always been a friend to our family."

"He's helped me beyond measure," Evan replied. "I'm forever in his debt."

He frowned at his own words. Although they seemed odd to his tongue, he found they were truthful.

"Let's go to the drawing room and have some tea," his mother said, placing a loving hand on his arm. "I've so many questions for you, and I'm sure you have some for me."

When they entered the room, his mother walked over to a table and picked up a figure of a horse. "Your father purchased this for me not long after we were married. I suppose you don't recall him, either?"

Evan shook his head. "Fletcher has told me that he was a good man, but other than that, I know nothing about him." The smile his mother gave him was somehow forced. "Was he not?"

Placing the figurine back in its place, his mother walked over and sat on the couch. "Your father had many good qualities, yes."

Fletcher entered the room carrying a silver tray. Once the tea was served, he gave a bow and left the room once more.

"Now," his mother said, splashing a bit of milk into her tea, "how have you been spending your days?"

Evan sighed. "Trying to remember anything, often with a great deal of failure. Miss Rose Follet, a lady friend of mine has been a great help." His mother frowned, and he quickly added, "Don't worry, she is staying in the guest cottage. You'll meet her soon. Or have you already met?"

"I don't recall meeting a Miss Follet, no," his mother replied, her frown deepening.

Strange, that. Why would he not have at least written to her about the woman he was courting?

He had hoped Miss Rose would join him in greeting his mother, but she had insisted that he do so alone. Although it had angered him at first, he saw her suggestion was for the best.

"May I ask you a few questions? Perhaps you can rouse my memory."

"Very well," his mother replied. "What would you like to know?"

"Why do you not live here at Tinsley Estate? Fletcher mentioned that you had already planned a visit before I fell, but why live elsewhere?"

His mother set down her teacup. "I'm on my way to our Cornwall Estate, just as I've done every year since your father's death. I currently live in a lovely home in Rochester, and I enjoy spending my days painting and reading. I'm not sure what more I can tell you."

"How long will you be staying?" Evan asked.

"I had only planned two days here before leaving for Cornwall, but I cannot help but feel as if I should stay longer."

Two days? Why would she choose such a short visit? Yet Evan did not ask the question aloud. He was putting her through much already. There was no need for rudeness. If only he could remember something—anything—about her, but he could not, and that brought about a sense of shame. What he wanted was for her to remain longer so he could get to know her better but doing so would likely make her suffer.

"No. There's no need for you to change your plans, Mother. If you usually only stay two days, then you should do so now. Perhaps keeping to what is normal will somehow spark a memory or two."

The smile his mother donned made his heart warm. "You've always been the persistent one." She patted her legs and stood. "Come. I wish to show you something."

He followed his mother to the ballroom. She led him to the middle of the room and turned to face him. "We hosted a party here six years ago to see me off to Rochester. Dozens of guests filled this room, many I had never met before. I don't even recall most of their names."

Evan's mind began to whirl. Was this the same party of which Miss Rose spoke? The same party with the woman in the red dress? He had hoped so but also understood that they had hosted many parties in the past. Why would it have been *that* party?

"I looked forward to a change of sorts," she continued. "Yet I was sad to leave you here alone. We didn't always get along, you and I. But I feel that, somehow, this time around we shall. That's why I wanted to talk to you here in this ballroom. That night meant a great deal to me, for I began a new life, and I believe you are beginning anew, as well."

Evan was confused. Their relationship was strained? But why? "Did we argue often?" he asked, not sure if he wanted to hear the answer. He had been under the impression that he and his mother got on well. That was what Fletcher had told him.

His mother sighed. "We did."

"I assume that's why your stays here are so short." Her sad smile told him his assumption was correct. "What were the topics of our arguments?"

"What difference does it matter now?" she asked.

"I must know. It may help me remember."

With a nod, she said, "Our most recent argument was over a gentleman friend of mine. In your last letter to me, you said I was far too old to have gentleman callers. That my time would be better spent working with charities rather than... How did you put it? 'Seeking a lover'. Yes, that was what you said."

A sense of despondency blanketed Evan. Why would he treat his mother with such disregard?

"I don't recall this, Mother, but you've my sincerest apologies for my deplorable attitude. Everyone is allowed to pursue love in his—or her—way. You've been alone long enough."

The words somehow eased his soul, as if a heavy weight had been lifted from his shoulders.

To his delight, his mother squeezed his hand, and tears glistened in her eyes. "You've no idea how long it's been since I've heard those words. I appreciate them more than you can no. But, I would also like to encourage you not to despair. One day, you'll remember everything. But you've been given a special opportunity, Evan, to do the right thing. Make yourself a better man."

A better man? Better than what? According to Miss Rose and Fletcher, he was already a good man. Was there more he did not know beyond an argument with his mother?

Yet he could not get himself to ask the question outright.

She snaked an arm through his. "Let's go finish our tea, my son," she said, smiling at him. As their conversation continued to other matters, worry crept into Evan's mind. What could have caused him and his mother to disagree? And what would make a woman travel so far only to visit her son for two days once a year?

But more than that, he feared his memory would never return, and Miss Rose would suffer the brunt of it. Her intentions, like her heart, were pure, but his inability to recall even the smallest detail would soon make her leave him. And the thought of being alone made him shiver.

Chapter Eighteen

The sound of the yellow fabric of Rose's dress filled the hallway as she made her way to the drawing room. After the debacle that took place in the parlor, followed by an awkward dinner in near silence the night before, Rose had made a hasty return to the cottage to retire for the night.

What a disaster it had been! Why had she weakened at Lord Westlake's touch? And that kiss! She should have been immune to his games by now. If not for the bolt of memories, it would have been far worse.

It was the pledge to her, however, that had bothered her greatly. One that waged war in her heart and mind. His promise to love her again. She had spent hours scolding herself a she lay in bed contemplating the possibility of a relationship with the baron. His words had made her feel complete.

The battle thus far had not been easy, but she reminded herself of her purpose for being at Tinsley Estate. He would be the one hurt, not she, no matter how unwavering her resolve became!

Now she had other problems at hand—the baron's mother.

Lavinia, Lady Westlake had arrived early that morning. Rose had purposefully avoided being in attendance for her arrival, explaining she did not wish to ruin the wonderful reunion between mother and son. Now she could use the situation to her advantage. As mother and son spoke together, Rose could listen in on their conversation without having to be a part of it. Both would be franker with one another, or as frank as they could be given the baron's current situation.

Furthermore, what if Lady Westlake began asking questions of Rose rather than focusing her attention on her son? Although Rose had concocted a number of stories, hearing his mother's questions ahead of time would help her be better prepared.

Once Rose was certain no one was about, she hurried to the door and lowered herself to peek through the keyhole.

Lady Westlake sat on the couch. She was as strikingly beautiful as she had been the night of her farewell party six years earlier. She wore a brown dress and a green ring, and her blonde hair still held most of its color.

"I think you're worried about your condition," Lady Westlake was saying. "Fletcher assures me the doctor believes you'll recover. And likely soon."

Although Rose could not see Lord Westlake from her current position, she could hear his voice.

"That's what I've been told," he replied. "But thus far only one memory comes to mind, one of a woman to whom I was attracted. I thought it was Miss Rose, but it was not." He sighed. "Now I sit here with my mother, who is but a stranger to me. Although she hides it well, I suspect that Miss Rose grows frustrated with me daily, and I cannot blame her. I've seen little progress, and I find myself taking my frustration out on her at times. I can only imagine how that makes her feel. I fear I'll never improve."

A surge of pity pumped through Rose. He spoke with such anguish, of such loss.

Is that not what you wanted?

It had been her greatest wish, but now guilt joined the pity. Had she gone too far?

No! she insisted. *What he did to you was far worse!*

"My son, have no doubt that my love for you remains whether or not you remember me. Your memory will return in time, I'm sure of it. Now, this woman, Miss Rose, tell me about her. I understand that she's a lovely lady."

"Do you not recall her?" Lord Westlake asked. "I would have mentioned her in my letters, I'm sure."

Rose smiled. She had nothing to fear. Fletcher had assured her the relationship between mother and son was strained. Any correspondence was brief and was always limited to matters of the estate rather than personal. How did he know this? She had asked.

"Because he typically asks me to write them," Fletcher had said. "After all, he only did so only out of a sense of responsibility and not because he for her."

Lady Westlake smoothed her skirts. "As I said before, we've not spoken, nor written, for some time."

"But why?"

"I assure you the reasons no longer matter. If this woman brings you joy, then she is the one for you. Now, tell me about her."

It became silent, and Rose could imagine the baron's frown. She found herself holding her breath while waiting for him to reason out the truth, which would lead to having her sent away, which would ruin all of her carefully laid plans.

"There is a poem I once read about a lost man and the woman he needs. Miss Rose is a light in my dark night, allowing me to see lest I stumble into oblivion," Lord Westlake said. "Every day, she has been by my side, guiding me and helping me to see who I once was. And although I don't remember her from before my accident, I know her now. Mother, she's a lovely creature and as wise as any sage. The way she laughs enthralls me. I cannot imagine life without her. She means everything to me."

Rose backed away from the door and wrapped her arms around herself. This was what she had wanted, to have the baron fall in love with her, to rely on her for everything. But now it was all…unsettling. Hearing his words sent a light wave of joy through her, but not in the way she had expected. Rather than the joy of setting him up for his destruction, there was a distinct pleasure for hearing that he felt as he did.

You are brainless! she chastised herself. *A bumbling, idiotic fool of a girl! If you're not careful, you'll fall victim to your own charade!*

She had heard enough.

Making her way to the library, Rose sat on one of the armchairs. She needed something to distract her. Taking the book that sat on a side table, she opened it to the title page. It was the same book of poetry she had recommended to Lord Westlake. The very one he had recited with such enthusiasm.

She slammed shut the book and smoothed her skirts. Why was she the one feeling guilty? Did she not have the right to exact revenge? "And eye for an eye," was it not? Then why did the idea that had sounded sweeter than honey now leave a bitter taste on her tongue?

Emotions swirled as a strikingly beautiful woman entered the room.

"You must be Miss Rose," the baroness said, smiling widely. "It's such a pleasure to meet you." She stopped and her smile fell. "My dear child, have you been crying?"

"Oh, no, my lady," Rose said, standing and dropping into a curtsy. "I'm just...inundated at the moment. There is so much to do."

"Come, let's go have a cup of tea together so we can talk."

She held out a hand to Rose, and for a moment Rose stared at it. Could she trust herself in this woman's company?

You knew this day would come, Rose Follet. No more being sheepish! You've had this planned for ages! There is no backing out now.

Taking the baroness's hand, Rose followed Lady Westlake to the drawing room, where they sat on the couch together.

After sending Mr. Fletcher for a tray, Lady Westlake turned and smiled at Rose.

Rose gripped her hands in her lap. Why did she feel like a child awaiting reprimand?

"Evan's correct, you're a lovely woman," Lady Westlake said and then frowned. "Have we met before? I feel as though I know you."

"I can assure you we have not," Rose said a bit too quickly. "That is, not that I can recall, and I'm sure I would have remembered."

"Evan told me about your parents. I recall meeting them once, years ago. But I must admit, my mind often fails me. You would think that a baroness would have the decency to remember everyone she meets, but, alas, that is not the case." She leaned in closer and lowered her voice. "Let me share in a little secret. Few of us truly remember everyone with whom we are introduced. We just pretend that we do."

Mr. Fletcher returned with the tea tray, poured, and left with a bow.

"He's a wonderful butler," Lady Westlake said. "And a dear friend to the family. I'm glad he's here to take care of Evan. And you, as well."

Rose offered a polite smile, wishing the awkwardness in the room would dissipate. Lady Westlake seemed a lovely woman, and Rose felt that tinge of guilt return for what she was doing to the lady's son. But if she only knew…

"Miss Rose, I've not seen my son in nearly a year. The last time we spoke, we departed in anger, just as so many times before." Lady Westlake placed her teacup in its saucer. "Our arguments seem to revolve around the choices he makes in his life. You understand my meaning, do you not?"

Rose new exactly what she meant. "I do."

"Then please, help me understand why you are here. Why would you want him to remember his past? Surely, you would prefer he did not?"

"It's difficult to explain," Rose said, unable to keep eye contact with the baroness. Silence filled the room, and she wondered what to say next.

Yet it was Lady Westlake who finally spoke. "My dear girl, I can see it as plain as day. Evan hurt you at some point."

Rose blinked back tears. She refused to weep again today, whether it be for Lord Westlake or for herself. "His lordship hurt me more deeply than I wish to share. As to why I'm here, I only wish to see him well and perhaps make him a better man than he was before."

She paused. Speaking those words aloud caused happiness to well up in her soul, which only led to confusion.

Before she could consider these strange emotions, Lady Westlake said, "In his younger years, Evan was a delightful boy. He looked upon life with vigor and wished only to help others. When he was six, I had to scold him for polishing the silver." She chuckled. "'Oh, Mother,' he had told me when I asked why he did it, 'why should Fletcher have to do all this work? Can't I do something to help him?'"

Rose could not help but laugh. "What changed?"

The baroness took a sip of her tea and then sighed. "His father had too great an influence over him, unfortunately. His love of the drink was only surpassed by his many affairs." She winced, and Rose's heart went out to her. Even after all these years, and with the man dead, his actions still pained her. A feeling Rose understood all too well.

"I overheard him speaking to Evan after they had spent a weekend in London together," Lady Westlake continued. "Evan was fifteen at the time. Where most fathers teach their sons how to conduct business, draw up contracts, and what it means to be a man of integrity, what my husband taught him was far less respectable. That was when my son changed." She gave a half-smile and set down her teacup. "I suppose there is no need to explain what his lessons consisted of, for Evan's actions tell it all."

Rose considered all the baroness had told her. Was Lord Westlake's faults truly his father's? How much responsibility should the son take?

"May…may I ask a question?"

The baroness smiled. "Of course."

Rose licked her lips. "Surely, what your husband did caused you a great deal of pain. Did his indiscretions not make it difficult to be near him?" She sighed. "I'm sorry, my lady. That is far too personal. Forget I asked."

"No need for apologies," the baroness said. "We ladies must stick together if we're to endure what men put us through. Indeed, I hurt daily, and I prayed for him to stop. I even considered having an affair of my own in retaliation, so he could see how badly he hurt me. To know what it was like to suffer as I had all those many nights I spent weeping for what once was and the hurt I held. I can assure you those tears are by far the worst." She shook her head. "I'm not sure why I'm sharing this with you. I've never told anyone. But, then again, no one bothered to ask. Too many others in my position have suffered thus, and we're taught to endure in silence. Perhaps if we spoke about it more, it would occur less."

The baroness's story was not all that different from that of Rose. How many pillows had Rose wet with her tears? Too many to count. This realization created a bond with this woman.

"What did you do about it?" Rose asked. "Did you take revenge on him in some way? If so, did it give you a sense of satisfaction afterward?"

Lady Westlake shook her head. "Although I felt justified, I remained a dutiful wife. I played my part and did my best to influence Evan as much as I could. It appears I failed in that arena."

"But why did you choose not to seek your revenge on him?" Rose asked, feeling a pinch of anger. "Did your husband not deserved to suffer?" Her heart raced and her breathing became heavy. What kind of woman would not make her husband pay for such outlandish disrespect?

"Because doing so would only make me the same as him," Lady Westlake replied. "If we use anger to fight anger, the only result is more anger. Evan would then have two parents destroyed rather than one."

Lady Westlake stood, and Rose did the same. "I'll not ask how my son hurt you, Miss Rose, for I suspect it looks very much like what his father did to me. But I'll say this. I'm only to be here for two days. If anyone is to help him, to make my son a better man, I believe it is you."

Rose shook her head. "But you don't know me, my lady. How can you be so sure I can make a difference?"

"There's a delicate glow about you when you laugh," the baroness said with a small smile. "A beautiful aura. I would venture to say, if you release whatever hurt you're feeling inside, that glow will only become brighter." She took hold of Rose's hand. "Evan once possessed an aura very much like yours, and I pray it returns. Promise me that you'll take care of him. Succeed where I failed. Make him the man he is meant to be."

Everything inside Rose told her to turn and run away. To stop this charade before the pity inside her completely replaced her anger. If it remained, if it did indeed take precedence in her thoughts, would it make her a fool? Although she had every reason to hurt Lord Westlake, Rose found the baroness's advice wise. The joy of seeking revenge no longer gave her a sense of reward as it once had. Doing so would damage not only the baron but herself, as well.

Therefore, she nodded in agreement. "I promise to remain until he is well," she said, unable to voice a promise that went beyond.

Chapter Nineteen

Had Rose made a promise she could not keep? Or rather, did she want to keep it? These thoughts and more puzzled her still three days later. Lady Westlake had left the previous day, and Rose had agreed to accompany Lord Westlake into Dunark. At least Leah and Aaron were accompanying them.

The baron had been unusually quiet since the departure of Lady Westlake. As they traveled to the village, he stared out the window, but his eyes were unfocused as if he were lost in thought. Perhaps he was already missing his mother. After all, he could not remember the strain of their previous relationship.

To her surprise, Rose wished she had the words to help ease his discomfort, but it was Aaron who spoke first.

"Lord Westlake," he said, holding up one of his wooden toys, "do you want to play with my dog?"

"Aaron, dear," Rose said as a knot of worry grew in her stomach, "I'm sure His Lordship would prefer to be left to his thoughts."

"No, it's all right. I would love to, thank you." Lord Westlake took the dog from Aaron, and a small smile crossed his lips. "This is a wonderful dog, Master Aaron. Have you named him yet?"

Aaron nodded. "I call him Fletcher."

The baron's laughter filled the carriage. For a moment, Rose found she enjoyed hearing the sound but then pushed away that joy.

"A wonderful choice! I suppose you named it after my butler?"

"Yep," Aaron replied. "I wanted to call him Lord Westlake, but

Miss Rose said that was rude."

Lord Westlake turned the toy in his hands. "She's correct, you know," he said as he looked at Rose. "Miss Rose is a very wise woman. It will serve you well to pay her heed."

Rose's heart skipped a beat, which was happening far too often as of late. His gaze remained on her as the carriage slowed, and she found herself unable to look away.

Soon, the door opened, and they exited the vehicle.

"So, this is the village in which I grew up," the baron said. "I'd love to visit every shop here. I'm sure the proprietors will welcome me with open arms, and my old friends will give me hearty greetings."

The winding street was filled with people moving from shop to shop. Carriages ambled past, a dog running alongside one, barking at its wheel.

Rose knew this day would come, the day Lord Westlake returned to Dunark. The question was, what would he learn?

According to Mr. Fletcher, few shopkeepers liked the baron. Oh, they enjoyed his money well enough, but the man himself was altogether another matter. Her initial reason for keeping him away had been to delay the return of any more of his memories. Now, however, she wondered what learning the truth would do to him.

"You look worried, Miss Rose."

She forced a smile to her lips. "Not at all, my lord. I'm very much looking forward to this outing." Although she was tempted to tell him all would be well, she found herself unable to speak that lie. "Let's hope for the best, but if your memories don't return on this first visit, don't fret. And those who know you may not be working today." As if the butcher or the cobbler could afford to hire help! She had to keep herself from rubbing her temples.

Lord Westlake offered an arm, which she took. "You'll see that your worries are for nothing. As you've said before, I'm a charitable man. People will return it to me in kind."

Leah gave Rose a warning look, but Rose could only offer a small shrug. When Lord Westlake had suggested they visit the village, try as she might, Rose could not think of a single excuse to keep him from going. Therefore, she had agreed. She had put off this visit long enough.

They stopped in front of Madam Trudeau's dress shop. "Is this where you purchased your new dress?" he asked.

Rose nodded.

"If you wish to order more, you may. I would be happy to cover the cost."

"That is kind of you, my lord, but I have plenty of dresses. But thank you, all the same."

He smiled. "Well, the offer stands if you change your mind. Whatever you want, it's yours."

They continued their stroll until they came to the butcher's shop. A man with a thick mustache slammed down a massive knife onto a side of meat. He did not smile when they greeted him.

"If you're here with a complaint about the last order, my lord," the butcher said, frowning, "I checked it myself before having it delivered."

Lord Westlake shook his head. "I'm afraid I don't recall making any accusations against you, sir." The butcher raised an eyebrow. "You see, I've lost my memory."

The man returned to his cutting. "Right. I heard something about that. So, I don't suppose you remember telling me that if I didn't give you a discount, you'd open another shop next door and take all my business, huh?"

"I threatened you?" Lord Westlake asked, his lips turned downward in a pensive frown.

The butcher set down his knife, leaned his hands on the counter, closed his eyes, and sighed. "Forgive me my rudeness, my lord. My daughter's taken ill, and it's been late nights without much sleep."

Rose placed a hand on Lord Westlake's arm. "There was a mistake with an order," she said. "You were angry, as anyone would be. But you came to realize that Mr...." She glanced at the man on the other side of the counter.

"Coleman," offered the butcher.

"Yes, Mr. Coleman had not made the mistake but rather a footman. Since then, Mr. Coleman returned to charging the normal rate. Is that not so, Mr. Coleman." She gave him a pointed look.

The butcher seemed to like the change the conversation was taking, for his frown became a smile. "That's right, miss."

"Still," Lord Westlake said, "I should not have threatened you. Never fear, I've no interest in opening a butcher's shop, let alone one beside yours."

Mr. Coleman's jaw dropped. "I...well, I appreciate you saying so, my lord. You know, I've the most wonderful pork that just came in today..."

As the two men spoke, Rose could not believe what she was hearing. Lord Westlake apologizing again? Or at least coming very close to doing so. Was the hard work she and Mr. Fletcher done seeing results?

Once they left the shop, they resumed their walk. Rose sneaked a glance at the baron, who was mumbling to himself.

"There's no need to get angry at yourself for losing your temper," she said. "You're not the first to do it, nor will you be the last."

"It's not that I lost my temper in the past that bothers me," Lord Westlake said as he came to a stop. "It's that my first reaction now to any given situation is to lash out at everyone around me, even if they have not done anything wrong. I've made every attempt to assuage my ire but hearing that man's words reminds me that I've a long way to go." He shook his head. "Coming here today was a mistake. Let's return home."

"No," Rose said, giving him a smile. A couple walked past them, and the woman's eyes went wide upon seeing Rose take hold of the baron's hands. Rose ignored her. "You'll remain and enjoy your time here. Retreating will not help you regain your memory."

He sighed. "I don't know. I feel as if this ailment is hindering me from returning to the man I once was."

"Even a gentleman can have his ire stoked, my lord," she said. "It's how you react to that anger that decides what type of man you are."

Lord Westlake nodded. "Thank you for your wisdom, Miss Rose. And you're right. I must stay."

Two hours later, they returned to the carriage. They had stopped at several shops, including the haberdasher, the apothecary, a tailor, and a jeweler. Each offered a cold reception. None of the shopkeepers were outright rude—Lord Westlake was of the aristocracy, after all—yet neither were they welcoming. Except the tobacconist. He had opened his shop only two weeks earlier and had yet to meet Lord Westlake.

Yet, with each encounter, the baron had smiled and graciously looked at whatever goods for sale at the particular shop, offering to purchase at one item or another for Rose or Aaron.

But Rose had refused outright. She would leave Dunark owing him nothing!

As she went to step into the carriage once they had visited all of the shops, the baron grabbed Rose's arm and pulled her aside. "Wait, I wish to speak to you," he snapped. "You two, get into the carriage. We'll be along momentarily."

Leah gave Rose a fearful look, but Rose nodded to indicate all was well.

Once they were relatively alone, Lord Westlake turned an angry glare on Rose. "I feel like everyone is keeping a secret from me, and I want to know what it is!"

Rose drew in a deep breath. "There is no secret, my lord," she lied. "I think you're just seeing problems where none exist."

"No," he growled. "It's more than that. It has been a month since my fall, and besides a memory of a woman I believed to be you but who was not, I recall nothing!" He tightened the grip on her arm. "Do you not see that I'm failing as a man?"

She gave a small cry of pain.

He released her, his eyes nearly covering his face. "I...I don't know what made me act so harshly," he said.

But Rose knew why—his name was Evan, Lord Westlake. His kindness today had all been an act. What a fool she was! She should have known better. Once a cad, always a cad. It was so far engrained in him, any attempt to change it was a waste of her time.

He sighed. "I've spoiled yet another outing, haven't I?"

Rage filled her. Oh, yes, she was a fool, indeed! "It's not the first time, I assure you," she snapped, unable to keep hold of the reins on her emotions as she stepped into the carriage. "Nor do I suspect it will be the last."

But as she took her place inside the carriage, the words of Lady Westlake came to mind.

"If we use anger to fight anger, the only result is more anger."

No truer words had ever been spoken.

Chapter Twenty

Something was terribly wrong. It had been six weeks since Evan's accident, and he was no closer to breaking down that wall that held back his memories than he was during his first week.

To make matters worse, the only person to call on him had been his mother. Did he have no family, no friends who wished to see he was recuperating? His cousin, Colin, Duke of Greystoke, wrote asking after him, yes, but where were the others? From what he understood, he had too many cousins to count!

Taking a sip of his tea, he surveyed the garden from the path on which he stood. Upturned soil filled the otherwise empty flowerbeds. Meticulously trimmed shrubbery crisscrossed the expanse of the area. Large trees, their half-brown leaves clinging to their branches, stood at attention at various points throughout. It was a lovely garden. Yet Evan paid it little heed.

Movement to Evan's right caught his attention. The cook's assistant—what was her name? Tilly? Yes, that was it. Tilly hurried down a side path that led to the guest cottage. Had she been to see Miss Rose?

No, she had no business calling to the cottage. And he put it out of his mind.

"My lord."

He turned as the butler approached. "Yes?"

"Lord Caney and Lord Downwick are here to see you, my lord."

Evan did not recall either name, although Fletcher had mentioned both men several times during their talks about his life. Apparently, they were frequent callers to Tinsley Estate. "Thank you, Fletcher. Bring them here. I don't feel like being indoors."

The butler bowed. "Yes, my lord." When he returned, two men followed in his wake. One was thin with a nose far too for his large face. He reminded Evan of a vulture. The other had stringy blond hair and a coat that barely closed around his large midsection.

"Jasper, Lord Downwick," Fletcher said of the vulture, "and Archibald, Lord Caney."

"Thank you, Fletcher," Evan said, handing him his empty cup. "Bring us some..." He turned to his guests. "Brandy, gentlemen?"

"Indeed," replied Caney, and Downwick agreed.

"Brandy, please," Evan finished saying to Fletcher.

The butler bowed and returned to the house.

"Well, gentlemen, it's a pleasure to meet you. I was just wondering if anyone planned to call. Your arrival has put that worry to rest. I thank both of you."

"Is it true, old boy?" Caney asked, taking a step forward and eying Evan as if he were some sort of rare creature. "Have you lost all your memory?"

Evan nodded. "Unfortunately, yes."

"And you don't know either of us?" Caney asked. "Not at all?"

Evan shook his head. "Not in the slightest, I'm afraid."

That familiar sense of frustration grasped hold of his mind as he tried to conjure any memory of either man to no avail. Since his mother's departure two weeks prior, he and Miss Rose had gone into Dunark twice, visiting what should have been familiar shops, but the proprietors greeted him as if he were a stranger. Granted, he was a baron, but their distant behavior was disconcerting. It was as if they were frightened of him. Which, of course, made little sense. Then again, perhaps what he was interpreting as fear was diffidence.

Well, he had no time to consider people who were not here. He had to concentrate on the two men before him.

"I'm sorry, but I don't remember a thing about either of you," he said with a sigh. "Nor anyone else, for that matter."

"You see, Downwick? I told you it was true. He's forgotten

everything. That columnist didn't lie." He chuckled. "Just like the ones before, she's writing about him."

Downwick eyed Evan with what could only be named as suspicion. "I suppose so. You realize now I'll have to spend the next month conceding to Eliza that she was right." He barked a hearty laugh.

Evan was not amused. "Who is Eliza?" he demanded. "And what column?"

"By God, you really don't remember, do you?" Downwick asked. Why did he sound angry? "Eliza is my wife. You've spent a great deal of time ridiculing me for marrying her. As you put it, 'her bloodline makes her opinion negligible.'"

Evan waited for the expected bark of laughter, but none came. A strange sensation washed over him. None of this made sense. "I said that? I must have been joking, surely? I heard we spend hours together laughing about all sorts of topics."

Downwick took a threatening step forward, but Caney put a hand on the man's shoulder. "Go easy on the man, Downwick. It's obvious you're upsetting him."

"Upsetting *him*?" Downwick sputtered. "For years I've been forced to endure his incessant ridicule of my wife, my children. My nose! Now I'm expected to be concerned about upsetting him? I knew I never should have returned here!"

He took a step closer to Evan, a vulture peering down at a dying animal, waiting to devour him. "The column—'News of the *Ton*'—is from The Morning Post. For months, it has been rife with stories about a baron who is detested by all and completely oblivious to it." He pulled a clipping from his inside coat pocket. "This was published three days ago. There's no doubt about it, Westlake. It's about you. So, you can end this charade of pretending you've lost your memory, for I know who you are. As does all of England!"

"Come now—"

Downwick turned a scowl on Caney. "I'll not stand here and play this silly child's game. It would not surprise me if one of the women he's deflowered and used hasn't come knocking at his door and is threatening to ruin his name! I'll wait for you in the carriage." With one final glower for Evan, he stormed away.

Evan's head spun. How could this be?

"Here, let's sit down." Caney led Evan to a nearby bench.

"Is what Downwick said true? Did I say terrible things about him and his family?"

Caney sighed. "I'm afraid so, old chap. You've never been one to bandy your words. And it's been a while since you've spoken kindly to anyone." He chuckled at this. "I wouldn't worry. He'll come around. He always does. Just give him time."

"I'm confused," Evan said, feeling more lost than ever. Could he trust this man's word? "Why have I been told differently about who I am? And what about this?" He lifted the clipping. "Is this truly about me?"

"Read it and then we'll talk," Caney replied.

Evan nodded and silently read the column.

Dear Readers,

Our Fanciful baron believes there is hope for a better day. But, alas, his future remains bleak. It is time that he takes responsibility for his mistakes—and trust me, there are many! Yes, he must pay for the pain he has inflicted on those who have put their trust in him.

If one is so inclined to place a wager on boxing, more so in a small village near Dover I cannot name, be cautious. Our baron and a member of his illustrious family have fixed the outcome of one of those matches, if not all of them. This pales in comparison to some of my other findings. but that, my friends, I must save for a later course in this delectable meal of gossip!

Until next time,
Lady Honor

Blood pounded behind Evan's ears. "Caney, is Fletcher being truthful when he says we—you, Downwick, and I—are friends?"

"Indeed," Caney replied. "For many years. Since childhood, really. We're a most unusual group, I must admit, but we've always kept one another's company, nonetheless."

Evan nodded absently. A gardener carrying a hoe walked past, bobbing up and down with jerky bows when he noticed them. As if he were frightened. "Then tell me the truth," he said once the man was gone. "Does this column speak of me?"

The sigh that his companion heaved filled Evan with shame. "I'm afraid so, old chap."

"I'm more confused now than before you arrived. I must know. Who am I? Because I'm hearing conflicting descriptions, and I've no idea which to believe."

Caney leaned back on the bench and crossed a leg over the other. "Where to start?" he said, rubbing his chin. "You're known for having very loose morals. You've admitted openly to Downwick and me that you've blackmailed not only enemies, but friends and family, too. You've never had a concern for whom you hurt."

"My family?" Evan whispered, his stomach twisting itself into knots. "So, that's why none have come to see me. And you're the first friends to call since my accident." This realization clung to him like lichen to a damp log, and he found breathing difficult. "And these women Downwick mentioned?"

"Both he and I saw you just before your fall," Caney said, brushing back a strand of hair from his face. "You were quite irate..." He paused and looked at Evan. "I'm not sure I should say more. I don't wish to agitate you more than I already have."

"Doctor Norman calls once a week," Evan said. "Each time, I must explain that I've made no progress. If I'm a beast of sorts, I must know." He turned a fervent look on the man who said was his friend. "Please, don't make me beg. What happened the last time we spoke?"

With a heavy sigh, Caney said, "Very well, I'll tell you. But don't hold it against me afterward."

"I swear," Evan replied. "I just want to hear the truth."

"You were quite drunk, which is not uncommon for you over these last years. And you're an angry drunk, Westlake. But that day, you were far angrier for two reasons. One had to do with that morning's Lady Honor column. The other was Miss Constance Haskett."

Evan frowned in thought. "Miss Constance Haskett?" he repeated, trying to pull up any image to match the name. "Is she a cousin? Or a friend?"

Caney chuckled. "Neither. She was a young lady you propositioned and failed to take to your bed."

Jumping up from the bench, Evan said, "No! That cannot be true! Miss Rose and I have been courting for some time now. Why would I do such a terrible thing to her?"

An image of an anguished Miss Rose sprang in mind. If he hurt her, he was unsure if he could live with himself.

"Miss Rose?" Caney asked, frowning. "Who is Miss Rose?"

"Miss Rose Follet," Evan replied, his head hurting from the confusion that filled him. "Surely, I've mentioned her? After all, we're supposed to be courting. She arrived the day following my accident and is staying in the guest cottage until I've recovered. Fletcher knows her well."

"My friend, you've never mentioned this young lady to me," Caney said, giving Evan such a look of pity it left him all the more dismayed. "Then again, I suppose you would have kept such information to yourself if she's a genuine interest. Anything you would deem as weakness you've always hid from others, including Downwick and me. But honestly, from what I know, the last woman you tried to take to bed was Miss Constance. Your anger was for failing to do so. Which I must admit—without praise, mind you—was a rare occasion."

With his head spinning, Evan stared at this man he did not remember. "Then...I'm a...a whoremonger?" The man must have been mistaken!

"In a word, yes," Caney replied. "I'm sorry to be the bearer of what surprisingly seems to be very bad news. It appears you had hoped to hear something different today."

Evan considered the implications of this information. If he was so consumed with Miss Rose, why would he seek the arms of another woman? Guilt tore through him. Was Miss Rose aware of his iniquities? If so, why had she chosen to remain and aid in his recovery? That explained why tears filled her eyes so often!

Oh, Evan, you scoundrel!

"I must apologize for cutting our time short," Evan said, leaping from the bench, "but I must speak to Miss Rose right away. I hope you don't mind seeing yourself out, but please, do call again soon. I've more I would like to discuss with you. And give Downwick my apologies for however I've wronged him in the past. Tell him I'd greatly appreciate him accompanying you when you return."

"Don't worry. I'll convince him," Caney said. "And, Westlake, for what it's worth, the man I see before me today is far better than the one I left a month ago. Whether or not you remember, let the new you emerge and leave the old behind. He really was a brute."

Although he did not understand completely, Evan nodded and watched as Caney walked away. He had to speak to Miss Rose! Yet, what would he tell her? That he was a cad and had hoped to take another woman to his bed?

And why had Miss Rose and Fletcher not told him about these terrible transgressions? Why had they painted a lovely spring picture when the truth was as bleak as any dark winter's night?

The realization of who he had been made him want to retch. Was he truly this vile man? If anyone would know the truth, it was Miss Rose.

Then again, what if she did not know the truth about him? Could he reveal this dark side to her? Perhaps he could keep this information to himself and they could carry on as normal.

He came to a stop as an image of Miss Rose's lovely features came to mind. She deserved to know the truth, no matter how much it hurt either of them. He was lower than the mud on his boots after a hunt, and when she left him this day, he had no one to blame but himself. The punishment of her leaving would be well-deserved.

It was the right thing to do, telling her the truth, and he was compelled to do just that.

Making his way down the stone path, he passed through the gate and looked at the cottage ahead. Movement to his left made him pause, and he turned to find Miss Rose standing beneath a tree. She stood smoothing the front of her dress, a nervous habit he had seen her do often.

Yet, as he gazed at her, the longing in his heart collided with his guilt. He had hurt her and would have no choice but to beg for her forgiveness.

With leaded feet, he approached her, following her gaze out toward the horizon. Low, green hills stood beneath a blue sky dotted with white clouds.

"What are your thoughts?" he asked.

Miss Rose started and turned to smile at him. "The past," she replied. "I think of it often. One would think the misery it brings would make me stop."

Pain filled her eyes, pain he somehow knew he caused. She knew about Miss Constance, he could feel it. And that thought paralyzed him.

You don't have to speak of it! he rationalized.

No, he had to make certain she knew how sorry he was for hurting her.

"Two of my friends called," he said, joining her beneath the tree. "Caney and Downwick."

"I remember them," Miss Rose said. "Quite the pair, I would say."

Evan frowned. "Caney claims to never have met you."

Miss Rose smiled at him. "And he's quite right. We've not met, but you've spoken of them so often that I feel as if I already know them." She tilted her head. "Has their visit distressed you?"

Evan found himself unable to look her in the eye. His guilt weighed as much as a horse. "Miss Rose, I've a confession to make. It will not be easy, but I must say it, or my shame will eat away at my soul."

Her brows knitted in worry. "What is it, my lord?"

Evan took Miss Rose's hands in his. "Before I make my confession, I must ask you a question. Have you heard of Lady Honor?"

Chapter Twenty-One

Standing beneath a tree within the grounds of the guest cottage, Rose stared at the horizon. Had she made a mistake in coming here? The past weeks were spent attempting to make Lord Westlake fall in love with her.

Yet, with each lie she told, every string she pulled, her frustration grew in equal measures to her guilt. Her point had been to take advantage of the baron's condition and teach him a lesson. To see him pay for the wrong he had caused her. But the truth was, she suffered far more than he.

The promise she had made to Lady Westlake did not help matters. In fact, it made them worse. But how could she forget what happened that evening six years earlier?

What bothered her more was the shame her current actions exhumed. Why had she trusted him that night? How could she have allowed him to enthrall her with his sweet words? To trust him to speak the truth?

And why did she believe there was hope for him now? He did not deserve it.

In all this, however, the letters she found in his desk haunted her more than she could have ever imagined.

It came as no surprise he had bedded other women. She had come to that conclusion years ago when he had not replied to her pleas. What was on her mind now was the letter he never sent. Had he truly cared for her? Had her previous size not mattered to him after all?

Then there was his only memory, that of a woman wearing a red dress standing alone along the far wall in the ballroom. Lord Westlake had believed it was her, but she was sure it had been someone else. After all, besides the color of the dress, his description of that woman sounded nothing like her. Now, her confidence eluded her. At times, she secretly wished it had been her.

"Miss Follet!" Tilly called, hurrying toward Rose. "I bought the new stockings you said I should buy. Can you believe it?" She spun around so the hem of her uniform lifted to show smooth silk on her ankles. "Me, having silk stockings! I don't think I can ever thank you!"

Rose had paid each of the house servants a small sum for the part they had to play in the ruse. All had refused outright, insisting that their employer's new outlook was worth it, but Rose would not take no for an answer. What she was asking them to do was risky. If it all fell apart, they could be out of a job for the part they played.

"I'm happy for you," Rose said, smiling. "You deserve it. I could not have done any of this without your help."

Tilly grinned. "Having His Lordship not shoutin' at us all the time is more than reward enough, I'll tell you. And you know what? The other day, he went to shout at me but stopped and covered his mouth! Maybe he saw I wasn't doin' nothing wrong."

She shrugged and dug the toe of her shoe into the dirt beneath the tree. "At this rate, I might start likin' my position here more." With a glance toward the house, she added, "I'd best go and see to my chores before Mrs. Moore takes up where His Lordship left off!" She threw her arms around Rose. "But I just had to come thank you!"

Bidding the girl a farewell, Rose returned her gaze to the horizon. It was apparent Lord Westlake had changed. Oh, his temper still flared from time to time, but now he did his best to control it.

Despite his changes, however, deep inside, she could not let go of her resentment.

Smoothing the front of her dress, she started when the object of her thoughts said, "Miss Rose, I've a confession to make. It will not be easy, but I must say it, or my shame will eat away at my soul."

Rose's heart pounded in her chest. Was he ready to admit what he had done to her? Did he finally remember? "What is it, my lord?"

He collected her hands in his. "Before I make my confession, I must ask you a question."

She had to swallow to add moisture to her throat. A confession and a question? Would he propose marriage? If so, how should she respond?

No! You did not come here to marry him. He is right where you want him. Now, take him down!

"Have you heard of Lady Honor?"

For a moment, she could do nothing but stare at him, stunned. Had she forgotten to return the newspaper clippings to their proper place in his desk drawer? No, she had made certain everything was in order before returning the key...

The key! Having gathered plenty of information, she had not returned to the office to replace the key to its small hidden pocket beneath the desk. Had he found it where she had dropped it?

"I've heard of her, yes," she said, surprised her voice was not shaking. "She writes a gossip column for the Morning Post, I believe. About the aristocracy, if I were to hazard a guess. Although she's not always clear about whom she is writing."

He produced a piece of paper. "Downwick gave this to me."

Rose took it and looked it over. It was a clipping of her most recent article.

"Do you believe it speaks of me?"

"Don't be silly," she said. "These are written in such a way that it can be assigned to any number of people. They are meant to create gossip, to make people speculate so they buy more newspapers." She folded the paper and slid it into the pocket of her dress.

"Are you sure?" His tone had an urgency about it.

"There is a married lady in London who has been showing an interest in a man not her husband."

Lord Westlake frowned. "Pardon?"

"Who do you believe it could be?"

"How would I know?" he demanded. "London is far too large, making it impossible to know given such little information."

Rose nodded. "Precisely my point, my lord. It could be any lady.

Such vagueness keeps people guessing. Trust me, this has nothing to do with you."

Guilt tugged at her heart like an undertow in the sea, but when he gave her a relieved smile, it nearly drowned her.

"I don't deserve you in my life," he said.

Rose felt sick. These lies were causing a canker in her heart she feared would never heal. Balancing her need for justice and the desire to comfort him was becoming a battle she might never win.

"I must go," she said, forcing a smile. "Leah and Aaron will return from the village any moment now and I had hoped to get in a bit of reading while they were gone."

As she turned to walk away, Lord Westlake took hold of her arm. "I must make a confession. I did something, or rather I attempted to do something that I should not have done. After you hear what I have to say, you may wish to leave, and I'll not stop you if you choose to go."

Rose turned to face him. What confession could he possibly make that was bad enough to send her away? Then again, if he had remembered something about his past, it could be any number of things.

"Go on."

"Are you acquainted with a Miss Constance Haskett?"

All words stuck in her throat. Without a means to respond, she merely nodded.

"It appears that right before my fall, I..." He drew in a deep breath and closed his eyes. "If what Caney says is true, which I've no doubt it is, I made an open proposition—a quite wicked one—to that young lady."

"I see." What could she say? If he learned this truth, why would he be willing to believe what she and Mr. Fletcher were telling him about who he was before he lost his memory? Did this mean that the ruse was over?

"I...I don't know how she and I became acquainted, nor how she came to be in my home unchaperoned. Nor do I understand why I would do such a despicable thing when I care so much for you." His face paled. "Caney says this was not an uncommon situation for me. What I would like to know is if you were aware of any of this."

Rose could only stare at the man she had once loved. She had sought to destroy him through trickery, but it appeared she there had been no need. Learning the truth about his past was doing that without her help.

Then a strange thing happened. Seeing him in such pain, Rose found the idea of driving the knife deeper into his heart, of twisting it until his soul seeped out onto the floor, no longer appealed to her.

"He did not lie," she replied. "You were a rogue. And about what happened with Miss Constance..." She swallowed hard. "I witnessed for myself your attempt to be with her."

"You were there?" he asked.

"I was. You were quite inebriated that night. You tried to woo her, but it failed."

He paled further. "And the other women with whom Caney says I've acted improperly?"

She nodded. "It's all true."

Lord Westlake took a step back and slumped against the trunk of the tree. "Why did no one tell me this before? I've been told that I was a gentleman, a charitable man. Not a rogue whose main ambition is to add to the number of women he has bedded!" He pushed away from the tree and turned away, his face red with anger. "I cannot look at you—nor myself—any longer."

"But, my lord, I believe—"

"I also learned that I blackmailed many people, including my family. Who does that? It's no wonder no one has called to see how I'm faring. All I've received is a single letter from a cousin I can't remember. Even the butcher clearly despises me!" He gave a maniacal laugh. "And how is it I care what the butcher thinks? Why should I care about the opinion of anyone? And yet, I do."

Then he turned toward her again, the corners of his lips dropped and his brows knitted. "Unless you and Fletcher have lied to me all this time. Did I hurt you somehow? And if so, why remain? Why help me at all?"

Seeing the hurt in his features confirmed what Rose had suspected. He was broken and teetered on the brink of total destruction. Oh, he would not weep, he was far too strong to shed tears. He had the look of a man mourning the death of a loved one—stoic and resolute yet guarded.

Then, Mr. Fletcher's words came to mind.

If you're willing to aid me in this endeavor, then let us work together to turn him into a better man and pray he never remembers his past. That can be your revenge.

At first, Rose had thought the butler's objective a waste of time, but now she understood how important it was. Pairing that with Lady Westlake's description of who her son used to be only made the outcome far more appealing.

Rose recalled the devastation she had endured, the heartbreak she had experienced.

Lord Westlake deserves every ounce of heartache he's suffering! Rose argued with herself. *He should have his wealth, his dignity—his very life!—stripped away.*

Yet she had played as much a part in her destruction as the baron. She had met with him, unchaperoned, of her own free will. He had not locked the door so she could not escape. He had not forced himself on her. Despite his deceptive words, the choice to give herself to him had been her own.

Now, here he stood, a man on the precipice of a deep well of anguish for deeds he could not even remember. Perhaps they both had paid far more than the required debt.

"Because inside you there was once a good person," she replied to his question. She recalled the unsent letter. "A man who has attempted to make amends but could not see it through. You were once a man who was good but became lost. Your mother still sees him in you, and I believe her when she says that man is still inside you. It's for that reason I remain."

And she found that what she said was the truth. But was she setting herself up as a fool once again? Would she be left bleeding and broken by the time this all ended, to the point her heart would never heal again?

"My Miss Rose," Lord Westlake whispered, "I betrayed you, but I did nothing with this Miss Constance. I made the attempt, but it did not happen. Surely, my hurting you justifies any anger you may have for me? Do you not wish to lash out and hurt me in return?"

She could not stop a tear from escaping her eye and rolling down her cheek. If he had asked this just days ago, she would have gladly honored his request. Now, she was not so sure.

"You'll never know how much you've hurt me," she said. She rubbed the tears from her cheek with the heel of her hand. "Therefore, I have a proposition for you. Beginning tomorrow, we double our efforts to truly you regain what you can of your memory. If it's possible, we'll see you become the man you're meant to be. But understand one thing. My time here is short. No matter what you recall, or how much, I'll be leaving in the end. That point is nonnegotiable."

The words did nothing to heal the pain in her heart, but it did ease it somewhat. The anger that had clenched her jaw for so long lessened, as did the guilt that tried to suffocate her at every turn.

"But about this other woman—"

"That no longer matters," Rose said. "You did not succeed in that particular venture, so we'll pretend it did not happen. Now, are we to put this all behind us and move forward?"

"I know you say you'll leave," Lord Westlake said. "And I cannot blame you for wishing to do so. But can you at least forgive me for the hurt I've caused you?"

Pity Rose could afford. Compassion she could give. But complete absolution of his transgressions? That could not be. At least, not today. And she doubted she could ever forgive him for the part he played on that night so long ago.

Yet saying so would not help him remember.

"As I said before, let's not speak of it any longer."

"You're as gracious as you are beautiful," he said. "I don't deserve your kindness, but I'm thankful for it."

Her heart skipped a beat as he took her hand in his. Then, to her bewilderment, he closed his eyes and brushed his thumb across the underside of her wrist. A wave of electricity coursed up her arm and down into the pit of her stomach. Could he feel her heart racing at his touch? Did he hear her strangled breaths?

When he opened his eyes, he smiled. "I may never know why you chose to remain with me, Miss Rose, but know this. I swear to you I'll never hurt you again. A new Baron of Westlake shall rise up and replace the man he had once been. I may not deserve your affection, but over these last weeks I've come to care very much for you. Your smile gives me strength. Your words stoke my soul and make me feel like a man. I've lost you through my own recklessness, but I promise to make it my mission to win you back and restore the affection we once shared."

Rose was dumbfounded. How could she respond to such a vow? The one he had made previously had been mean to destroy him. Now, however, it was very different. He needed to understand, the last thing he should do was love her, for she could never return it. She no longer wished to see him hurt anymore. And had she not made that clear in her promise to leave as soon as his memory returned?

Before she could remind him of this fact, however, Aaron came bounding over to them. "Miss Rose, we saw five dogs playing in a field!" He wrapped his arms around her waist.

"Five?" Rose asked, giving him a quick hug. "How wonderful."

"Hello, Lord Westlake." Aaron tilted his head and crinkled his brow. "Why do you look sad?"

The baron smiled and ruffled the boy's hair. "I had thought I was lost, but Miss Rose showed me the way." He looked back to her. "I'll speak with you later."

She watched him walk away, a stone filling her heart. Why could this not have been the man to whom she had given her love all those years ago?

With a sigh, she returned her attention to Aaron. "Did you have fun?"

He nodded. "Miss Leah said I was good."

"I've no doubt you were," Rose said. Leah approached and Rose smiled. "Go along and play, Aaron. I would like to speak to Miss Leah."

Without any urging, the boy ran off, leaving Rose and Leah alone. "Matters have changed," Rose said. "I've a new plan."

For some time, she explained the next steps to Leah, Aaron running from bush to bush, his laughter filling the air. When she was done, she said, "We'll remain here for a short time only, in hopes of helping him regain his memory or to acclimate himself to his new life if it does not return."

"And what's brought on this sudden change, miss? If you don't mind me asking."

"Let's just say that I no longer feel the need for revenge," Rose said as she watched Aaron roll around in the grass. "Leah? Does giving up my quest make me weak?"

"Not at all, miss. I think it makes you human."

Rose nodded and turned to her friend. "We'll stay, and I'll help him remember his past. Let's just hope the man he recalls is the one his mother remembers, for I've no idea who he is. I only want what is best for him."

"Oh, Miss Rose, what you're doing is what's best for everyone. You'll benefit from this new venture as much as he will. You'll see."

"What do you mean?" Rose asked, confused.

Leah laughed and took her hand. "I'm hoping that by helping him, you'll remember that girl you once were, too."

Chapter Twenty-Two

The carriage pitched to the left and Rose let out a relieved sigh when it corrected itself a breath later. She and Lord Westlake were on their way to see Mr. Harold Brunsworth, whose name appeared often in the baron's ledgers.

Rose had gone through the accounts again, this time to compile a list of names of men with whom the baron had made any sort of a contract or trade. After conferring with Mr. Fletcher, she had whittled the list down to a select few he felt would do the most good.

It was Rose's hope they would spark any sort of memory for Lord Westlake. Another trip to the village had done little more than frustrate him further, and no matter how many strolls he took through the house or around the property, he had no recollection of anything before his accident. With each passing moment, he grew more despondent.

She glanced in the baron's direction from the bench across from him. In the three days since they spoke beneath the tree outside the cottage, an air of awkwardness remained between them. Now that her intentions had changed somewhat, she was unsure around him. How strange it was that she was less comfortable now than when her goal had been to bring him to his knees.

"I cannot help but think that I've angered this man somehow," Lord Westlake said, breaking the silence in the carriage. "What shall we do if the last time he and I met I had cheated him or made some sort of attempt to ruin him?"

"Then, I imagine we'll not be offered tea," Rose replied with a smile.

The baron snorted a small laugh. "I suppose that is one way to view it."

Rose could feel his discomfiture rolling off him in waves as he shifted in his seat again. Without warning, her gaze dropped to his broad chest, and she brought her hands to her stomach to smooth her dress. She really should stop thinking of what he looked like devoid of that coat and shirt. That likely played a part in the awkwardness she felt in his company...

"I realize everything you see at this moment is foreign to you," Rose said. "But you must endure the unfamiliar—both good and bad—if you wish to remember the past. Whether or not the man accepts you into his home remains to be seen, but you'll not know for certain unless you make the attempt to speak to him."

Lord Westlake peered out the window. "I suppose so. I can see why I relied on you so much in the past." He turned to look at her, tenderness in his blue eyes. "I can never repay you for all you've done for me."

Rose laughed. "You may regret those words after Mr. Burnsworth throws us out of his house."

For the first time since that moment under the tree, Lord Westlake barked a true laugh. Rose found she adored that sound, yet it was made more beautiful when her laughter joined his. It was a lovely musical chord written by the most skillful composer.

The carriage trundled to a stop, and they alighted from the carriage into the warm sun. The house was simple—a two-story square building of gray stone covered in ivy. A gardener pruned a nearby tree as another dragged away the fallen limbs.

"Well," Lord Westlake said with a resigned sigh, "let's hope for tea. He'll at least do that, will he not?"

Rose placed a comforting hand on his arm. "Who knows? Perhaps we'll be invited to stay for dinner."

They walked up to the front door and applied the knocker. The door opened to a short, liveried butler with tufts of blond hair on the sides of his head.

"Lord Westlake and his cousin, Miss Rose Follet, to see Mr. Brunsworth," the baron said. They had conceived the idea of traveling as cousins as a way to keep at bay the question of their traveling alone. Given the size of the Remington family, no one would give their story a second thought.

The butler bowed. "He's been awaiting your arrival, my lord. This way, please."

They followed the man through an open set of double doors and into what appeared to be a drawing room or parlor of sorts. With a low ceiling and dark wood on the walls and furniture, it gave Rose the sense of entering a cave. In one of the chairs sat an elderly gentleman well into his seventies or eighties, and upon seeing Rose he struggled to pull himself to his feet, balancing on a brown-stained cane topped with ivory.

"Lord Westlake and Miss Rose Follet," the butler said before stepping aside to allow them to pass into the room.

"Thank you, Timmons," the older man said in a shaky voice. "Please, bring us tea, will you?"

Upon hearing the word tea, Rose turned to find Lord Westlake wearing a grin that matched her own.

"I'm glad to see that having tea still brings smiles to faces," Mr. Burnsworth said with a chuckle. "Please, sit, my lord. And accept my apology for not bowing. I'm afraid my back does not move that way anymore."

Lord Westlake smiled. "There is no need, Mr. Burnsworth, I assure you."

They took the seats on the sofa across from the chair in which Mr. Burnsworth lowered his hunched form. "Miss Follet, I must admit, when I received your letter, I believed it to be a prank. But I've since come to learn that His Lordship's ailment is true." He turned to face the baron. "Do you remember me, my lord?"

"I'm afraid not, Mr. Burnsworth."

The old man laughed. "Oh, don't look like that. I'm not mocking you. It's just that you always used to call me simply Burnsworth. Before that, when you were only a young lad, you called me Harold. But it was never any of that mister stuff for you." He leaned forward on his cane, his eyes narrowed to slits as if trying to see the baron better. "Still, it's fascinating. You don't remember anything?"

Lord Westlake shook his head, and Rose felt a bit of sympathy for him. "Mr. Brunsworth," she said, hoping to get on to the matter at hand, "we were hoping that calling on you today would help bring back any recollection, no matter how small."

"You alluded to as much in your letter," the older man said.

The butler entered with a tray heavily laden with a silver tea set and three teacups. Once he had poured them each a cup, he left the room.

Once everyone had their tea, Mr. Burnsworth returned his hands to the top of his cane and looked at Lord Westlake. "Well, what would you like to know, my lord?"

"How long have we been acquainted?" Lord Westlake asked. "You mentioned me being a young lad, but how young?"

Mr. Burnsworth crinkled his brow in thought. "Well, you were maybe six or seven when we first met, but we didn't really get to know one another until your father passed. You were what? Fifteen or sixteen when that happened?"

Lord Westlake nodded. "Sixteen, yes."

"Thought so. Well, I'd done a bit of business with the late Lord Westlake, and once he was gone, you and I made several agreements. Mostly in sheep, but we jointly own a copper mine. That's what keeps us going."

The baron turned his cup in his hands as he stared at it. "I remember nothing of it." He looked up at the older man. "And what can you tell me about my reputation?"

Mr. Burnsworth took a sip of his tea from a trembling hand and replaced the cup to its saucer. "Perhaps that can wait until another time, my lord." He glanced at Rose. "It's a bit of uncivilized talk some of what I'll say."

Rose smiled. "Say what you wish, Mr. Burnsworth. I'm not as frail as I seem, I assure you."

"I don't know…" The old man eyed Rose once more. "I'd hate to upset a lady's good senses."

"Trust me, Burnsworth, she's much more resilient than she appears, my cousin. I doubt anything you say can upset her any more than I already have myself."

"Well, if Miss Follet doesn't object," Mr. Burnsworth said. "I'll not tread lightly, my lord. Just know that."

"Please, I need as much truth as can be said."

The older man sighed heavily. "If you say so. Well, in a nutshell, you betrayed everyone you know. Well, there was one exception. Do you remember anything about your cousin, Mr. Markus Remington?"

The baron shook his head. "I've heard his name often, but I don't recall the man himself."

"Well—and forgive me for my bluntness, you being a baron and all, my lord—but the two of you've done more unscrupulous business than any pair I've ever known. You've burned many bridges, my young sir. Angered most you've traded with or with whom you've made agreements. Mainly because you broke those agreements. You've used everyone, friends and family included, all to your own gain."

Lord Westlake paled with each word. "And…have I done this to you?"

Mr. Burnsworth chuckled. "The last time you were here, six months ago if I remember right, you called me an old fool and threatened to convince the miners to strike just to spite me." His story sounded as if he were speaking of a humorous moment between good friends.

After watching Lord Westlake's shoulders droop, Rose said, "You said you began working with His Lordship when he was sixteen. Was the man you encountered six months ago the same as the younger?"

The bushy gray eyebrows on the old man's head rose. "Not in the least."

"How was he—or rather I—different?" Lord Westlake asked.

"Well, you were a gracious young man in the beginning, quite enthusiastic, really."

The baron frowned. "And when did you begin seeing a change?"

Mr. Burnsworth scratched his chin. "I don't feel comfortable speaking disparaging words, my lord. After all, we still have several contracts together."

"No," Lord Westlake said, sitting up straighter. "Speak freely. I give you my word I'll not use whatever you say against you in any way."

"Your word?" Mr. Bursworth asked, arching an eyebrow.

"Yes, I suppose my word is not worth much these days," Lord Westlake murmured.

Rose smiled. "But you have my word, Mr. Burnsworth. I'll not allow him to retaliate in any way. No matter what you say."

"Well, if you're willing to vouch for him, Miss Follet, I suppose I can speak truthfully. But it may be a bit painful to hear, my lord."

"Even so, go on," the baron replied.

"I'd say it was maybe two years later or so. I heard you began attending all sorts of parties—questionable gatherings, or so they say. After that, you began to change."

Rose said, "What you're saying then is that His Lordship was a decent, respectable gentleman at some point?"

The older man nodded. "Oh, most assuredly, Miss Follet. I don't know what brought on your change, not exactly, but there was a time when you were respectful to everyone you encountered, and you had a desire to help others. That was what convinced me to continue doing business with you after your father died."

He shifted in his seat and leaned on his cane once more. "You know, what seems like a curse now may be revealed later as a blessing. Perhaps you've been given another chance to return to doing right rather than…well, what you've become better known for these past years. Few her given such a wondrous opportunity. I pray you don't waste it."

Lord Westlake smiled. "I thank you for your forthrightness, Burnsworth. But I'd like to ask one more question. Or rather ask for a bit of advice. How do you suggest I right my previous wrongs?"

Mr. Burnsworth stroked his chin once more. "I suppose all you can do is offer to put right any wrongs mentioned to you. No matter if it was business or personal. But I'd suggest you not allow the weight of your past to burden your present while you attempt to make amends. Rather, focus on being who you were before your troubles set in."

"That is what I want," Lord Westlake said. "But I must admit that I'm more than a little disconcerted that I won't be able to find him."

"I see him before me now, my lord. You'll see him soon enough, I'm sure. If you want it bad enough. Now, you must forgive me." He pulled himself to his feet with the aid of his cane. "I must have a nap. At my age, I find myself resting at least twice a day." He leaned in and lowered his voice. "Not that I'm complaining, mind you. It beats the hours I spent sitting at my desk pouring over my accounts or going out to that old mine of ours."

Once outside, Lord Westlake smiled. "For the first time since waking last month," he said as they stood beneath the small overhang outside the front door, "I feel there is hope. Hope that I'll find the man I truly am. The man I once was before I became one others despise."

Rose sighed and placed a hand on his arm. "It's apparent Mr. Burnsworth does not despise you. Nor do I."

It was as if a weight had lifted from her shoulders and breathing became easier for the first time in years, for that was the truth. The burden of her past had lessened.

"I already believe you're becoming an even better man than the one you were all those years ago."

"You've no idea how much that means to me," Lord Westlake said. "Mother would often say the same. I cannot count the number of times she said that Father corrupted me and that—" He paused and turned to Rose, his eyes glinting. "That Father had twisted me with his thinking! Miss Rose, I can remember her saying that! I was twenty at the time, and we had argued during dinner together!"

Before she could stop herself, Rose wrapped her arms around him. "How wonderful! I'm truly happy for you."

"We must celebrate," Lord Westlake said, still grasping her waist. "Tonight, we'll dine together, all of us—you, Aaron, and I—and feast as never before!"

Rose nodded, stunned that he had yet to release her. His touch was comforting, and her heart soared. Yet she knew she could not allow old feelings to resurface. Not now. And certainly not with him.

"I know Fletcher will be pleased to hear it," Rose said, stepping away from him. The disappointment on his face said he did not like that, but Rose could not encourage another embrace. They were supposed to be cousins, for goodness' sake! "Let's go so we can inform him."

Once back at Tinsley Estate, Rose looked on proudly as Lord Westlake relayed the memory to Mr. Fletcher. As he spoke, she considered her time there at the estate. What had begun as a way to hurt him had turned into helping him. Who would have thought it possible? Certainly not she!

"With that said," Lord Westlake said once he finished with his exciting news, "I believe I'll take Mr. Burnsworth's advice and take a nap. I'll see you this evening at dinner."

They watched him ascend the staircase, and once he was out of sight, Mr. Fletcher turned to Rose.

"May we speak in private a moment, Miss Follet?"

"Of course," Rose replied. "Is everything all right?"

The butler made no response as he led her to the parlor. He turned to her, a stoic expression on his features. "I found a letter last week you forgot to post, and I must admit I was curious when I saw it was addressed to a certain newspaper in London. I've asked you before, but I must ask again. Are you Lady Honor?"

"I...that is..." Did any excuse exist that would get her out of this predicament? How could she have left that letter where anyone could find it? Perhaps because she was tired of the lies. "Yes, I'm she. But you must understand, that letter was to ask them to stop publishing any new columns until they hear from me."

"Can you not simply stop writing them?"

Shaking her head, Rose replied, "I've sent them a half dozen already. That way, if I'm delayed for whatever reason and unable to do any writing, they at least have something to publish."

Mr. Fletcher groaned and pinched the bridge of his nose. "Miss Rose, what other lies have you told me? I believed you were here to help His Lordship become a better man, but now I realize you meant to sabotage him in some way. Tell me I'm wrong."

The truth was the only option left. Enough deceit! "You're not wrong," she said with a deep sigh. "The night you arrived at my cottage, I had lied to you. I wished to do as much harm to him as I could. But over these last weeks, I've seen a kind side of His Lordship, which is why I made my request to the newspaper."

"You must understand my reluctance to believe you. How do I know you're not simply saying this so I'll allow you more time to trump up more lies? This revenge you sought, is it settled?"

"It is."

Mr. Fletcher pursed his lips. "What could he have done to make you write such horrid things about him, true or not?"

Rose took a moment to consider this question. How could one convey what the baron had done to her? She could not. "Mr. Fletcher, I would ask that you allow me what little dignity I have remaining, but if you require me to reveal my secrets in order for me to remain here, I will tell you."

After all she had been through, after all she had given up, was this the end? Yet the thought of leaving the baron bothered her even more, and she was unsure why. How had the hatred she had felt for him turned into caring?

They're opposite sides of the same coin, that's why.

"No, I won't force you to tell what you would prefer to keep to yourself, Miss Rose," Mr. Fletcher said. "If you promise to continuing helping him, then I'll trust you. And hopefully a better man emerges after all this."

"Thank you," Rose said, relief filling her. "It means much to me. And I do believe there is a chance for him. In fact, I feel it."

The kind butler bowed. "There's always a chance, Miss Rose. Even for someone like His Lordship. I think you've helped me see that, too." With a small nod, he turned and exited the room.

Rose considered his words as she walked over to a window that overlooked the gardens. It made her happy that Lord Westlake recalled a memory today. Yet, the more he remembered, the shorter her time here remained. For the day the baron remembered everything in his life, her mere presence might be the very thing to unravel all the good work they had done.

Chapter Twenty-Three

Evan was being followed. The footsteps coming from behind him grew in fervor the further into the woods he moved. At a fork in the path, he made to go right but, at the last moment, hid behind a bush to the left. He held his breath, listening as the heavy breathing of his pursuer grew louder.

Then a twig snapped. Trouble had arrived. He had been caught.

"Found you!" Aaron cried.

Evan hung his head in defeat. "How did you find me?"

The young boy beamed. "I can find anyone! Want to play again?"

Dropping to one knee, Evan smiled. Aaron was the most well-behaved and delightful child he had ever met. Not that he had much experience with meeting children, of course, but the fact still remained. Well-mannered, considerate, charming, the boy would have a bright future ahead of him.

"I would love nothing more than to continue with our game, but Miss Rose and Miss Leah will be waiting for us. Would it be fair if we remained here playing while they were home alone?"

Aaron's face scrunched as if he had eaten a green gooseberry. A memory flickered in Evan's mind. He had seen a boy much like Aaron many years ago making that same odd face. Had he been a cousin, perhaps? Or a friend?

"No," Aaron replied after much thought, "it's not nice to ignore them. But when Miss Leah sews, she makes me stay." He leaned in closer and added in a whisper, "Girls are boring."

Evan could not help but laugh.

"Will you carry me back, please?" Aaron asked.

"I think that's a marvelous idea," Evan replied, turning so his back faced the lad. Once Aaron had his arms securely around Evan's neck, Evan said, "Now, hold tight. I'm prone to stumbling." With a grunt, he stood and began the short trek back to the place where a picnic had been set up.

It had been a week since calling on Mr. Burnsworth, and although no new memories came to mind, Evan was not worried. His relationship with Miss Rose, as strained as it had been, was much more improved. She laughed more often, and their conversations were much more substantial. Yes, life was much better than it had been after his fall.

Yet Evan was also a pragmatist. He knew the day would come when she would leave him, and rightfully so. Still, he wanted to prove he had changed. And to tell her what he truly felt for her.

His affection for Miss Rose grew with each passing day. He found her the loveliest creature he had ever known, and he suspected his opinion would not change once he regained his memory. Her intellect intrigued him, but her courage to remain with him endeared her to him the most. Although he could not recall his former life, he knew one thing. She was a far better woman than he had been a man.

"Don't forget to stumble," Aaron said in Evan's ear. "It's boring up here."

"Boring you say?" Evan said, grinning. "We can't have that now, can we? I'll make this much more exciting."

Gripping the boy's legs, Evan moved and pitched his torso to the left, Aaron cheering as he did so. Small twigs snapped and leaves rustled beneath his feet as they pressed forward. Then he pitched to the right, emerging from the woods to the glen where Miss Rose and Leah sat.

"Miss Rose!" Aaron called. "His lordship dropped me four times!"

Evan pretended to tumble onto the blanket that had been spread across the ground, which caused everyone to laugh.

"Did you have fun?" Miss Rose asked. She turned to Evan. "And did he behave himself?"

Evan brought himself to his knees and placed his hands on the boy's shoulders. "Young Master Aaron climbed a tree so tall, I was unable to see him." Aaron covered his mouth in a failed attempt to hide his giggle. "Thankfully, a rather large bird—I believe it was a crane—took hold of his ear and brought him down to me safe and sound."

Miss Rose stood and placed her hands on her hips in mock exasperation. "Well, at least you're safe. And where is this bird so I can thank him?" She peered around as if searching for the crane.

Aaron threw his arms around her waist and laughed. "There was no bird, Miss Rose. We're only teasing!"

As she gathered him into her arms, Evan felt joy at being a part of their lives. If his former self had not been so idiotic, he could have enjoyed a future with them. Yet, he held little hope that would happen. Miss Rose was resolute about leaving once she felt he was well enough.

"I think we'd best get you cleaned up," Leah said, taking Aaron by the hand. "We'll see you back at the cottage, miss." She bobbed a quick curtsy. "My Lord."

"That boy is a joy to be around," Evan said as he sat on the blanket across from Miss Rose. "What a wonderful day it must have been when you took him on as your ward."

Miss Rose smiled and looked out toward the forest, her eyes unfocused. "I'll never forget the day I first saw him." She sighed and smoothed out her green skirts before offering him a glass of wine, which he accepted. "I'm glad he likes you."

"And I like him," Evan said. "Oh, and I've had another memory."

"How wonderful!" Miss Rose exclaimed, her smile widening. "Do tell me what you recalled."

"Aaron and I were speaking, and he made a face like this." He mimicked Aaron's expression from earlier, making Miss Rose laugh. "I remembered seeing a boy do that many years ago. It must have been a cousin, although which still evades me. Apparently, I have hundreds."

She gave a polite nod, and his gaze dropped to the small plate of food before her. Much of what she had been served remained.

He frowned. "Miss Rose, you should eat. You cannot starve yourself. If you suffer from a lack of appetite, perhaps I should send for Doctor Norman."

"I don't need a doctor!" she snapped. She took a sip of her wine and looked away. "Forgive me."

Evan was unsure what to say. He had not meant any disrespect. "But if you're ill, or simply not feeling well, I would like to help if I can."

She shook her head. "I'm not ill. You would not understand. The woman I am now looks far different from the woman she once was."

"Do you mean you were heavier?" Evan bit his tongue and closed his eyes. What an absurd statement to make! "I mean, you looked different? Is that what you're saying?"

"My father termed it 'unusually large'," she replied, dropping her gaze. "It was his greatest disapproval of me and why men never gave me a second look. Why friends stopped inviting me to tea. So, I made a vow to make myself beautiful to catch all men's eyes!" With each word, her voice became harsher.

She set down her glass and allowed it to topple over, the wine spreading a red stain on the blanket. "Oh, you can never understand! A woman's plight is very different than that of a man. If I were to regain even an ounce of the weight I lost, I would become ugly again! Seen as unbearable company. Disgusted with myself again, just as I am now!" Her voice was filled with angry pain, and Evan felt helpless to relieve it.

Before he could respond, she stood and walked over to a nearby tree.

She was right. He knew not the first thing about women or their mode of thinking. How could he possibly help her? Then an image came to mind, of a particular habit he had witnessed often over the past weeks.

Rising, he went to stand behind her. He wanted to hold and comfort her, but she needed something more than simple affection.

"I've seen you smooth your dress many times," he said. "Is this a habit you formed when you...looked different?"

He thought she might not answer, she waited so long to respond.

"Yes."

"If I could advise you, I would. But I know nothing about the subject of women's beauty. Or at least none that I can recall. I suppose if I did, I would worry all the more."

She gave a small laugh, and he placed his hands on her shoulders. "What I do know is that you're a very beautiful woman, Miss Rose. Does your figure contribute to it? I won't lie and say that I haven't noticed your lovely form, for I have. Nor shall I say that I haven't noticed what a beautiful face you possess. But it's your strength of character more than anything that garners my attention. That is what brings out your beauty. That is what I've come to cherish most about you."

She slowly turned to face him. "Truly?"

Evan nodded. "The fact that you've remained here after I hurt you? That's beauty. The way you care for Aaron as if he were your own child is equally so. The way you speak to the servants. Even Fletcher's day is better because of you. That kind of beauty is a gift, and you have it. But it doesn't matter how I see you but rather how you see yourself. Just as no single memory can bring the forgiveness I so need, no particular waist size will every make you happy. You must recognize that you're beautiful no matter how you appear. Only then will you see you for who you truly are."

Her lower lip trembled as she placed a gloved hand on his chest. When their eyes met, he leaned forward and kissed her. Her lips were soft and tasted of wine. The last time he tasted them had been in lust. Now was different, for he suspected he felt for her what he once had.

The kiss slowly came to an end, and Evan searched her face. "I do care for you, Miss Rose. I may even say that I love you."

Apparently, that had been the wrong thing to say, for she took a step backward, her face bathed in agony. "No, you can't love me, my lord! Please, you mustn't say such things!" She wrung her hands and turned away. "This has been a terrible mistake. I believe it's time I return to London. Tomorrow, in fact."

A strange sense of panic washed over Evan. "Miss Rose, please, don't make me beg you to stay. I fear what my life will be without you in it." Could she not see how hard he was trying? Could she not forgive him for what he had done?

"I'm sorry, my lord," she whispered. "This is how it must be."

She walked past him, leaving Evan standing on ground that swayed beneath his feet. "Please, don't go!" he called out after her. "I'm sorry for hurting you yet again. It was not my intention."

But rather than the words placating her, Miss Rose let out a sob, lifted her skirts, and hurried back toward the cottage.

Hanging his head in defeat, Evan lowered himself to the blanket.

You fool! he thought. Things had been going well until he opened his mouth. Of course, she did not believe he cared for her, not after what he had attempted to do with Miss Constance. What a mistake it had been believing himself worthy of her love.

Taking a gulp of his wine, Evan considered the day thus far. What had begun as an enjoyable afternoon had ended in frustration. And like his memories, he had no idea what would come next.

Chapter Twenty-Four

The ballroom was empty.

Evan glanced over the grand area, trying to recall something—anything—but failed. Why did that boundary around his memories refuse to fall?

He turned toward a wall, and a shiver went through him. A woman had stood there once. But who was she? Miss Rose had alluded to it being another woman, but Evan now questioned whether that was the truth. Yet, Miss Rose would never lie to him. Would she?

"It no longer matters," he said aloud, his voice echoing around the room. "Tomorrow, she leaves, and I'll still have remembered nothing of importance."

How frustrating it was! He could count his memories on one hand.

"My lord."

He turned to where Fletcher stood in the doorway. "Yes? What is it?"

"Doctor Norman to see you, my lord."

"Yes, yes, send him in," he said offhandedly.

The doctor entered, his bag in hand.

"Thank you for coming out in this weather, doctor."

"It's no bother at all, my lord. Just a light mist out there, really. Now, have you recalled anything since the last time we spoke?"

"Nothing more than a few fleeting images of faceless people I don't recognize. I'm beginning to believe that this will be my life from now on."

Doctor Norman sighed. "I'll not lie to you. It's possible your memories may never return. That does not mean they won't, but you should know it is a possibility. Now, I did receive word from that colleague of mine I mentioned before. He suggested you visit any places you may have enjoyed in the past, such as a church or some other location that might be of significance."

Evan could not help but laugh—a very rueful laugh. "How do you expect me to know where to go if I can't remember where I've been?"

"I would recommend asking Mr. Fletcher for advice in that arena," the doctor said. "He's been employed here for quite some time. He would have several helpful suggestions, I'm sure."

"Yes, of course," Evan said with a sigh. "Thank you, doctor. I do have one question before you go. If I do happen to recall my former life, and I learn it's as terrible as I've come to understand it was, what then?"

Doctor Norman stared at him. "I'm not sure I understand the question, my lord."

"I've come to learn that my former self was not a very kind man," Evan replied. "Is it possible that I may become him again if my memories return?"

"Ah, yes, I see now." A small smile playing on the doctor's lips. "May I ask what you've heard exactly?"

"Blackmail, lies, deceit, the usual sins," Evan said. "I've considered that the only way to save my soul may be to commit myself to a monastery."

Or never leave my estate again, he thought wryly.

"I see," the doctor said. "Well, my lord, I cannot offer much in way of advice except this. Whether or not your memories return, you may choose what direction your life takes from here on. The choices you once made need not be repeated. Remain steadfast on the course you've set for yourself."

"It's that simple?" Evan asked, surprised.

"Indeed, my lord. Life is nothing more than one choice after another. You are the only one who can decide where your life leads you." Doctor Norman chuckled. "Perhaps I should stick to giving medical advice rather than any of a philosophical nature."

"Not at all, doctor. And thank you. Your words encourage me. Allow me to walk you to the door."

Doctor Norman smiled. "That won't be necessary, my lord. I can see myself out."

Bidding the man a good day, Evan considered his advice. Perhaps the doctor was correct. Evan had to simply make better choices. And that included the vow he had made to right his past wrongs. Whether it be monetary or other means, he would make every attempt to atone for what he had done.

The problem was, he would still lose Miss Rose. No amount of words or actions could convince her to stay.

"My lord?" Fletcher called from the doorway. "Which wine would you like served at dinner this evening? Or would you rather I choose?"

"You, please. And this will be Miss Follet's last evening with us. She's returning to London in the morning."

"I'm sorry to hear that, my lord. I was unaware. Her presence has been a treat, I must say, even for me."

Evan nodded. "My world will become dimmer once she's gone. But it doesn't matter. She'll leave, and I'll continue my pursuit for my memory. Doctor Norman suggested that I return to familiar places, such as a church. Can you give me any suggestions as to places I've frequented in the past?"

"Not likely a church my lord," Fletcher said with a light chuckle. "When you were young, you spent a great deal of time at the fair in Conley. As it so happens, the fair begins today and lasts the entire week."

"Conley...Conley...and where is that?"

"It's an hour carriage ride at most, my lord. Prague knows how to find it." He spoke of Evan's driver, who seemed to know where everything was located.

"I'm going for a walk," Evan said. "I've many things to consider, but I do wish to go to the fair. Perhaps after Miss Rose has left."

The butler bowed. "Very good, my lord."

Thick clouds gathered on the horizon as Evan stepped outside. A fierce storm was coming, one he wanted to avoid if possible. Yet it was far enough away he would be able to enjoy a nice stroll and return well before the heavy rains arrived. A little water never hurt anyone.

He walked out to the main road and turned right, wandering without purpose as he contemplated his future. A light mist surrounded him as he considered the days ahead. Would he be forever grasping at fleeting images?

Thunder rumbled in the distance, and the sun disappeared. Evan turned back around. The storm was traveling much faster than he had anticipated. Soon, water was dripping from his hat, but he ignored it. Was that not what hats were for?

If he had a way to convince Miss Rose to stay, he would. Yet he had hurt her in the worst way, and no amount of pleading would do any good. Why he knew that, he could not say.

Another peal of thunder made him hurry his steps.

"Ah, Westlake," came a voice from behind Evan, "we've been looking for you."

***

Light rain plinked off the window in the guest cottage, Rose's breath fogging the glass. What was she doing? Tomorrow, she, Leah, and Aaron would return to London, leaving Lord Westlake to find his way alone. It was not what she wanted, but it had to be done. For the sakes of everyone involved.

"He's finally asleep," Leah said as she came to stand beside Rose. "I'll begin packing now. Would you like me to leave something out in particular?"

Rose gave a small laugh at the thought of traveling in the red dress she had ordered during her stay here. No, that would be packed away and never worn again.

"Forgive me for asking, Miss Rose, but…are you sure you want to leave?"

Sighing, Rose turned to the woman who had become her closest confidante despite the differences in their stations. "I've done what I came here to do. He's admitted that he loves me, and I cannot have that. Therefore, it's best that we leave."

Leah took out a selection of shawls from the wardrobe and placed them on the bed. "Are you sure your plan hasn't changed?"

Rose frowned. "What do you mean? Of course it has not."

"I'm not so sure, if you don't mind me saying, miss. You wanted him to fall in love with you and then you were to destroy him. Well, here you are going back to London, all so he's not hurt. Seems to me that he's not the only one who's developed feelings in this."

Anger flared in Rose. "I suppose you think I'm foolish for leaving," she snapped. "Well, if you believe that, you've forgotten what he did to me! I'll not risk being used again. Not by him or anyone!"

"It doesn't matter what I think, miss," Leah said, undaunted by Rose's anger. "This has always been about you finding a way to make peace with your past. Yet even you've admitted to changing your objective and helping His Lordship become a better man. From what I've seen, he's achieving that objective. If you leave, he may resort to his old ways. All because he'll not have someone here to remind him who he's become."

Rose shook her head. "Again, you put his life in my hands. He's not my responsibility. I've done enough for him when I could have easily walked away."

Leah placed a hand on Rose's arm. "Yet the anger you brought with you remains. Leaving for London tomorrow won't make that disappear. Whether His Lordship learns the truth from you or from someone else is one matter. But letting go of your anger for him is something you've yet to face."

Rose pulled her arm from the maid's hand. "I've made myself a rug on which he may walk for far too long! Your advice is not wanted or needed. Pack my things, and I'll inform Fletcher that we'll be dining here tonight."

Guilt tugged at Rose's heart as the maid gave a sad nod and resumed her duties. She had not meant to speak so sharply, for Leah had always had her best interests at heart. But Rose struggled to untangle the knots that were her feelings.

As she passed the standing mirror, Rose ran a hand down the front of her dress, and Lord Westlake's words came to mind.

You must recognize that you're beautiful no matter how you appear. Only then will you see you for who you truly are.

Over these past years, many men had given her a second glance, but none made her feel beautiful. What little joy she gained by such attention was short-lived.

"His Lordship once told me that words of admiration nor dresses can ever make me beautiful," she said, looking at Leah's reflection in the mirror. "He said that my greatest beauty is inside me and that I'm blinded to it. And he's right. I cannot remember the last time I felt pretty. Shall I leave here with unresolved anger? Indeed, I shall. But at least I'll leave here knowing he taught me something, as well."

Without waiting for a response or indicating her destination, Rose left the cottage. A light mist filled the air, and she hurried to the house, where Tilly signaled her from the corridor.

"You're not going to believe it!" the maid squealed. "His Lordship's increasing our wages!" She threw her arms around Rose. "And it's all because of you. You've turned him into a nice man. I'm so glad you're here!"

"I'm pleased to hear such wonderful news," Rose said as the embrace broke. "But my time here is done. I'm to return home tomorrow."

Tilly's jaw dropped. "No! You can't do that! What'll happen if he needs you and starts remembering more and turns back into his old self? No lord's going to listen to a kitchen maid."

Rose smiled. "I'm sorry, but I do wish you the best."

She found Fletcher in the dining room polishing the silver. "There you are, Fletcher," she said. "I wanted to—"

He lifted a fork to inspect it and began speaking as if she had not spoken first. "In all my fifty years of employment in this house, I've seen all sorts of things. Family members who have lived and died. Children grown into adults. Fights and tears and many servants sacked." He put down the fork and picked up a spoon. "But I must say, a woman pretending to be a servant and later becoming a love interest of His Lordship has been the most peculiar."

"I'll not argue that point," Rose said, smoothing her dress and chuckling. "It has been an interesting journey, I must say. Though I'm afraid it has come to an end."

"The newspaper responded," he said, moving a folded napkin to reveal an envelope. "I've not read it, of course, but I suspect what it says."

Rose opened the letter and began to read, her jaw clenching tighter with each line. "He says he won't stop printing the articles I've already sent him."

"As I thought," the butler said. "What will you do?"

She tapped the edge of the letter in the palm of her hand. "I must speak directly to Mr. Green. I'll go into the newspaper office the day after tomorrow and make him see reason."

Mr. Fletcher smiled. "I assumed as much. But will you truly leave? You've come so far and yet you're willing to simply walk away? You can see how close we are to victory, can you not?"

"Be that as it may, I've no choice but to do so."

"Forgive me, Miss Follet, but you do have a choice. That is the strange thing about life. Troubles come and go, sometimes by no fault of our own and sometimes because of decisions we've made, and often they are quite painful. But we always have choices."

Rose dropped her gaze. "You don't understand. Sometimes the pain lasts far longer than we hope. No matter what we do, some pain will always remain."

The butler shook his head. "Although I disagree with your assessment, I'll not argue with you. But I do wish you would remain. You're needed, Miss Follet. You've certainly made my days pleasanter." He put down the spoon and leaned his forearms against the edge of the table. "Or you may leave. I'll hold no judgment in the choice you make. But no matter what you decide, I do wish you the best."

"Thank you, Mr. Fletcher," Rose said, smiling. "We've a very unique friendship, you and I, and I, for one, shall never forget it."

"I'm pleased to hear it. Now, you came here to say something?"

"Yes. I'll be taking dinner at the cottage tonight."

He gave her a nod. "I'll inform Mrs. Moore."

"Is His Lordship in the drawing room?" Rose asked, looking over her shoulder. "I must speak to him about arranging a carriage."

"He went for a walk and has not yet returned," Mr. Fletcher replied. "I doubt he went far. You may find him in front of the house."

"Thank you," Rose said.

If only speaking to Lord Westlake would go as smoothly, her leaving would be less cumbersome.

Chapter Twenty-Five

Evan turned to find three men on horseback, one with dark hair beneath a brown cap. He wore a brown woolen coat over beige slops. The other two were similarly attired with green and blue woolen caps.

An uneasiness crept over Evan. "Forgive me, gentlemen, but I've had a recent accident that has resulted in a bout of amnesia. I'm afraid I remember nothing."

The brown-capped man barked a laugh that was echoed by his companions. "You hear that, boys? The baron don't remember nothing. Convenient, wouldn't you say?"

"I'd say so, Flatrick," said the man with the green cap, his brown mustache twitching above a toothy grin.

Evan's heart skipped a beat. Something was wrong.

"The paper let slip that you fixed a fight," the man named Flatrick drawled. "That cousin of yours was supposed to win, not lose, Westlake. That was our agreement. Now you're saying it was an accident? Or that you somehow forgot?"

"But you must understand. I remember nothing about any agreement!" But before he could repeat his story, the man lifted his booted foot and struck Evan on the chin, sending him flying to his back on the muddy road.

With the world spinning in his vision, Evan tried to rise, but the man's companions stopped him once he reached his knees. Placing their large hands on his shoulders, they held him in place as easily as a child.

Flatrick glared down at him. "You owe us money," he said. "Six thousand pounds, to be exact."

Evan was stunned. "Six thousand pounds?" he managed to repeat before pain erupted in his head as the man's fist made contact with first Evan's eye and then his jaw.

"Six. At least it's not as much as that cousin of yours, Markus Remington."

"How much does he owe?" Evan asked.

The green-capped man spat on the ground. "That ain't none of yer business." He lifted a fist to strike Evan again, but with a small wave from Flatrick, he lowered his arm.

Although Evan did not recall who Markus Remington was, he wanted to do right. "I'll pay his share if you've been unable to collect," he said, hoping this would appease the men.

The trio barked several guffaws, and Flatrick said, "Well, that's awfully obliging of you, seeing as Markus had an accident of his own when he tried to run away from us. Now he's dead." This had the others laughing all the more.

Evan needed no explanation of what sort of "accident" Markus had.

"It don't matter, though. We'll collect what's ours from his estate. But what're we going to do about yours?"

"If I owe you money," Evan said, "allow me to pay my debt. I don't have it on me, of course, but if you will meet me at the bank in Dunark tomorrow, I'll see you have it."

Flatrick grabbed Evan by the hair and pulled back his head. "Tomorrow morning at ten, Westlake. If you're late, you may as well run 'cause if you're anywhere but there, it won't be good for you. And if you think you can show up with any magistrates or the like, you'll learn what it's like to make me angry."

Evan managed a nod.

"Now, boys, give him a reminder of the time."

"I won't forget," Evan rasped before all the breath was forced out of his lungs by a carefully planted punch to his stomach, doubling him over in pain.

By the time the men were mounted and gone, Evan was pulling

himself from the ground once more. His face ached, his head throbbed, and his sides hurt when he breathed. Likely from a broken rib.

He let out a deep groan as he stood. "It's a shame they didn't punch harder," he mumbled, clutching his side. "It might have helped you remember more."

With painful steps, he stumbled up the drive and made his way toward the house. By the time he reached the carefully trimmed lawn, he dropped onto the ground and rolled to his back, unable to go further. Plus, the cool mist felt good on his aching face.

Gasping for breath, he considered what had happened. The incident only brought up more questions than answers. He could only assume they meant boxing. Fighting in itself mattered little, but the fact he participated in corruption around the sport was an entirely different matter. Just another shameful memory he had conveniently filed away.

With a sigh, he rolled over, raised himself to his hands and knees, and crawled toward the house. Each attempt at movement made his body scream in pain, but he could not remain outside in the rain. Yellow circles of light glowed on the mist outside the windows.

Then, ahead of him, through the droplets of water, he saw Miss Rose. Just like the fleeting memory in the ballroom, she wore a red dress. Was he hallucinating?

The pain in his side worsened, and his sight went dim as he collapsed on the grass.

"My lord?" he heard her gasp. "What happened?"

Then she was sitting beside him, pulling his head into her lap. It was not a dream, his Miss Rose was there. He was thankful for her touch. As she stroked his hair, he explained about the three men and their treatment of him. With each word, she kissed his head and his cheeks.

"Here, let me help you stand," she said.

He draped an arm around her shoulders. Together, they ambled to the front door of Tinsley Estate. Each step sent a shot of pain into his side. He had no doubt one of his ribs was broken, if not two.

They stopped beneath the overhang of the portico, and even with her soaked dress and matted hair, Evan had never seen anything so beautiful. Unable to stop himself, he took her hand, closed his eyes, and moved a thumb across the underside of her wrist.

"Thank you for all you've done for me," he said. "I'll miss you."

As he held her hand and felt the smoothness of her skin, Evan, Lord Westlake, knew one thing. Miss Rose Follet might deny it, but she had been the woman he had seen in the ballroom all those years ago. He felt it. Yet the question still remained.

Why did she insist it was someone else?

***

Rose pulled her wrap closer as she exited the house. The fog had thickened, leaving a fine mist in the air. Would she be able to find him in this? Surely, he had not gone far in this weather.

She walked a short distance down the drive, but given the conditions, she did not dare go too far. Perhaps she should wait inside.

A sudden groan made her turn toward the grass. She gasped at the sight of a man on all fours, his head hanging between his arms.

"My lord?" she whispered. Lifting her skirts, she hurried to his side. What she saw made her skin grow colder than the mist. Bright bruises were already forming around an eye and on his jaw. Blood dripped from his nose and mouth.

Lord Westlake turned toward her and gave her a half laugh. "I'm afraid my past has finally caught up with me," he said. "It appears the charitable acts you mentioned were greatly exaggerated." Unable to hold himself up, he dropped back into the grass.

Rose sat and pulled his head into her lap. "What happened, my lord? Who did this to you?" Her heart was filled with worry at seeing him in such physical pain.

"Not a clue," he replied with a grunt. "I was set upon by three men to whom I apparently owe money. Six thousand pounds, to be exact."

"For what?" she asked, smoothing his hair in an attempt to comfort him.

"That gossip column about the baron who fixed a fight? Do you remember?"

Rose's heart skipped a beat as she whispered, "Yes."

He gave another agonized chuckle. "Well, I learned by way of fist and boot that I'm that baron."

"I'm so sorry, my lord." She kissed his forehead. Never had she imagined that her words would bring him physical harm. Now that it had, guilt hung heavy on her.

When Lord Westlake looked up at her, the pain in his eyes, partnered with the bruised face, brought tears to her eyes.

"It appears I'm not the only Remington to be involved, either. Apparently, my cousin Markus is dead. It's not clear if they were the ones who caused his death, but a man has died, nonetheless."

Rose felt sick. She had not caused the man's death, not directly, but she did feel responsible. "What will you do?" she asked.

"I'm to meet them at the bank in Dunark tomorrow. They'll be paid and I'll be left alone. At least, that was the agreement. I see no reason not to take such fine gentleman at their word." He chuckled again and then moaned as he gripped his side.

"I'm so sorry, my lord," Rose said, tears mixing with the wetness on her cheeks. "I didn't mean for this to happen."

"It's not your fault," he said with a bewildered look. "How could you have known? Still, we should get out of this rain. Will you help me stand?"

Rose nodded. With his arm around her shoulders, they both stood.

"You see?" he said. "It's like I told you before. Without your help, I'll fail."

Worry dug at her insides as they began the difficult and slow trek back to the house. She struggled beneath his weight, but not once did she allow him to fall.

As they walked, the only sound an occasional grunt from the baron, Rose considered all that had happened during her stay here. The earlier picnic, the dinners, the laughs, the tears. Could she truly leave now? The baron had made wonderful progress, not just with his memory but with his character, too. He was becoming the man he had once been. Or at least the man Mr. Fletcher and Lady Westlake had known all those years ago.

As the mist turned to light rain, Rose knew she had to stay. For both of them.

But what about his confession of love? And what did she feel for him? She could never return his admiration, but maybe she could continue on as she had been. If she guarded her emotions, she could keep her promise to remain until he regained his memory.

Then, I'll leave, she thought resolutely. After all she had endured over the past years, surely she could finish this quest.

At the front door, Lord Westlake took Rose's hand in hers. He closed his eyes and moved his thumb over the underside of her wrist. "Thank you for all you've done for me, Miss Rose," he said. "I'll miss you when you're gone."

"I…" Rose swallowed hard. Should she?

Yes, she should.

"I'll remain for now, my lord, but only if you understand that I'll certainly leave once you're well. I care for you, but I can never return your love."

He looked down at her and smiled. "That is the first time you've expressed that you care for me and I've believed it. No, it's more than that. I can now feel it."

Chapter Twenty-Six

Peeking out the carriage window, Rose searched for any sign of Lord Westlake. She had insisted on joining him for this meeting with the men who had hurt him. After arguing for what seemed like ages, he finally relented under the condition she remain in the carriage while he entered the bank.

Now she considered going back on her promise to go in search of him.

After tending to his numerous wounds the previous evening, Rose had found sleep evasive. What if the scoundrels attempted to hurt him again? They did not sound like men who would simply accept his payment and go on their merry way.

What good can you do if you were there? she asked herself. It was not as if she had the ability to stop them from causing him further harm.

To her relief, Lord Westlake appeared. Memories of the first time she saw him came to mind. His swagger was gone but his steps still gave an air of confidence. Or at least that was what she saw.

He stopped to say something to the driver before climbing into the carriage. "If I'm to take them at their word, which for some reason I'm inclined to do, that is the last we'll see of those men."

Rose worried her bottom lip. "Are you certain? What if they try to come after you again and demand more?"

"From what I gathered while speaking to them this morning, Markus was the primary target of their anger. He died in a carriage accident, not by their hand."

Rose let out a relieved sigh. At least she had not caused the man's death.

"He was the one who lied about the outcome of the match," Lord Westlake continued. "Apparently, I wasn't involved in the fights until recently, and that particular match was my first and only."

Rose frowned. "Does that mean you may not have known about what your cousin was doing?"

"It's hard to tell. It appears this Markus has fleeced many men, fixing fights left and right. Regardless, they've been paid. Now, all I must do is wait for the next angry mob to come after me."

He gave her a sheepish smile, and she laughed. At least he had not lost his sense of humor.

Yet she could not shake the guilt for what he had been forced to endure. Although she wanted him to suffer at one point, physical harm had not been in her plans.

"Let's hope they are the only ones," she said as the carriage moved forward. She looked out the window and frowned. "Are we not supposed to turn right to return home?"

Lord Westlake grinned. "Indeed, but we're not going home. Not yet. I'm taking you somewhere special today, a form of reward for your willingness to help me."

Rose looked down at her hands in her lap. "You owe me nothing, my lord. And what about Leah and Aaron? They will worry if we're gone too long."

"Ah, but I've already taken care of that," the baron said. "Forgive my boldness for ordering your maid, but I did want you to come with me today."

Rose was taken aback. "You mean, after all your arguing with me yesterday, you meant for me to accompany you after all?"

"That is correct."

"And I suppose you've no plans to tell me where we're going."

He shook his head. "Not in the least."

She shot him a mock glare. "At least tell me how far away our destination is."

"An hour or so," he replied, stretching out an arm and placing it over the back of the bench. His face twisted in pain, and he lowered his arm once more. "I really must remember to watch how I move."

"You must remember everything," Rose said.

The baron laughed but then doubled over with a moan as he grasped his side.

"Oh, my lord, I'm so sorry!" she said, leaping over to his bench to make sure he was all right. Just as she sat, the carriage turned right, sending her tumbling into his lap. Rather than push her away, he wrapped his arms around her and pulled her closer.

Looking up into his face, a longing came over her, to kiss his face, his lips, his neck. To run her hands over the hard muscles of his arms and chest. To have him hold her as he once had...

Scolding herself inwardly, Rose pulled from his hold and settled back into the opposite bench, her face hot. Why would leaving his arms make her feel empty?

They rode in silence for some time, each staring out his or her respective window. Soon, she caught the baron's gaze upon her.

"The men last night reminded me that someone close betrayed me," he said. "Whoever is informing this Lady Honor about my business interests is employed by me. I'm thinking it may be Tilly. I've heard her gossiping far too often to believe otherwise."

"Tilly?" Rose said, a stone forming in the pit of her stomach. "I can't believe she would do such a thing. Are you sure it's not someone with whom you struck up a bargain in the past, someone with a grudge against you perhaps?"

"I've considered that, yes, but as I have no recollection with whom I've done business—besides a list of names of men I don't remember—I can't investigate it." Lord Westlake sighed. "Last night I was so angry, I considered confronting the girl. But as I was dressing for bed, I decided against it."

Rose's curiosity piqued. "Oh? Why?"

"I recognized that I was allowing anger to drive my decisions, which would benefit no one. Therefore, I decided to wait until I had definitive proof before I make any outright accusations." He smiled. "And do you know what? I fell asleep almost immediately for the first time since I can remember." He chuckled at this attempt at humor.

Pride swelled in Rose. This time spent with him had not been in vain. He truly was becoming a better man. "I'm very pleased to hear you're thinking before acting. I've no doubt that you are—and will continue to be—a fine gentleman."

Lord Westlake beamed like Aaron receiving praise for performing acrobatics across the lawn. It was charming to see.

"I believe I should go to London soon," he said.

"Why?"

"To speak to the editor of The Morning Post. I want to learn who's supplying the information for their 'News of the *Ton*' column."

Rose's breath caught in her throat. "No!" she blurted, causing the baron to frown. "That is, they'll never reveal their sources. Or so I've heard. I'm sure you have better ways of spending your time than chasing fairies."

"Chasing fairies?" Lord Westlake asked, his eyes narrowed. "You act as if I should allow these people to write these things about me." He waved a frustrated hand at her. "Forgive me, I know you mean well, but even if they are unwilling to tell me, I can at least ask them to stop printing the rubbish."

Panic filled Rose. It was unlikely that Mr. Green would betray her, but one could never tell. This could end in disaster if she did not put a stop to it! Perhaps it was time she told him the truth.

But even as the thought entered her mind, she pushed it aside. Revealing all to the baron after working so hard to earn his trust would negate everything he had accomplished. Not a single excuse seemed adequate enough to stop him from going.

Well, she would not allow him to go alone. Although Mr. Green would likely keep the identity of Lady Honor to himself, Rose could not take the chance that he might buckle under pressure.

"I've a house in London," she said as the carriage slowed. "We can go together and take Leah and Aaron with us. I'll accompany you to confront these people."

Lord Westlake shook his head. "I should go alone. It might become unsavory, and I'd rather you not witness it."

Rose reached out and took his hand. "Please, allow me to be there for you. Besides, you'll want to wait a few days before leaving. Unless you want everyone to see your bruises."

The baron laughed. "That is a great point," he said as the carriage stopped. "There's no need to supply the papers with more fodder. I'll write to them, requesting a meeting. But I shan't mention that you'll be accompanying me." Rose went to argue, but he raised a hand to silence her. "I'll not have your name attached to mine. It's the least I can do for all you've done for me."

Rose forced a smile. She appreciated his consideration, but she, too, would send Mr. Green a letter. He had to be forewarned to keep the fact he knew her to himself.

The carriage came to a stop, and when the door opened, Rose gasped upon seeing Leah and Aaron there.

"Miss Rose," Aaron said, bouncing on his toes, "there's a fair! We'd better hurry or we'll miss it!"

Rose turned a surprised smile on Lord Westlake. "A fair? And you failed to mention that they would be meeting us here."

"I thought I would surprise you," he said with a wink. "We should go as young Master Aaron has said or we'll miss it all."

Alighting from the carriage, Rose took Aaron by the hand.

With Lord Westlake on her left and Aaron on the right, Rose was filled with happiness. What the baron had done was a wonderful surprise, indeed.

Yet she prayed Mr. Green would agree to keep her columns from the newspaper. If Lord Westlake were to learn she was Lady Honor, it would hurt him.

And for the first time in six years, Rose found the idea distasteful.

Chapter Twenty-Seven

The village of Conley reminded Evan of worn leather. The shops were lifeless forms with faded and peeling paint, warped doors, and signs long faded from weather and sun.

The majority of the people matched the town with their threadbare, plain clothing. But the smiles on their tanned faces said they found the fair as exciting as Evan did.

Few of the nobility took the time to visit, but those who did wore smiles that matched their lesser-means counterparts. Rich and poor alike applauded as a man with a painted face juggled three apples. Beside him, a small wooden booth displayed a puppet show.

The smell of freshly-baked goods filled the air, mixed with the unfortunate odor of cattle and sheep brought for sale. Crafted goods and household necessities mingled with all sorts of entertainment—tumblers, posture-men, and dancing dogs—made for an enjoyable environment. And more so for those in Evan's company.

Aaron bobbed on his toes, moving from left to right, and then huffed. "Lord Westlake, can you lift me up? I can't see."

Evan grinned. "I'd be happy to." Yet when he leaned over to grasp the boy, his side screamed in pain.

Miss Rose turned at his gasp. "You're going to hurt yourself again, my lord. We can move to a better place."

Surveying the crowd, Evan shook his head. "I'm afraid there is nowhere else. Besides, I don't mind." He lifted the boy into his arms and settled him onto his hip. A bad move, that, but he refused to give into the pain. It would only concern Miss Rose more.

Watching Aaron fixated on the puppets with his hands clasped together sent a bolt of joy through Evan he doubted he had ever experienced. A sudden urge to take care of the boy, to make sure all his needs in life were met, took over him.

As he thought of this, he glanced at Miss Rose, who was speaking with Aaron. Her love for the boy was unmistakable. Not for the first time, Evan admired her strength for taking on a child not her own.

"I'd like to give the man a coin," Miss Rose said. "I'll be back in a moment."

She pushed through the crowd toward the puppet booth, but before she was halfway there, a scream filled the air.

As one, all heads turned toward the sound, and a murmur rustled throughout the crowd. Then, as if the Red Sea were parting, the crowd split, people running in either direction as a pair of hefty bulls drove through the throng, running down anyone in their way.

Clutching Aaron against him, Evan pushed through the mass, grasped Miss Rose by the waist, and pulled her back just as the animals bolted past. The warm breath of one of the bulls told him how close she came to being one of the many casualties.

"Are you all right?" Evan asked, trying to ignore the blazing pain in his side as he lowered Aaron to the ground. "You're not hurt, are you?"

"No," Miss Rose replied, her hand to her breast and her face the color of chalk. "I...I don't know what happened. My feet refused to move. If not for you, I would have been trampled."

Everything around them disappeared. All sounds of the babbling crowd, the weeping of the children, the angry rants of the men, all muted as he stared down into her lovely face. All he wanted to do was kiss her. To let her know that nothing, not even he, would ever hurt her again.

"Oh, I'm so glad you're safe, miss!" Leah said, and the moment dissipated. "I went to speak to a woman about her scones and saw those beasts running right at you!"

"Yes, we're safe," Miss Rose replied. "Thanks to His Lordship." She turned back to him. "Are you all right? You're holding your side."

Evan nodded as the puppet show started again. "It hurts a bit but nothing about which to worry. We should keep moving. There's still much to see."

Miss Rose dropped a coin in the hat in front of the puppet show, and they walked ahead, passing a man playing a lively tune on a Dutch organ.

"Behind these drapes," called a man in his fifties with patched trousers and coat and a brown wool cap, "is the words most confounding science one will ever see! For inside you'll find a man born three hundred years ago but who's never aged a day!"

Aaron gasped. "Oh, I want to see him! May I, please?"

Evan chuckled and leaned in close to Miss Rose. She smelled of lavender. "They had this very same exhibit when I was a child. What you'll find is a young boy he hired to sit on the other side."

Miss Rose's eyes went wide, and she smiled broadly. "You've had another memory, my lord! How marvelous!"

Taken aback, Evan said, "You're right! How strange I didn't even realize it." He turned to the husker. "You're Charlie the Charismatic, aren't you?"

The man placed his thumbs in the armholes of his waistcoat and grinned with pride. "That's right. The most honest man you'll find in all of England."

This had the crowd laughing riotously, and several people joined the queue to see the marvel behind the curtain.

"I'll take him," Miss Rose said, taking Aaron by the hand. "We'll return shortly."

As she walked away, Evan pondered the hope that filled him. Not only had he recalled coming here as a child, but he also remembered a name to a face. He could not wait to tell Fletcher how right he had been. The fair had proven to be a wondrous tool to unlocking his memories.

"The old man looks like me!" Aaron said as he ran up to Evan several minutes later, his eyes wide with awe. "Three hundred years old. I can't believe it!"

Evan roared with laughter. "It's truly remarkable, indeed. Let's find some food and you can tell me all about it. Would you like a hot pie?"

Aaron took no time to devour his pie, exclaiming about the "young old man" between bites.

"I would like to go look at the wares," Miss Rose said. "Leah, will you mind Aaron while I'm gone?"

"Of course, miss," Leah replied. "He mentioned he'd like to see the dancing monkey, so I'll take him there."

Miss Rose turned to Evan, a splash of pink spreading across her cheeks. "I really should be accompanied by a gentleman. Do you happen to know someone who can fulfill that responsibility?"

Bowing, Evan replied, "As a matter of fact, I do." Soon, they were strolling past the food vendors. Just being beside her made him feel...whole.

"May I ask why you have not offered me your arm?" Miss Rose asked. "Am I so repulsive that you would prefer those around us believe we are not together?"

Her smile told him she was teasing. "I'd thought...Well, I didn't want to impose on you. My bruised face is gaining more attention than the jugglers. But if that does not bother you, I would be honored if you took my arm."

She snaked an arm through his. "You saved me earlier. Being seen in your company is the least I can do to repay such gallantry."

He grinned down at her. "If this is my reward, perhaps I should save you more often."

The goods vendors' stalls lined one section of the many paths. Miss Rose stopped to inspect a display of aubergines and beetroot before moving to the next stall. Once she had passed the fourth, Evan wondered if she had any intention of making a purchase.

"A woman will send an estate into bankruptcy if she's left to her own devices."

Evan paused. His father had made that statement concerning women and their shopping habits when Evan was ten.

As he went to tell Miss Rose, however, he bit his tongue. Saying that aloud where others, particularly women, could hear would likely bring him more harm than the three men who had set upon him ever could.

"What a handsome couple," the elderly woman said in the next stall. Her gray hair was pulled into a long, single braid that lay upon her shoulder. Wrinkles filled her face and she greeted them with a toothless grin. "I see the admiration you have for the young lady in your eyes, my lord. Would the lady like to inspect my shawls? They're the finest you'll find anywhere."

"This white one is lovely," Miss Rose said as she ran a hand over it.

Evan could only gape. Miss Rose had not put the old woman to rights about their relationship. Had she changed her mind? Or did she simply not want to embarrass him by correcting the old woman?

"Well?"

Miss Rose had placed the shawl over her shoulders. She smiled up at him, stroking the fabric of the wrap. Evan's breath caught in his throat. What he experienced now was not the primal urge he had felt when they had kissed before but rather a need to protect her. As he had done earlier. He would do anything to keep her—and Aaron— safe. The yearning for her threatened to burst from within him.

If only he could hold her, seek her forgiveness. Tell her he cared.

"My lord?"

Shaking his head, Evan said, "You look lovelier than any lady in all of England. It would be a crime not to purchase it."

"'Tis right what he says," the old woman said. "And a gentleman in love never lies."

Miss Rose removed the shawl. "I'll take it," she said.

After the money exchanged hands, Evan offered his arm again, breathing in a sigh of relief when Miss Rose took it. An awkward silence fell between them.

Wanting the silence to end, Evan said, "It's a lovely shawl."

"Quite lovely," Miss Rose replied, not looking at him.

As they approached the next stall, Evan's eyes widened when he recognized Downwick, one of the two men who had called on him right after his accident. Had Evan truly teased him about his nose? Surely not. The thought made his stomach writhe. That was one relationship he had to mend.

Downwick was in the company of another man Evan did not recognize. He wore an impeccable suit of dark blue and had a rather long neck.

"Downwick," his companion said, a sneer on his face, "it's not difficult to spot you in a crowd, I must say. Does your nose get bigger each time we meet? Perhaps you should consider working for one of the Astley's rejects that tour the country. I'm sure you'd fit right in!"

Evan clenched a fist and took a step between the two men. "Is my friend's nose a bother to you?" he demanded of the long-necked man.

"And who are you?"

"Does it matter? All you need to know is that you've insulted a friend of mine. Now, apologize at once."

"It's fine, Westlake," Downwick said with a sigh. "Jenkins teases me every time we meet. It's no bother, really. He doesn't mean any ill will."

"Westlake, is it?" Jenkins said with a snort. "You of all people want to tell me right from wrong? And with your face all marked up with bruises? I'd love to hear that story! I'll buy the drinks since it's likely extraordinary. I've heard all sorts of tales about you, my man."

Evan glanced at Miss Rose. "You were right. My name is tarnished." He returned his attention to Jenkins. "Well, I'll say now that what you say to Downwick here may be in jest, but it's not taken as such. A quip may be humorous once, perhaps even twice. But when it becomes repetitive, it loses its flavor. I believe it's because those of us who tell it are insecure with ourselves." He was uncertain how he had drawn such a conclusion, but it made sense, nonetheless.

Jenkins reached up, touched his own nose, and sighed. "I suppose you're right." He turned to Downwick. "Apologies, my friend. I didn't consider my words before speaking them." With a bow, he bid them all good day and walked away.

"Downwick, may I present Miss Rose Follet, a friend of mine. Miss Follet, Lord Downwick."

To Evan's surprise, the man gave a sardonic laugh. "Friend? You've no friends to speak of, Westlake, only those you use for your own gain. I appreciate you putting Jenkins in his place, but know this. I put up with your belittling for far too long. And this charade of losing your memory does not fool me!"

"Excuse me," Miss Rose said. "His Lordship is not playacting in any way. Regardless of what you thought of him before, I can assure you he is no longer that man. I've seen the changes he's made with my own eyes." She raised her eyebrows. "Unless you believe me to be a liar?"

"Look, Downwick, I truly am regretful for any words or actions I used against you. I don't doubt what you say about who I was is true, but I'm truly trying to make amends."

Downwick ignored Evan. "Miss Follet, I mean no disrespect, for we've only just met. But I would advise you to watch your step with this one. Don't fall for his tricks. If I were you, I'd run away. Far away!"

Evan pinched the bridge of his nose as Downwick stormed away.

"He'll come around," Miss Rose said, placing a hand on his arm. "He just needs time to understand the new you."

The high spirits Evan had enjoyed plummeted. Every step forward ended with him taking an extra step back. Would everyone from his past abandon him?

Then Miss Rose gave his arm a reassuring squeeze.

No. Some would remain, most assuredly. The question was, would Miss Rose be one of them?

Chapter Twenty-Eight

The simple facade of Rose's Mayfair three-story home was not as grand as those on Grosvenor Square. No front garden welcomed her. No wrought iron gate separated the house from the world, for the single step before the entrance touched the pathway. But it was lovely, nonetheless, with its brown bricks and arched entryways. It was home.

This had been the very house where she had planned the destruction of Lord Westlake. It was where she had received her letter offering her the position as maid at Tinsley Estate. She had been sure that her return here would be in triumph, that she would have exacted her revenge on the man who had ruined her life.

Indeed, she had returned a victor of sorts, but in a way far different than she would have ever expected. For the man who stood beside her was changed. She had witnessed how he had come to Lord Downwick's defense. How he addressed his staff with calmness rather than rage. And, for the first time, Rose considered truly forgiving him.

It had been a week since their excursion to the fair, and with each passing day, Rose found Lord Westlake's company all the more enjoyable.

"I suppose I should leave for the hotel before your neighbors begin gossiping about us," Lord Westlake said, breaking Rose from her thoughts. "The last thing we need are rumors that I'm courting you. That would cause quite the storm since that is no longer the case."

Rose laughed as she placed a hand on his arm. "There are worse things they could say." She removed her hand as if he were a hot stove. "I'll see you here tomorrow evening. Seven, correct?"

She had sent a letter to Mr. Green, warning him that the baron would be going in to speak to him, appointment or not. In that correspondence, she had made two things clear. One, he would make no acknowledgment of ever knowing her in any way.

The second had been a warning that Lord Westlake was quick to anger and any refusal of stopping the column might result in harm. Of course, the last was a lie—or so it was now that he had changed— but Rose wanted the editor to put a stop to the column. Or at least the articles she had sent him about the baron.

Within two days, she had received a reply with a date and time. Because it was she who had set up that meeting, she used it to convince the baron to allow her to attend.

"I'll be here at seven exactly," Lord Westlake said, bowing. "Oh, and tell Aaron that if he still would like to go to the park with me, we can go this Sunday." He shut the door to the carriage and leaned out the window. "You may accompany us if you would like."

"I'll consider it," Rose said with a smile.

As the carriage pulled away, Rose longed for him to return. Which was silly seeing as he had just left. Yet the more she considered it, those girlhood feelings rose inside her. She had always thought the baron handsome, but now she saw it more so than before. The writings of love she had penned as a girl came to mind, poetic ramblings of one who fancied herself in love. The memory made her cheeks heat. Thankfully, her parents never saw them.

The sudden thought of her parents sent a twinge of sadness through her. They, of course, never met Aaron. Nor would they see the woman she had become. A woman of whom she, herself, had become quite proud.

"There you are," said a familiar voice.

Rose turned to find one Lady Fanny Lockhart marching toward her, the skirts of her white walking dress swishing around her ankles.

The woman was two years younger than Rose but spoke with the authority of an older sage. Tall and thin with dark red hair, dark-brown eyes, and a quick tongue for gossip, she had been a wonderful source for several of Rose's columns.

"I was just saying to Lewis that I thought you had moved away." She held Rose's arms out to her sides. "My, but don't you look refreshed. Did you enjoy your holiday? And who was that man?" She gasped. "Are you engaged?"

"He's only a friend," Rose replied with a smile. "An old friend who was kind enough to allow me the use of his carriage."

Lady Fanny glanced around and sniffed. "The way you smiled at him tells me more," she said and then sighed. "But it's apparent you don't wish to share with me." Before Rose could respond, Fanny continued. "Have you heard the latest on the Remingtons?"

Rose shook her head. "No. What have you heard?" She prayed it was not about Lord Westlake.

Lady Fanny leaned in closer and lowered her voice. "Lewis and I were at Lady Lymington's last week. It was a bore, my dear, so you were lucky to have missed it. Who has their child sing before the party begins? It's so seventeen hundreds, I tell you. Anyway, I leaned that Miss Katherine Haskett returned home, rejected. And by a duke, no less! Can you imagine?"

"Haskett?" Rose asked, her mouth suddenly dry. "She has a sister, does she not? Miss Constance?"

"Oh, yes! Rumor has it that she was at the home of Lord Westlake just two months ago." Lady Fanny gave a derisive sniff. "And it's quite clear what she was doing there. To think she gave herself to that man! Pray she doesn't wait for an invitation to my next party, for I'll not have some hussy in my home!"

An image of Miss Constance came to mind, a woman who was nearly seduced by Lord Westlake but had been able to walk away. For all the gossip Rose had spread through her column, she had never considered the harm she might have caused others. Except Lord Westlake, of course. And even that no longer held any appeal.

"Perhaps Lady Honor will write about it soon," Lady Fanny continued. "I, for one, believe Miss Constance should be outed and shamed. Wouldn't you agree?"

"I met Miss Constance recently," Rose said, making Lady Fanny gasp. "I can assure you that those are only rumors. Whatever people are saying, it did not happen."

Lady Fanny frowned. "Are you certain?"

"Quite," Rose replied. "Miss Constance is a very respectable young lady. She's far too wise to fall for a man's sweet words." She smiled. "She mentioned you and the parties you've hosted and did nothing to hide her enthusiasm for them. If I were you, I would reconsider leaving her off your guest list. She does have a vast circle of friends."

Lady Fanny raised her eyebrows. "Then I must invite her to my next party." A frown crossed her lips. "But I'll be leaving Miss Howard off the list. She was far too familiar with Lewis at dinner last week at the home of Lord Bullips."

As Lady Fanny continued her deluge of gossip, Rose considered further the part she played as Lady Honor. It was time she informed Mr. Green she no longer wished to write that column. Gone was the appetite for gossip. If anything, it made her stomach churn.

"Then, Lewis said that the new chambermaid is far better than the one she replaced. Of course, that reminded me of Lord Emmerton's maid, the one who carried his child? I couldn't help but wonder if Lewis has plans to bed the girl. Shall we fill our house full of servants who are really Lewis's children?"

Lady Fanny drew in a lungful of air, her first thus far, and Rose used the interim to speak.

"Lord Lewis loves you and the children," she said. Although Lord Lewis was a wonderful husband, he trembled in the presence of his wife. He was far more likely to stand up for himself than to have an affair. "I imagine that he is pleased with the maid's performance of her duties and nothing else. Now, if you'll forgive me, I must see that Aaron is behaving himself."

"Oh, do tell him that his Auntie Fanny misses him," Lady Fanny called out after her. "If he wishes to come play with Gregory, he may." Gregory was Lady Fanny's youngest son, a quiet, soft-spoken child who resembled his father in every way.

Assuring the lady that she would relay the message, Rose entered the house and closed the door behind her. Sighing with relief, she greeted the butler.

"It's good to see you again, Miss Follet," Morton said. In his mid-fifties, dark still spotted his otherwise silver hair. He had deep creases across his forehead and around his blue eyes, but a smile always erupted on his lips whenever Rose walked into the room. He had been in the employ of the Follet family since Rose was a girl.

"And you, Morton. Is there anything that needs my immediate attention? I would like to rest before dinner."

"Mrs. Follet is waiting for you in the sitting room, miss," the butler replied, speaking of Rose's aunt. "Shall I bring you a tray?"

"No, I think we should be left alone for now, but thank you."

Rose had written to Aunt Jean about her return to London and, therefore, was not surprised to find her there waiting.

Sighing, she walked into the sitting room where her aunt sat in a white chair edged in gold. Wearing a blue gown and jewels on her fingers and neck, one would have thought she was prepared for the first party of the Season.

"There you are," her aunt said, turning as Rose entered the room. "Until I received your letter, I was unsure that you would ever return." Although her aunt was only sixty, she appeared far older as her health worsened. Gone was the glowing skin, replaced with a sallow tint. Her once-glinting eyes were now dulled.

Rose leaned over and kissed her cheeks. "I'm sorry I didn't tell you I'd be leaving," she said as she took the chair across from her aunt. "I knew you would not approve, which is why I sent a letter."

Her aunt smiled. "My dear, my approval no longer matters. You're an adult now and must make your own decisions. But I am curious. Is the man with whom you were speaking outside just now the same baron?"

Rose absently smoothed her skirts. "He is."

"Then it's evident your plans did not go as expected. What caused you to deviate?"

"I believed at first I wanted to hurt him," Rose said, sighing. "Then, he had an accident." She went on to explain all that had happened from her employment as a maid to why everything had changed.

"Rose, are you saying that you care for him?"

"Yes," Rose replied with a huff. "But I don't know why! Only a fool would allow herself to have feelings for a man like him."

Aunt Jean raised her brows. "But are you speaking of the man he was before or who he is today?"

Rose buried her face in her hands. "That's the problem. I detest who he was before, but the man today? I care for him! So much so that it frightens me."

Shame filled her for admitting this, both to herself and aloud. He had become an important part of her life, but she had to put a stop to it.

Did she not?

"You must think me as foolish as the child you took to the Continent," Rose said, leaning her head against the back of the chair and closing her eyes.

Her aunt laughed. "Oh, dear, you were never foolish. You really must stop being over-critical of yourself."

"But, Aunt Jean, you know—" Her aunt raised a hand, and Rose clamped shut her mouth.

"What did you do that was so terrible? Did you make a mistake? Perhaps so, but it has made you into a stronger woman."

"You don't understand," Rose said. "If anyone learned the truth, it would ruin me."

Aunt Jean pursed her lips. "I don't understand? If you allow that single night to haunt you, you'll be the one who ruins yourself. Oh, tongues will wag and invitations will stop arriving, but does that truly matter? You've a healthy allowance you could live on even if you chose to remain a spinster. But in all that, one question remains. What do you live for? I don't think it's the approval of others."

"Aaron," Rose whispered. "He's my life now. He's my reason for living."

"Then, live it with pride," her aunt said. She pulled herself from the chair. "Six years ago, you believed your life was over. Now you have a chance to change that night into something beautiful. To finally rid yourself of the hurt." She patted Rose's hand. "But that, my sweet child, is for you to decide."

"Thank you, Aunt Jean," Rose said, hugging the woman. "Will you stay for dinner?"

"I'm afraid a Mr. Percival Templeton has invited me to dine with him," her aunt said with a smile. "Why else would I dress so formally? Even at my age, a lady must look pleasing to a gentleman."

"You're terrible," Rose said, laughing.

"I know that, dear," Aunt Jean said. "Since I've no lady's maid, I'll be going alone. Let the tongues waggle with gossip about me!"

After her aunt was gone, Rose considered their conversation. Aunt Jean was right. Rose had as much a choice to make as Lord Westlake. Could she turn that night from six years ago into something beautiful?

It was an interesting thought, and one she deliberated into the late hours of the night. Yet, as pleasing as it sounded, Rose knew some things simply could not happen. And giving her heart once more to Lord Westlake was one of them.

Chapter Twenty-Nine

A heaviness clung to Rose. Tonight, she would inform Lord Westlake she would not be returning with him to Tinsley Estate. The decision had not been easy, but no matter how much he had changed, she could not let go of the past. It would hurt him—as well as her—but it was best for both of them to part ways.

Aaron sat in the sitting room, listening to Leah read him a story. Rose pulled closer the white shawl Lord Westlake had purchased for her from the fair. It matched her gown, and with her white gloves, she felt beautiful.

Her thoughts returned to that day at the fair and the old woman. She had said she could see the admiration in Lord Westlake's eyes. Although Rose had made no comment, the words had sent a thrill through her. She considered the picnic. The numerous times the baron had played with Aaron. Teasing Lord Westlake on the couch. Dressing his wounds.

Yes, there had been good memories, but some could not be forgotten. Such as one from six years earlier. Or two months ago.

Sighing, Rose adjusted her gloves. The clock struck seven, signaling it was time to leave. Yet was she ready to give Lord Westlake her decision?

"Morton," Rose said as she entered the foyer, "I'll be back no later than nine. I don't expect any callers, but if Lady Fanny comes by, just tell her I'm visiting my aunt."

"Of course, miss," Morton replied with a bow.

A knock came to the door, and the butler answered. Lord Westlake entered, and Rose took in his well-fitting breeches, tailored tailcoat, and perfectly tied cravat. His smile was warm, and his eyes raked over her, gleaming with not lust, but rather pleasure. When he removed his hat, he revealed wavy blond hair. Oh, but he was handsome!

"Good evening, Miss Rose. Are you ready?"

Rose hesitated. Was she ready? Should she say instead that she was feeling unwell? That she wanted to put off the inevitable for just a bit longer. "I am," she replied, despite her reluctance.

Dark clouds hung over the horizon, creating a wondrous sunset as Rose followed Lord Westlake to the waiting carriage.

"We have plenty of time," the baron said. "Would you consider walking with me rather than riding?"

Thunder rumbled in the distance. "Let's take the carriage there and walk back after. I've something I would like to discuss with you after your meeting, and a nice stroll together may be the perfect setting."

Lord Westlake gave a nod and motioned to the waiting footman to open the door. "You really should be careful how you say things," the baron said. "You have me worried you plan to say you're leaving me."

Rose forced a smile as she allowed him to hand her into the carriage. Afraid he might inquire into what she wished to discuss with him, she said, "You must be happy to end this debacle with the newspaper."

He gave a snort. "More than you can imagine. Though, I must admit that showing up after my bruises have gone may not lend credence to my story." He gave a grunt to indicate that although the bruises were gone, his ribs were not yet healed.

Rose watched the passing buildings. How odd it was to think about her reason for leaving London two months earlier. And now she sat in the same vehicle as the man on whom she had meant to exact her revenge.

"May I ask what you're thinking?"

Rose turned to look at Lord Westlake. If he only knew. Well, perhaps she could be partially truthful. "I was thinking of you," she said with a firm nod. "Does that satisfy your curiosity?"

The baron laughed. "Not in the least. Now I'm more curious." Her breath caught as he leaned forward. "Miss Rose, today will be another way I'll right my wrongs. I'll make this man see reason with words, not by coercion. My old ways are gone. He'll see the new Baron of Westlake and will have no choice but to honor my request." He placed a hand atop hers. "And all because of you. These coming months will be so much better. Together, we can do anything!"

Rose's heart ached as the carriage began to slow. "I think we're here," she said, trying not to allow her voice to break.

Signs gently swayed in the breeze above shops closed for the night. Two men entered a pub across the street, laughing and bantering with one another until their voices ceased behind the closed door.

The baron knocked twice on the red door, and Rose prayed Mr. Green would not give her away.

The lock clicked and the door opened.

"My lord," Mr. Green said, his brown hair sticking up in various places as it always did. "And what's this? I didn't expect you to bring a guest."

A short, pudgy man, the editor of The Morning Post was in his late forties with dark circles under his eyes from too many late nights at the paper. And he was grinning far too widely for Rose's liking.

"Well, it doesn't matter," he said, moving aside. "Please, come in."

"Thank you for seeing me," Lord Westlake said as they stepped into the small entryway. "I hope we're not keeping you too late."

"How could I possibly refuse, my lord?" the editor asked. "It's not often a baron calls on me. And it's not too late, I assure you. I rarely leave before nine. Let's go to my office."

They walked past the main room that held several large tables to a room at the end of a short corridor. A plaque with "Mr. Nathaniel Green, Editor" was attached to the wall to the left of the door.

"Please, have a seat," Mr. Green said, indicating two chairs in front of an old desk.

"Do you print your newspaper here, Mr. Green?" Lord Westlake asked as he sat in the chair beside Rose. "I cannot imagine where you would put a printing press."

Mr. Green chuckled. "No, this is just the main office. We type up the articles, do the final proofing, and design the layout here. The printing is done elsewhere. Now, what was it you wished to discuss with me, my lord?"

Rose held her breath. Mr. Green had promised to hold his tongue about her, but he was as stubborn as they came. If he got it in his mind, he could decide to oust her as Lady Honor if Lord Westlake became overly zealous.

"I've a concern about a gossip column that appears in your newspaper," Lord Westlake said.

Mr. Green leaned forward. "I would prefer that you use its proper name, my lord. News of the *Ton*. But please, go on."

Lord Westlake sighed. "Regardless, there have been several articles pertaining to me. Therefore, I would be very interested to know who Lady Honor truly is and to ask her to stop writing about me."

Rose's heart skipped a beat. She glanced at Mr. Green. He would not give her up, would he? She had doubly expressed her wishes in the letter she had written.

Thunder rattled the panes and rain tapped the window. Why was he taking so long to respond?

"Allow me to address your first concern, my lord," Mr. Green said. "We receive dozens of letters every day, informing us of particular goings-on. I can assure you, your name has never been mentioned— not in the letters nor in any articles. Rest assured I've not printed anything slanderous against you. As I said, our information comes from many sources, and never is a name given."

Rose swallowed hard. "At least we now know, my lord."

Lord Westlake shook his head. "At the risk of offending you, Mr. Green, I find your explanation lacking. I've been told, in the past when I've been faced with situations such as this, I often resorted to using the Remington name or my title to coerce others to do my bidding. I would hate to whisper in the King's ear that some of what you've printed is about him."

Mr. Green's smile fell, and his face paled. "There is no need for such drastic measures, is there, my lord?" the editor stammered.

Rose held her breath. Was the old Lord Westlake reemerging? Had all her work been for naught?

"No, I suppose not," Lord Westlake replied. "For those ways are behind me. I would prefer to appeal to your good nature and ask that you listen to my story."

"Of course, my lord," Mr. Green said. "Go on."

"Last week, I was accosted by three men." As Lord Westlake told his story, Rose's heart swelled with pride. His voice remained calm, and he spoke eloquently. "So, Mr. Green, I come to you not as a baron but as a fellow man to ask for your decency to stop printing articles about me. You can say that no names are mentioned, but I've no doubt about whom the latest columns have been."

Rain now pelted the window as clouds covered the sun. Rose did her best to convey with her eyes that Mr. Green should do the right thing.

After what felt like hours, the editor said, "These articles sell many papers, my lord. How about this? If I do print anything from this particular source, I'll see that the column be more general than it has been as of late. It won't mention anything about your current condition, for how many barons can we say have lost their memory?" He chuckled and then his eyes went wide. "I don't mean to make light of your ailment, my lord. I do hope you recover soon."

"I appreciate you saying so, Mr. Green." Lord Westlake stood and glanced at Rose. "There have been those who have come to my aid. Without them, I would never recover."

"Miss Follet appears to be quite the friend, my lord," Mr. Green said as he walked around his desk. "I do wish you the very best in the days ahead."

"Are you certain you cannot give me the name of the person who gave you your information? If I promise not to repeat it, can you tell me who this Lady Honor is."

Rose's heart constricted. They were so close to walking out the door! Everything had been going so well. Would she be found out at the very last moment?

Mr. Green shook his head. "There have been no names, as I said. Even about you. But I will say this. Most of Lady Honor's sources are scorned business partners, ex-lovers, disgruntled servants, that sort of thing. Those willing to give their names, that is. Otherwise, I cannot give you a particular name to match a particular article."

"Well, I suppose I'll have to be more careful with who I keep close," Lord Westlake said, looking at Rose.

Her breath caught in her throat. Had he figured out everything? No, how could he? Nothing pointed to her being the culprit.

"We can see ourselves out, Mr. Green. Good evening to you."

They stopped into the entryway, and Lord Westlake placed a hand on the door handle. "Miss Rose, it's about time you admit the truth."

Rose thought her heart would burst out of her chest. "The truth?" she whispered. Her legs grew weak and her hands trembled.

Lord Westlake nodded. "I saw how you glared at that man. You wanted to scold him!" He grinned. "Tell me I'm lying."

Rose laughed. "Indeed. I had to bite my tongue several times."

"I'm glad you did," Lord Westlake said. "For it allowed me to be a rational man, and you were there to witness it."

Smiling, Rose stood back as the baron opened the door for her. Rain blew in as thunder rumbled.

"I should not have sent away the carriage," Lord Westlake said, frowning deeply. "Would you like to wait here while I call for a hackney?"

Knowing this would be their last night together, Rose placed her hand in his. If this was to be their last night together, let it end pleasantly.

"A bit of rain won't hurt us," she said. With a grin, she hunched over and hurried out into the rain, dragging a reluctant Lord Westlake behind her.

Chapter Thirty

C an laughter be louder than thunder?

Rose believed so as she and Lord Westlake passed the darkened shops hand in hand along the footpath. A gust of wind sent another wave of pelting rain against them. The street glowed like ten thousand candles with each flash of lightning. Everyone with sense had already retreated inside for protection from the storm.

They skipped from one side of the street to the other, avoiding large, undisturbed puddles on the street.

That is, until Lord Westlake stepped in one.

"Oh, bother! Now my boot will be ruined," he said between chortles.

Rose clutched at a stitch in her side, unable to stop her giggles of happiness. Rain dripped from their noses and chins.

"You find it funny, do you?" he asked.

Rose glanced at his foot, still ankle-deep in water, wondering why he decided to leave it there. "Indeed, I do!" she said. "Oh, my lord, what a sight you are standing there in a puddle! You really should get out of the water."

"I?" he demanded, although his lips quivered. "What a sight *we* are!" Before she could work out what he meant, he grasped hold of her waist and pulled her into the puddle beside him.

"My lord, no!" If they were wet before, now they were soaked.

A sudden flash of lightening made Rose scream.

The baron pointed behind her. "There!" he shouted to be heard above the rumble of thunder that followed. "That archway!" He grabbed her hand and pulled her after him.

They hurried across the street, rain splattering the gathering water around them and splashing onto their already soaked legs. Not only would her shoes be ruined, but Rose feared her dress, wrap, and gloves would be, as well. Why had she not chosen clothing more suitable to the weather?

Because you never considered you would be traipsing through London in the rain!

The archway turned out to be the entrance to a small walkway that connected the footpaths between the street on which they were now to the one behind the line of shops. The shops on either side had been built around it, creating a tunnel-like space that protected them from the elements.

Leaning against the gray stone wall, Rose removed her gloves, wrung them out, and set them on a crate beside her. She then did the same with her shawl. She turned to Lord Westlake, who had removed his coat and was shaking out the excess water.

"This is all your fault," she said, pointing at him.

"Mine?" he said with a laugh. "You were the one who said the rain would not hurt us. But I have to say, I don't remember having so much fun."

Rose shook her head. "That's not saying much considering how much you remember." She grinned, letting him know she was teasing.

Then her breath caught in her throat and her mouth went dry as the baron came to stand mere inches from her. Her heart pounded in her chest, not out of fear but rather as a reaction for the feelings she had for him.

A gust of wind howled through the walkway, and she swiped at the wet hair that clung to her cheek.

"I know you've no plans to return home with me," Lord Westlake said.

Rose could not help but gape. "How?" The only person she had told was Leah, and that was just before the baron had come to collect her.

"Earlier, when you said we needed to talk, somehow I knew. I could feel it."

She swallowed hard. "I can explain."

Lord Westlake shook his head. "There is no need. I've come to learn that some things cannot be forgotten. Or forgiven. My only hope is, one day, I remember what we once had."

Tears brimmed Rose's eyes as a surge of emotion swept through her. She never considered that ending what she had begun would be this difficult.

He took her gloveless hand in his. "I want to share something with you, Miss Rose. A secret of sorts. I'm sure you've notice when I do this?" He moved his thumb on the underside of her wrist.

"I have," she said, struggling to bring air into her lungs.

A flash of lightening highlighted his strong jaw and handsome features. Thunder boomed around them, and a gust of wind rushed past. Yet Rose was unafraid.

"When I close my eyes," Lord Westlake said, doing just that, "the touch of your skin is like a sea of light washing over me. A wave of memories swirl around me, begging to be released. They are so close, yet I cannot find them. I cannot find you. And therefore, I remain lost. But there is something deep inside me, a feeling that wants to emerge every time I touch you. Or whenever I think of holding you in my arms. You're a treasure to be honored and protected. I may remember very little, but this I know for fact." He slowly opened his eyes once more. "I've no doubt that I love you, Miss Rose."

Rose turned her head away as the tears washed down her cheeks, mingling with the rain that still dripped from her hair. Her mind and heart went to battle. Her mind told her to run away—far away—but her heart begged her to remain. Her soul was being torn in half, and she could do nothing to stop it.

Then the words of her aunt Jean came to mind.

"Six years ago, you believed your life was over. Now you have a chance to change that night into something beautiful. To finally rid yourself of the hurt. But that, my sweet child, is for you to decide."

The time had come to reveal the truth. Or at least a portion of the truth.

"I've a confession to make," she said, looking up at him through her eyelashes. "A secret of which no one save my aunt and Leah are aware."

Her hands shook, but Lord Westlake gave them a gentle squeeze. "Go on, please. Nothing you say can change how I feel about you."

Taking a deep, soothing breath, Rose nodded. "I didn't save Aaron from a poor family while I was abroad."

The baron's brow knitted. "Do you mean he came from a family here in England?"

Rose shook her head, praying her heart would remain in her chest. "I once loved a man, and I believed he felt the same. I gave myself to him in hopes of sealing that love forever. Although Aaron is a gift of that love, at least on my part, I've held a grudge against his father since."

A horse and rider passed by, splashing water in their wake. Another burst of thunder threatened to shake the very bricks around them.

Lord Westlake nodded. "If that man were standing here before you right now, what would you tell him?"

Rose pulled back her hands and wiped the tears from her eyes. "You've no idea what you ask," she said. "Some things cannot be said."

"But they must," Lord Westlake insisted. "I assume it's because of this man that you refuse to eat a full meal? That he's the reason you refuse to see yourself as the beautiful woman you are? He never came for you after your...encounter, did he?"

"No, he did not," Rose replied, the old anger swelling inside her. "So many nights, I wet my pillow with my tears. I wrote to him, hoping he would respond, but he never did." Her breathing became ragged as the rage grew, and before she knew it, she was shouting. "I starved myself because I believed it would make me happy, but more so because I believed doing so would make him look upon me with affection. So I could pay him back for his abandonment of me."

She began to sob as the long-suppressed emotions tore down the dam she had built to hold them back. Her fist pummeled his chest of their own accord. "I hate him! For what he did! Do you hear me? I hate him! I hate him with every fiber of my being! I've hated him for so very long!"

Gasping for air, she looked up into the face of the man she had hated for so many years. The man who had tricked her into believing he cared for her. The man who had made her feel beautiful all those years ago. The pounding of her heart lessened, as did her fists on his chest. As did her tears. And a sense of calm washed over her. How could she have not seen it before?

"I...I forgive him."

And it was true.

As Lord Westlake pulled her into his embrace, the anger she had carried over the past six years washed away with the tears she wept, and a serenity settled in their place. Air returned to her lungs, clean and pure. The ache in her jaw ceased.

The wind continued to blow past them, and the rain fell on the street as she realized what all she had said. There was still more she had yet to tell, but that could wait for another night. For now, she relished being in the baron's hold, listening to the beat of his heart.

Rose looked up into the face of the man she had hoped to destroy but for whom she had come to care. For whom she likely had never stopped caring.

"I love you," she whispered.

His arms tightened around her. "And I love you more than you can know."

Their lips met in the most wonderful kiss Rose had ever known. For it was not in deceit but rather in love, a love that beat within her heart. There was an urgency to that kiss that told her he felt the same.

As the kiss ended, they turned to look out onto the street, their arms wrapped around each other. Rose considered revealing everything, starting with Lady Honor. Or who she and Aaron truly were. Instead, she savored the moment, wishing it would remain thus forever.

Tomorrow was a new day, one when she could share everything with him. But, for now, she would enjoy the feel of his arms around her.

Yet a seed of doubt crept into her mind. After all they had been through, what they had shared this night, what if Lord Westlake remembered his former life? Was she willing to tolerate the man he once was if he reemerged?

Well, that was a risk she was willing to take, and she prayed her heart would not be broken a second time.

Chapter Thirty-One

Evan sat up in bed with a start. Rubbing his eyes, he took in his surroundings. A wardrobe, a wash basin, a single window that looked out onto the street. Oh yes, he was in a hotel room in London.

As he stood from the bed, he caught his reflection in a standing mirror. He attempted to flatten his unruly blond hair as thoughts of the previous evening came to mind.

Never had he enjoyed such a wonderful evening. Or least not since waking after his accident. The kiss they had shared confirmed what he voiced. He did love her.

They had stood there beneath that archway for nearly an hour watching and waiting for the storm to pass. Today, they were to meet at ten so they—he, Miss Rose, and Aaron—could spend the day together.

All seemed well, but Evan felt an uncertainty. Something he could not identify tugged at the back of his mind.

"That's ridiculous," he said with a snort. Something was always tugging at his mind. It was likely another memory.

He had experienced his first moment free of worry while standing there with Miss Rose. And the meeting with Mr. Green had gone much better than he had anticipated. Of course, the man had denied knowing his sources, but sound reasoning had convinced him to see reason.

Still, something about that meeting did not sit well with Evan. As he paced the room, he replayed everything that had happened. The editor had greeted them at the door. They had walked down a short hallway to an office in the back. There was a bit of back and forth, and then he, Evan, had shared about the men who had accosted him. Mr. Green had wished him good luck…

A cold shiver ran down Evan's spine.

"Miss Follet appears to be quite the friend, my lord,"

Had he given Mr. Green Miss Rose's name? No, he had gone to great measures to keep her identity safe. Then, how did the editor know it?

An uneasiness swept over Evan as he saw to his morning ablutions. Were Miss Rose and Mr. Green acquainted? If so, why did she keep it a secret? Perhaps the editor had learned that she was staying at Evan's estate.

After tying his cravat and buttoning his coat, Evan went in search of his driver. People filled the hotel lobby, and he ignored their scraps of conversation as he moved past them. Once outside, he stopped and glanced around. The sun shone brightly, and a few white fluffs of clouds dotted the otherwise blue sky. A few puddles were the only evidence of the rain from the previous night. But Evan barely noticed.

Had Miss Rose betrayed him? No, not after all they had been through. But who had? Fletcher?

The carriage arrived. "I wish to return to the newspaper office," Evan said before stepping inside, his mind still churning. With each *clip-clop* of the horses' hooves on the cobblestone street, his anger grew. Mr. Green and Miss Rose knew one another, they had to have. But how?

Then he recalled her hatred for the man who was Aaron's father. Could it be the lowly editor? Evan did not believe so, but anything was possible.

By the time the carriage arrived at the newspaper office, Evan had come to a decision. If Mr. Green was, in fact, the boy's father, he would make him pay for ignoring his son. What kind of man would do such a thing?

The vehicle stopped several doors down from the newspaper office, and Evan exited without waiting for the door to be opened for him.

His eyes narrowed when he caught sight of Mr. Green standing at the red door, fumbling with a key.

"Mr. Green," Evan called out. The man turned, and Evan could feel the fear radiating from him even from this distance. "We must talk."

"I'm sorry, my lord," the editor called back. "You'll have to make an appointment. I'm afraid my diary is already filled for the day."

He managed to unlock and open the door, and Evan took off running, throwing his body against the door before it closed.

Mr. Green let out a cry and stumbled backward, his hands raised in fear. "Please, don't hurt me!"

Slamming shut the door, Evan kept his eyes on the editor. "Last evening, you addressed my friend by name. Why?"

"Did I?" Mr. Green squeaked.

"Yes, you did. But I never mentioned her name. How did you know it?"

The man glanced toward his office, and Evan stepped in front of him. "Don't bother thinking you can somehow barricade yourself in there. I'll get in, I assure you. Now, how do you know her?"

Mr. Green swallowed hard. "We...we met at a party. A lovely woman, though that was several years back. I'm sure she'll not remember a simple man like me."

Evan took hold of Mr. Green's coat. Thoughts of pummeling him came to mind, but Evan brushed them aside. That was not who he was. But that did not mean he would not frighten the man.

"My patience is running thin. You don't want to know what happens when it runs out. Now, tell me what you know of her."

"I've known Miss Follet for well over a year now," the editor croaked. "She writes...for the paper."

Evan tightened his grip on the man's coat. "As?"

"Under the pseudonym of Lady Honor."

"That cannot be!" Evan gasped.

"But it's true, my lord! She's been writing about man in the Remington family. Including...including you, my lord."

"But why?" Evan demanded. "What has compelled her to do such a thing?"

Mr. Green shrugged. "She never explained her reasons, my lord."

"And what exactly has she said about me?"

"She…she wrote that you've had amnesia and that she's pretending to be a love interest. She writes the columns, my lord. I only print them!"

Evan released Mr. Green, feeling ill. Miss Rose had betrayed him. Everything had been an act. All she wanted was fodder for her column.

His rage must have shown on his face, for Mr. Green dropped to his knees and put together the palms of his hands as if in prayer. "Please, my lord, I know what you're capable of, and I beg for mercy. Don't hurt me!"

With a derisive snort, Evan said, "I'll admit the idea of flogging you is appealing, but I'll not lower my standards to such a degree."

Without another word, he exited the building. "Mayfair, Prague. To the home of Miss Follet."

As the carriage lurched forward, Evan fought down the anger and hurt at the deception of the woman he had come to love.

What an imbecile he was allowing her to look at his business ledgers! That explained how the newspaper learned of his supposed involvement with fixed fights. Had she done all this because of what occurred with Miss Constance?

No, that made no sense. The columns had been written long before that unfortunate incident. He thought of her bouts of anger, the night when she had tempted him with kisses and then scolded him for wanting what she offered. The ruffians who had come to hurt him. Because of her!

He knocked on the door, and Miss Rose smiled at him. "My lord, what a pleasant surprise you've arrived early. Aaron is beside himself with excitement…" She fell silent and tilted her head. "Is something wrong?"

"I learned who Lady Honor is," Evan replied. "Would you like to hear about her?"

"I…I don't think there is a need," Miss Rose said. "Why don't you come inside."

Evan ignored her, forcing his hands at his sides to keep them from massaging his temples. "She's a woman who's like a snake, slithering into people's lives. Weaving tales of heartache to get people to trust her. For me to fall in love with her."

"If you'll only allow me to—"

"No. You're allowed nothing, Miss Follet," he spat, putting all his anger—all his frustration—into his tone. "All this time, I believed you were on my side, but now I know better. To think I came to love you only to learn who you truly are. You disgust me."

He turned and signaled to the footman to open the carriage door. Pain guided his steps as Miss Rose hurried to his side.

"My lord, please, you must listen!"

Evan stopped and turned on her. "Listen? To what? Your lies? I can see why your lover refused to see you again. I'll not be made a fool of any longer. Goodbye, Miss Follet."

Ignoring her sobs, Evan stepped into the carriage, dropped onto the bench, and closed his eyes. He opened them long enough to glance out and see tears rolling down Miss Rose's cheeks.

"I'm sorry," she called out. "My objective had been to hurt you at first, my lord, but I changed. As much as you have changed."

Evan forced his gaze away. He could not take in her pain, for his was far more than he could bare. How had something so beautiful turned into something so ugly?

He was angry at being tricked, for being deceived, yet he could not help but still care for her. Despite that, he vowed never to see her again.

Chapter Thirty-Two

Sitting at her desk at in her Mayfair home, Rose stared at the final column she would write as Lady Honor. With each passing moment since she last saw Lord Westlake over two weeks ago, her heart ached for him more. They had been gifted a beautiful moment, but it had quickly fallen to ruin.

She had written late into the night, spending the better part of the morning revising and editing the piece. This was by far her best article, for it came from the heart. But that had also made it her most difficult.

As she waited for the last of the ink to dry, she sat back in the chair, regretting not revealing all beneath that archway. She had considered writing him to explain, but no words could express her regret, her sorrow for what she had done.

Movement had her turn her chair to find Leah entering the room. "Miss Rose, it's time that you give up your suffering. You must move ahead, just as you've done in the past."

Rose nodded. "I've spent a great deal of time thinking about my past. About Lord Westlake, Aaron, even you. The things we've lived through, the pain, the heartache. You and I weathered it all together."

Leah walked over and knelt beside Rose. "You're right. I've experienced all that at your side. Do you remember that first night on the ship to Spain? You believed your life was over. That you wouldn't ever feel happiness again. Then, you had Aaron, and I know he changed your mind about that."

"He did," Rose said, allowing a small smile to form on her lips. "But I also kept my heart sealed from every eligible man. With each inch I lost around my waist, the more men wished to call on me, but I refused them all. I believed that hurting Lord Westlake was the answer, but I learned that I never stopped loving him. Now he's gone forever because I lied to him."

As Leah had done so many times before, she held Rose, assuring her all would be well. Yet Rose knew the truth. All would not be well. She had opened her heart again to the very man who had crushed it before. The nightmare was repeated, and she had no one to blame but herself.

When their embrace broke, Rose sighed. "I've cried on your shoulder so often, I'm afraid I can never repay you for always being here for me."

Leah smiled. "What is done in friendship carries no debt. Now, shall I have tea brought to you?"

"No, thank you," Rose replied, picking up the parchment. "I must give this to Mr. Green. It's Lady Honor's final article. Would you like to read it?"

Leah nodded and took the paper from Rose. As her eyes danced across the page, Rose prayed that somehow Lord Westlake would learn of it.

"It's brilliant," Leah said, handing back the paper. "I'd say it's your best yet."

Giving her friend a hug, Rose folded the article and placed it in her reticule. Aaron bounded down the stairs as she entered the foyer, throwing his arms around her waist. "Will Lord Westlake come back and see me? I do miss him."

This was not the first time Aaron had asked this question. It was about time she told the boy the truth. Or a part of it. "I'm afraid we'll not be seeing him again."

Aaron gave her a hurt look. "Is it because I wanted to hide in the park?" he asked. "You can tell him I'm sorry. We don't even have to play at all if he doesn't want to."

"Now, you listen to me. You did nothing wrong." Rose squatted beside him. "You see, Lord Westlake is a good man, but I hurt his feelings."

"Did you mean to?" Aaron asked, frowning.

Rose shook her head. "Not in the end. But regardless, I did. So, he is hurt because of me, not because of anything you did. I promise." She kissed his forehead. "I have some errands to run, but when I return, we'll go to the park. Would you like that?"

Aaron placed his hands on her face, his eyes conveying all the innocence of the world. "Even if you hurt my feelings, I'll still love you, Miss Rose."

Rose fought back tears. "Thank you for saying so, Aaron. I love you, too. More than you can ever imagine."

Leah took Aaron's hand, and Rose stood, dabbing at her eyes with a kerchief. He was such a good boy. How could she have been so blessed with such a wonderful child?

The weather was warm with no sign of rain, so Rose decided to walk to the office. Once outside of her neighborhood, she encountered row upon row of shops. Couples strolled together, laughing with one another. Children clung to the hand of their mothers or governesses.

Time seemed to have stood still when she arrived at the archway where she and Lord Westlake had sheltered from the rain. And where they had confessed their love for one another.

With a sigh, she continued on. That moment was in the past. It would do her no good to dwell on it. Not if she hoped to be happy. Or at least content. Happiness was far too out of reach.

She knocked on the familiar red door, and it opened to Mr. Green.

He stuck his head out the door, looked left and right, and then pulled his head back inside. "Are you alone?"

Rose frowned. "I am. May I…may I come in?"

Mr. Green heaved a sigh. "I don't think that's a good idea, Miss Rose. I'm sorry I gave you up, but I can't handle anymore scorn in my life."

With a nod, Rose said, "I'm not angry with you, Mr. Green. Please, I need only a few moments of your time and then I'll leave you alone."

With a resigned nod, he moved aside and closed the door behind her. They walked to his office, where he offered her a chair as he took the one behind his desk. "Now, what can I do for you?" he asked.

She pulled the folded piece of parchment from her reticule. "I've written Lady Honor's final column. I'd like you to print it in tomorrow's paper."

"No, no, no," Mr. Green said. "The last thing I need is for that man to come back here and threaten me again." He leaned forward and whispered, "We both know the kind of man he is."

Rose placed the paper in front of the editor. "Read it."

Mr. Green sighed and leaned back in the chair. "Very well. Let's see what you have to say." After several moments, and with his eyes wide, he set the paper back on his desk. "Are you sure about this?"

Rose nodded. "I'm absolutely sure. Will you print it for me?"

Sighing heavily, Mr. Green replied, "I shall, under one condition. Explain to me your reasoning. Why Lord Westlake of all people? What did you hope to gain by pretending to be his love interest?"

Rose considered that question before responding. It was about time she told the truth. "Because I wanted him to love me, so I could, in turn, crush his heart. In the end, however, I was the one who was hurt." She stood. "Goodbye, Mr. Green."

"Goodbye, Miss Follet," the editor replied as he took the parchment back in his hands.

Once outside, Rose drew in a lungful of air. Although her life ahead would be without Lord Westlake, she had Leah and Aaron. And it was thoughts of them that made her hurry to go see them.

Chapter Thirty-Three

The ballroom was empty.

As Evan stared at the place he believed Miss Rose once stood, try as he might, he could not inspirit the image beyond that brief appearance. As a matter of fact, he had not recalled anything new since his last encounter with Miss Rose a month earlier.

He was lost without her. With each passing minute, he felt more alone. And afraid. He also missed her small entourage. Leah had been a delight on their outings, kind and considerate in everything she did. And Aaron! What a wonderful chap he was! At one point, Evan had considered his part in raising the boy. Every boy needed a man to teach him about life. Not like his father, of course. He would show Aaron that life required a man to have integrity and honor. Or rather, he would have shown him if he had not thrown it all away in a fit of rage.

Again, his temper had gotten the best of him. How did he function in life before his accident? He failed at every turn if he erupted at the slightest provocation!

As angry as he was with her for her deception, he could not rid himself of the love he had for her. Had her heart truly softened or was that a part of her ruse?

All this thinking was making his head ache.

Fletcher entered the room, carrying a small silver tray. "A letter arrived for you, my lord."

Evan took the envelope. "Thank you." He slid his finger beneath the wax and perused the contents. "Good news. Mr. Burlington is arriving tomorrow to take a look at my accounts. I suppose I should go over them first. I must give at least some semblance of knowledge."

"Very good, my lord. May I assist you with anything?"

Evan made to shake his head but thought better of it. "Yes. Miss Follet... Do you find the house empty without her?"

Fletcher smiled. "Indeed, I do, my lord. She brought with her a felicity that was missing." He cleared his throat. "May I speak freely, my lord?"

"Please."

"Whatever she intended when she first arrived, my lord, she enriched all our lives. Yours most of all."

Evan chuckled. "You're right there, Fletcher. Thank you. That will be all."

The butler gave a bow and left the room.

With one last look in the direction of that fleeting memory, Evan sighed and made his way to the study. He had spent no time in it since he and Miss Rose went their separate ways. Now, he needed to take up the work she had completed during her stay. The very same work she had used to betray him.

He dropped into the chair, sending a sheet of parchment floating to the floor. As he bent down to retrieve it, something black caught his eye.

How strange. How did a key end up beneath the desk? And what did it open? He glanced about. There was no chest in the room, nor did he see a box...

"Well, hello," he murmured when his eyes fell on the keyhole in the top drawer of the desk. He inserted the key, turned it, and opened the drawer. "What do we have here?"

Inside lay a collection of newspaper clippings. He took them out and began reading them. They were all from the "News of the *Ton*" column written by Lady Honor. Miss Rose. All told tales of various people of some notorious family—the Remingtons, he assumed—but most pertained to a particular baron, one who had a very nasty disposition. At least according to the author.

One article in particular made his heart race. "The Baron Time Forgot," he read aloud.

As a dam breaking, images flooded his mind. He was standing at the top of the stairs, drunk and enraged. But at whom was he shouting?

Closing his eyes, Evan tried to recall his words.

No one will ever forget my name! Do you hear me? No one will forget the name of Lord Westlake!

Evan dropped the clippings. "Fletcher," he whispered. He had been arguing with the butler, that much was certain. But why?

He closed his eyes and concentrated on that single moment. Because he had spoken ill of his mother. Yes, that was it. And how had Fletcher reacted?

"He had defended Mother's honor," he murmured. "Did he threaten me? Yes, he did."

His head spinning, Evan stood and took three ledgers from the shelf. The air in the room was pressing in on him. Did he want to remember? For so long, that was all he wanted. Now he was not so sure. Not if these memories were any indication of who he had been. Yet he could not stop the questions from coming.

Why had he been so angry?

His stomach knotted. *Because Miss Constance had rejected me.*

Now the memories flowed freely. He and Fletcher had argued. Then Evan had stumbled and fell. Fletcher had reached out to him...

"I beg your pardon, my lord..." the butler said as he entered the room, making Evan start. Fletcher hurried to the desk. "Are you all right, my lord? You look as if you've seen a ghost."

Wiping a bead of sweat from his brow, Evan said, "I'm well. What is it?" He looked past the butler to see a familiar figure in the doorway. "Downwick?" He stood. "Please, come in."

Fletcher dipped his head and left the room.

Downwick frowned as he flipped back the tails of his coat and sat in one of the chairs Evan indicated. "Is all well? You aren't ill, are you? You're very pale."

Evan sighed and lowered himself into the twin chair beside Downwick. "Some of my memories are returning, and to be honest, I wish they would not. I don't think I like the man I used to be."

Downwick sighed. "Never have I heard you speak more honestly. I see a broken man before me. Although I have every reason to rejoice in your suffering, I shall not. When I told Eliza about our encounter at the fair, she—in her infinite wisdom—advised me to forgive you your past transgressions. I realize you don't respect her opinion, but I do. And this is the best thing for both of us."

Evan gave a sad nod. "You're so right, I showed her no respect whatsoever. Now I see how ignorant that was. You've a wonderful wife, Downwick, a strong woman who has a good head on her shoulders. That makes you far wealthier and a far better man than I. For all I've said and done against you, I truly am sorry."

To Evan's surprise, the man offered his hand. "I thank you for the apology and accept it wholeheartedly. You were a good friend at one point. I would be pleased if we returned to that time and begin anew. And if I can be of help to you, all you need to do is ask."

"I appreciate you saying so," Evan said. "Now, would you like some tea? Or perhaps a brandy?"

He desperately needed a friend at the moment.

No, he needed Miss Rose.

"I would love nothing more, but I'm afraid I have plans. Eliza and the children are waiting in the carriage. But next week I'll return. I'll even bring Caney with me and we'll make a time of it."

Evan smiled. "See that you do."

As he placed a hand on the door handle, Downwick stopped and turned back around. "Oh, I nearly forgot." He reached into his inside coat pocket. "I think you should read this. It helped me reconsider my opinion of you."

Taking the offered paper, Evan thanked his friend. It was a newspaper clipping, very much like those he found in the desk drawer. Well, he had read enough gossip for one day. Perhaps he would read it later when his head was not aching as it was now.

Setting it aside, he opened the first ledger. Mining. Wool. He even dabbled in a bit of speculating. Now *that* was very much like the Lord Westlake he knew over the past years.

Time ticked by as he moved through the second ledger, which

contained the household accounts. Much less interesting, to be sure.

With a sigh, he glanced at the open drawer and frowned upon seeing a bundle of letters. Taking the top one, he began to read.

"As per our agreement, I've spoken again to Miss Constance. She has agreed to allow you to call on her…"

As the letter continued, the pounding in his head worsened. Had he used his cousin's good name, and his aunt—a duke and duchess, no less!—to get admittance to Miss Constance?

"All so you could bed the young lady?" he murmured with all the incredulity he could muster. His stomach churned at the memory.

The next letter was no less harsh.

"I thought you should know, I find my stable hand a far better lover than you."

The next made him pause. It was from Miss Rose. *"I fear you've used me. Why have you not replied to my letters?"*

The churning in his stomach worsened as he set that letter aside and opened another, also from Miss Rose.

"I leave for the Continent in ten days and wish to speak to you before I go. Please, I beg of you, whatever has caused you to turn away from me, give me the opportunity to rectify it. Send word as to when and where we can meet, for I have so much I wish to say."

The world around Evan began to tremble. Another surge of memories exploded in his mind. Miss Rose in the drawing room, his hand outstretched to her. She had been so beautiful, though her face was rounder than it was now. Whisper of love and promises made as he led her to the couch…

Evan gripped the desk and swallowed back bile. Then his eyes fell on another letter, this one in his own hand. He did not need to read it, for he knew what it said. It spoke of apologies for how he had treated her and the feelings he had for her that he could not bring himself to speak aloud. And it had gone unsent.

Pushing the letters away, one fluttered to the floor. Yet he ignored it as he looked upon the sea of horrible memories that now flooded his mind. His mother pleading with him to change his ways. His father telling him that only a true man betrayed the sacred vows of matrimony. That it was his right. That every woman was a conquest and worthy to become…

"A trophy," he growled in horror.

He dropped his face into his hands. He no longer wanted to regain the memories, for he could not fathom the man he once was. A scoundrel. A rogue. A wretch. Everything Lady Honor had said he was.

Looking for anything to distract him from this realization, his gaze fell on the newspaper clipping Downwick had given him. Well, it could not be any worse than his memories.

What does it mean to be remembered? Or even worse, forgotten? Either by the ones who have hurt us or by the ones we love? Both can be devastating in their own way.

I must admit that I often wonder what we can do about those who have hurt us. Do we forgive and forget as the Good Word commands? Or do we allow our pain and anger to fester like a sliver left beneath the skin?

I have spent a great deal of time writing to you, my dear readers, about a particular baron, one who has been a thorn in the side of many. Although he has suffered from a terrible ailment, I took it upon myself to retaliate against his past deeds, to make him pay for his past transgressions. Let us just say that I chose to play both judge and jury as a way to seek restitution for what had been done against me.

Yet being in his company changed my way of thinking. It is not the mistakes of others in our past that hold us back. It is the refusal to look forward to a better day. Holding on to bitterness harms no one but ourselves and those closest to us. Never does it change what has already happened. Never does it heal old wounds. And never will it lead to peace of mind.

I learned something from our once unscrupulous baron. It was not his past misdeeds that were important but rather his desire for repentance in the here and now.

This is to be my final column, and I would like to leave you with a little piece of advice. I once stated that in generations to come, let this nobleman, this man who wronged so many, let him become the Baron Time Forgot. Now, I say there is a better course, a more gracious way to see a man who has seen the error of his ways. Let him be the Baron to be Remembered.

The page fell from Evan's numb fingers. A broken saucer. A humble maid. A young girl standing by herself in the ballroom.

Blackmail. Deceit.

Love, Laughter.

Accusations of hurt.

A drawing room. A private time together.

In all that, Baron Westlake, remembered everything.

The Baron Time Forgot

A void settled in Rose's heart. A month had passed, and still, Lord Westlake had not called or written. Would she ever see him again? Likely not. Yet, as Leah had counseled, life would continue. And Rose was thankful she had Aaron and Leah with whom she could spend that life.

Yet the void remained.

Thunder rumbled in the distance, and the wind gusted. Rain had not yet fallen, but it soon would. Rose had once enjoyed the rain. Now, she wished to never see another drop for the remainder of her life.

It was a good thing the elements paid her little heed. The poor plants would wilt and die if they chose the weather based on her moods and desires!

"You're going to be soaked if you go out in that," Leah said when she caught sight of Rose in the foyer. "Would you like me to go instead?"

Rose thought back to the night Lord Westlake had pulled her into the puddle. What a wonderful evening it had been. A walk in the rain would do her good.

"No," she said. "I'll return well before it begins to rain." Neither she nor Leah believed that, but the maid did not try to stop her.

Indeed, the first spits of rain fell as Rose hurried down the footpath, her head lowered. She should have at least put on a head covering, but they could be so confining. She preferred to go without. Let the tongues wag. They would wag whether she wore a hat or not.

As she turned right on the footpath, a familiar voice made her stop in her tracks.

"It was you in the red dress that night."

Rose turned, her heart soaring at the sight of Lord Westlake. He was more handsome than she remembered. He, too, wore no hat. My, but they both not a pair of rebels!

Yet his eyes were filled with pain. "That one fleeting memory that escaped me back then has returned. I know it was you."

"It was. Do you remember everything about that night?" She was unsure how she wanted him to answer. If he did not, he could still be redeemed. If he did, it was difficult to say what the results would be.

Lord Westlake nodded. "And every day before and after." He shook his head and glanced at the door to her house. "I know why you lied to me, at least at first. You had every right to."

"No, I should not have—"

"Yes. You had to."

He walked up to her, his nearness making her heady. "I've considered all that I've done," the baron continued. "Who I am. The reasons for the choices I made." He sighed heavily. "I read your final article. It gives me hope for a better future. It will not come easy, I'm sure, but I think I can achieve it."

Rose smiled. "I know you can. You have the strength of character to achieve whatever you put your mind to."

"Perhaps I do, but I got that from you. That night six years ago, I remember seeing you standing against the far wall, alone. If you believe anything, believe this. No matter what others said, you were the most beautiful woman in the room. I cared nothing about your size or any such trivial matters. I saw that strength in you even back then. You stood proud despite others speaking about you behind their hands. You carried a smile while I knew inside you were hurting. You shone brighter than any star in the sky."

Rose blinked back tears. His words eased her heart. "I often tried to smile through the pain."

"You see? That is the strength of which I speak," Lord Westlake said. "All I knew was I wanted what you had. To have your strength rather than the weakness that consumed me. I know I hurt you. What I did, no words can ever erase. I just want you to know that I'm truly sorry for hurting you. If I could turn back time and return to that night knowing what I know now, I would have done things very differently. I once believe that what my father taught me about being a man was true. What I've come to understand is that he taught me to be a coward."

"I can see the truth in your eyes." She tapped her chest. "And I feel it here."

He reached up and wiped away a tear on her cheek with his thumb. "You taught me what courage is, and it's why I stand before you today. Thank you for teaching me that. I just wish you would find it in your heart to forgive me for what I've done. To tell me you will allow me to call, to return to where we were before my memories returned. But I know I've hurt you far too much to be forgiven. I cannot blame you for wanting your life returned to you. Therefore, I'll honor your request. Goodbye, Miss Rose."

He turned to leave, and a flood of emotions washed over Rose. Never had she imagined that Lord Westlake, the baron who had betrayed her, had used her, had lied to her, would become the man who stood before her now. Gone was the vain and wicked man, and in his place stood a man of honor and decency. Could she return to her life without him? Could she face a future where he was not in it?

No, she could not.

"Wait!" she said, taking hold of his arm. "Don't leave me." He turned around, and she placed her hand in his. "For years, I harbored anger and conceived every way possible to cause you pain. What I came to realize was that doing so only hurt myself. Yet it's more than that. I wanted to be accepted for who I am. To be called beautiful. As my waist became smaller, men took notice. Yet I found that it never made me feel any better. New dresses, jewelry, hats, shoes, all were but fleeting moments of joy. But the despondency remained."

She looked up into his blue eyes. "But the day we ate beneath the tree, you said that I had to see myself as beautiful before I could believe it when others commented on it. And you were right. Now, after all these years, I finally do. I no longer push away my plate in shame. I even enjoy a slice of cake from time to time." She let out a small laugh and wiped wetness from her cheeks. "I've learned that even if I return to the size I was before, it won't matter. For I'm beautiful regardless. I see that now, and nothing more can change that. And for that, I thank you."

As the rain fell upon them, the love Rose had for this man swelled. He was willing to stand beside her beneath the storm clouds and speak from his heart. She could not ask for anything more.

"If you can believe there is any decency in me," Lord Westlake said, "allow me to prove it. To show you how much I love you."

"Oh, Evan, you already have." She placed her hands on either side of his face. "Now, kiss me and then we can go inside and see your son."

He gave her no sign of surprise. Apparently, he had worked out that truth already.

Gathering her into his arms, he pressed his lips to hers. It was a powerful kiss, one that told of the love they shared for one another, that filled the void that had been inside her for so many years. Life would be different after this moment, far better and more fulfilled.

When the kiss ended, her mind turned to all that had transpired over these last years.

Feeling shame for her size.

A baron who had broken her heart.

A journey abroad to hide from possible scandal.

The gift of a child who brought her joy.

Laughter, tears, and heartache that all came back to a man and woman who stood holding one another in the rain.

Leah had once told Rose that Lord Westlake would not be the only one who remembered. Rose now understood the maid had been right. For she finally remembered who she once was. A girl who was happy. And in love.

Epilogue

The ballroom was full.

Lords and ladies alike had come to Tinsley Estate for the engagement party for one Evan, Lord Westlake and Miss Rose Follet. Just as it had been six years earlier, Rose wore a red gown and stood along the far wall. This time, however, she did not do so in shame but rather because it provided a prime spot to watch her fiancé as he chatted with his friends Lord Caney and Lord Downwick.

As she observed the guests, Rose could not help but smile. Some things had not changed. Gossip still filled the air, as did the drunken laughter. Women still wore the latest fashions. Men still boasted of sport and their latest conquests—although Rose saw no difference between the two. Not really.

One change that was certain was the very handsome and quite dashing blond-haired gentleman who looked her way. Her cheeks heated and her skin pebbled pleasantly under that steady gaze. She did not doubt that he loved her as he made his way through the crowd to join her. His words assured her of that. The way he continued to right his wrongs said as much. How he spent time with Aaron, his son. The smile he now wore. All indicated what he felt for her.

"Miss Follet," he said with a sly smile and a bow, "I could not help but admire you from afar. May I say you're strikingly beautiful and I would love nothing more than for you to accompany me."

Rose laughed and placed her hand on his proffered arm. "I would be honored to walk with you, my lord."

They smiled at one another as only those in love do. Then, Evan leaned in and whispered in her ear, "I do you love, Rose."

She gave an admiring sigh. "And I love you."

Unlike six years earlier, they did not sneak away. This time, they joined the other guests to engage in conversation together and to toast their engagement.

It was later, when the last guest had gone, that Rose found herself alone in that same ballroom. So many memories, both good and bad, but more good now. In fact, the painful ones had turned out beautiful.

She gave a start when arms encircled her, pulling her back into Evan's chest. "What is on your mind?"

"Our engagement. Marriage. The day we shall tell Aaron the truth about us." She could not help but sigh. Keeping the truth from her son had been the most difficult of all, but it had been necessary. Rose had not wanted to see him suffer for her mistakes. And suffer, he would. Society did not take kindly to children born out of wedlock. Yet they both agreed he had to know the truth once he was older.

She turned to face the man she loved. "It's truly beautiful, is it not? The love we have for one another?"

"I believe so," Evan said. "And is it not fascinating that when I'd forgotten everything, I still remembered my feelings for you? Why is that, do you think?"

Rose sighed. "Because it's love. And love never leaves us."

As Evan dipped his head and touched his lips to hers, Rose's legs grew weak, just as they did every time they kissed. When it ended, and they walked away hand in hand, Rose knew their love—like the new Lord Westlake—would never be forgotten. No, it would always be remembered.

Forever.

Extended Epilogue

Mrs. Tabitha Remington feared for her life. Such a feeling was not uncommon when one was married to Mr. Markus Remington, a man who used words, physical strength, and fear to control her life. No matter how hard she tried, no matter what attempts she made to appease him, the brunt of his anger was taken out on her.

Although she had come to accept Markus's behavior as a way of life, a new wave of fear had come over her in the last hour. Harm was coming. Yet who would bring it was still uncertain.

Sitting alone in the drawing room of her Barstow estate, Tabitha drew her shawl closer in an attempt to find comfort. Thunder rumbled, making the crystal shake with fervor in the panes of the windows.

At least the children were not here or they would have been running into the room to ask if they could cuddle close to her to ease their fears. She had sent the children to the home of her parents the previous week after Markus came barging into the room as she worked on her embroidery.

"That blasted Lady Honor will be the death of us all," he had bellowed. "Trouble is coming and we've no way to avoid it."

Tabitha recalled the name of the gossip columnist who had written about various members of the Remington family. Oh, they were not named outright, but every Remington would recognize himself in her words. As of late, however, the articles had focused primarily on one cousin in particular.

"Do you mean Evan?"

As soon as the words left her mouth, she wished she could have pulled them back. Her husband rounded on her, his face red with anger. "Yes, you stupid woman! Who else would I mean?"

Tabitha lowered her head lest his open hand meet her cheek again. He had struck her all too many times as of late, and never for anything she had done. To him, she was there only to take care of his children and to have someone on whom he could take out his rage.

"We're in trouble," Markus said, beginning his pacing once more. "No, it's worse than trouble. We may all be dead."

Tabitha's heart began to race. Dead? Whatever did he mean? He had been ranting thus since his return to his family home in Wiltsworth, a trip he made twice a year. Although his excuse was to see his sisters, Evelyn and Caroline, Tabitha knew better. Markus had arranged for one of his many lovers to meet him while he was there. He had no other reason to visit Redstone Estate without her.

"We'll send the children away at once."

Tabitha could not stop herself from leaping from her chair. "But why?" Her children were all she had left. They were why she got out of bed in the morning. If she could not have them with her, she would collapse and never rise again.

With two swift steps, Markus grabbed her by the arms and shook her. "Don't you see? Because of that column, they know we fixed one of the boxing matches! Lady Honor may as well have said it outright. Now I've learned that they are searching for me! If Evan's already dead, I won't be surprised. Christopher surely is, though that's no loss to the family name." He spat in the fireplace to punctuate his words.

"Christopher? Christopher Remington?"

A costly utterance, that. Her regret was instantaneous as Markus grabbed her jaw and squeezed it until her lips puckered.

"If you ever speak his name again, I'll cut out your tongue," he said before shoving her back onto the couch. "With all the problems I must face and his name has to fall from your lips? Do you see why I'm always angry? You're to fault!"

"I'm sorry," Tabitha whispered as she brushed away tears. "I'll never say it again."

Long ago, she had learned it was best to apologize, even if she had done nothing wrong. If she did not, his temper only worsened.

Markus rubbed his temples as he towered over her.

Tabitha closed her eyes and offered a silent prayer he would not hurt her.

"The children will leave for your parents' house today and are to remain there until I ask you to send for them," he said finally. "I'll leave soon after. Don't expect me to contact you until this is settled. It may take months. I've no idea how much they truly know, but I'm sure they'll want money."

Tabitha had no idea who this mysterious "they" were, but if they were anything like Markus, she wanted nothing to do with them. What she did understand was that Markus had betrayed them and put his family in danger. Again. He clearly owed them money, of which they had plenty. Why did he not simply pay them? Yet she was not willing to ask that question. The last thing she needed was the children—or her parents—seeing bruises on her face.

"I'll pack before waking them," she said. "I'll need several trunks brought down from the attic, one for each of us, if we're to be gone for some time. It should take me no more than an hour—"

Markus barked a laugh. "No, you'll remain here with the servants, for that's all you're worth. You can let them take their wrath out on you." He looked her up and down and scowled. "Perhaps using you for their pleasure can ease their anger. Hopefully they'll take your life in payment. I've been wanting a new wife anyway."

Two hours later, Tabitha held back tears as she kissed her children goodbye. Upon returning to her room after their departure, she had wept late into the night. Marrying Markus had not been her decision, but her parents had hoped they could make a solid connection with the Remington family. Doing so would allow them the opportunity to mingle with those of the wealthy class. Or so they had thought.

What they had learned was that Markus had little to do with parties and mingling. Instead, he was an unscrupulous man who spent more time with thieves and scoundrels than the type of whom her parents approved. But by the time they realized this, it was too late.

Not only had her parents been deceived, but the man Tabitha had loved, whom she had hoped to marry, was left heartbroken. She had not seen nor heard from him in nearly ten years.

That is, until today, a week after Markus had sent away her reason for living.

The sound of footsteps echoing in the hallway broke Tabitha from her memories. The butler entered the room. "Mr. Keats to see you, madam."

Tabitha stood. "Send him in, Carter."

The man who entered the room was quite tall, even compared to other men. Numerous pale scars marred his leathery face and silver topped his head. Tabitha had never met Mr. Keats, but she had heard of him. He worked for various members of the Remington family, seeing to things that many would otherwise deem unsavory. His arrival today had not been her doing but rather that of Mary Ann, Dowager Duchess of Greystoke.

"Good afternoon, Mr. Keats," Tabitha said with forced politeness. "Would you like me to send for tea? Or perhaps something stronger?"

The man shook his head, and Tabitha signaled to Carter to leave. Once the door was closed, she said, "What can I do for you? Her Grace told me you wished to inquire about my husband. I'm afraid he's not here."

Mr. Keats blinked twice but otherwise remained stoic. "I've been sent to inform you that your husband is seeking a divorce. Mary Ann wanted you to be aware of this and has extended an offer for you to join her at her residence if needed."

Tabitha stared at the man for a moment. Had he referred to the dowager duchess by her Christian name? Yet Mr. Keats did not appear the type of man to be questioned, so she made no comment. Learning that her husband wished to divorce her came as even less of a surprise. At least the dowager duchess cared enough to send this man to inquire after her.

"I see," Tabitha said. "Would you care to sit, Mr. Keats?"

"No, I prefer to stand, thank you."

"As you will. Is there anything more?"

He nodded. "On my journey here, I stopped at an inn. There, I learned a man had died in an accident. That man was your husband."

His words lacked even an ounce of emotion.

Tabitha winced in pain. Not for the loss of her husband but rather for her children who would now be without a father. "Do you know how? I know there have been men looking for him."

"I didn't ask for details," Mr. Keats replied in that same flat voice. "I'm available for hire if you'd like me to return there to find out."

Tabitha shook her head. "It doesn't matter. Markus is dead."

"You say that as if you're relieved," he said. "Don't worry. I haven't a care for who lives or dies."

Tabitha bit at her lower lip. With Markus gone, her life would be forever changed. For the better. But if this stranger noticed that the death of her husband did not matter to her, the family would, too. She would have to practice at playing the mourning widow. Markus may have been a devious man, but the Remington family backed every one of its members, no matter how much—or little—integrity they possessed.

But for now, there was someone else to consider.

"My husband believes..." She paused and corrected herself. "Believed the men to whom he owed money would enjoy taking out their revenge on me in...various ways. Do you think there is any truth to that?" Speaking the words aloud brought forth the same images her husband's words had, making her shudder.

"I can't say for certain," Mr. Keats said. "I'd think not, though. Most men like that are more interested in business than pleasure. Even the worst of men can often have some set of morals." He gave her a grin that made her blood run cold.

Tabitha walked over to a bookshelf and removed a particular tome. The inside had been carefully cut out to create a hollow space where she had hidden as much money over the years that she could save without raising Markus's suspicions.

"Her Grace mentioned to me in her last correspondence that you are a man she trusts. I would like to hire you, but I must ask that you tell no one. Not the dowager duchess, not anyone."

He gave her a cold smile. "No one would hire me if I spilled my secrets willy-nilly, madam."

"True," she said. "I'll write to the dowager duchess now to inform her of Markus's death. What I would like to know is if you're able to find people."

"Yes."

"Anyone?"

"Yes."

Lightning flashed, filling the room with sudden light and highlighting the tall man dressed in all black.

"I would like you to find Christopher Remington," she said. "I've no idea where he is nor anything else about him. Except that he's been involved with fighting for pay. Markus mentioned that men were after him because of a fixed fight. I'd like to know why Christopher turned to such a livelihood and if there was anything Markus used against him to make him act in such a cowardly way."

With a trembling hand, she pushed forth the notes taken from the book. "I believe this will be more than enough to cover your expenses. If more is required, send word and I'll find a way to get it to you."

Mr. Keats thumbed through the notes. "This should be enough for now," he said, placing the money into his pocket. "I'll post a letter if I need more. Now, one last thing. If I do happen to find Mr. Christopher Remington, is there any message I'm meant to give him?

Tabitha walked over to the window and watched the rain trickled down the panes. Memories of years long gone came to mind. Laughter, picnics beneath a never-ending blue sky. A promise made. Why had Christopher involved himself with Markus and Evan of all people? Was he now like them?

"Mrs. Remington?"

She turned back to face Mr. Keats. "No, no message. I would prefer he not know that I sent you."

With a nod, Mr. Keats left the room.

As the hour grew late, Tabitha continued her silent vigil at the window. She thought of Markus and his fate. Not only would their children be heartbroken, so would Evelyn and Caroline. Yet knowing she was free of him, that her face would never be bruised again, Tabitha Remington did something she had not done in more than ten years outside the company of her children.

She smiled.

About the Author

Jennifer Monroe writes Regency Romance you can't resist. Her stories are filled with first loves and second chances with dashing dukes and strong heroines. Each turn of the page promises an adventure in love and many late nights of reading.

Other Series by Jennifer

Those Regency Remingtons

Sisterhood of Secrets

Victoria Parker Regency Murder Mysteries

Secrets of Scarlett Hall

Regency Hearts

Made in the USA
Monee, IL
22 July 2022

10177521R00154